ICE AND SKY

ENA OF ILBREA, BOOK THREE

MEGAN O'RUSSELL

Ink Worlds Press

Visit our website at www.MeganORussell.com

Ice and Sky

Cover Art by Sleepy Fox Studio (https://www.sleepyfoxstudio.net/)

Editing by Christopher Russell

Interior Design by Christopher Russell

Printed in the United States of America

To the ones who fight for change.
Generations will remember you.

ICE AND SKY

I am not innocent.

I have killed. I have harmed. I have tried to do good and ended up hurting the people I cherished most.

I cannot argue any punishment the stars torment me with. I deserve to burn.

I have waited for the sky to turn to ash as the gods declare my guilt.

I am waiting still.

There are legends of people living deep beneath the stones of the eastern mountains. I had heard the stories long before I knew the Black Bloods were real.

But somehow, even after all the magic and monsters I'd seen, I didn't believe the tales to be true.

I was wrong.

I did not understand how terrible my mistake had been as I journeyed through the darkness. The only sounds in the black stone tunnel were the soft plodding of my feet and the rhythm of my own breathing. There was no sign that any other living person existed.

I don't know how long I walked down the high-arched corridor before the walls began to sway and exhaustion finally won the battle against my own will to escape.

I lay down on the ground, gripping my lae stone in one hand and my knife in the other. I nestled into my coat and pressed my back against the wall as sleep swallowed me.

I don't know how long I slept. When I awoke, nothing had changed. There was no sun to judge time by. As far as I could tell, there was nothing in the world beyond the little pool of blue light cast by my lae stone.

My throat burned from thirst, and my stomach longed for food. But I didn't know if I'd been asleep for hours or for days.

Finn might have made it to the camp before I woke up. Or he might have been taken by the Guilds. There was no way for me to know.

I clutched my lae stone tight, trying to convince myself the answer to that question was worth journeying through the darkness.

My legs trembled as I stood up. My feet ached as I kept walking down the tunnel.

There was no change in the walls, no slope or corner. There was nothing but darkness and moving forward one step at a time.

The pounding in my head began before my hands started to shake.

I had once seen bare bones in a passage created by the mountains. I hadn't thought to ask Finn if he had seen others who had been left to decay far below the ground.

As my fingers began to feel too thick to grip my weapon and light, I wondered if the person who had been trapped had been like me—whisked away from Death's embrace so the mountain might torture them more. I wondered if anyone would find my bones, and what they might think of my fate if they did.

"I'm sorry." My words crackled in my throat. "Whatever I've done to offend you, I'm sorry."

I stopped and leaned back against the wall, resisting the temptation to lie down and sleep. Warmth radiated from the stone. I pressed my palm to the heat.

"Actually, I'm not. Punish me if you like. I am willing to die if that is the price you demand, but I am not sorry for saving those children." My breath caught in my chest. "For trying to save those children."

I thought of the four of them—Evie, Gwen, Dorran, and Cinni—captured by the Sorcerers Guild, trapped in the stone tower in Ilara. I shut my eyes, sending a plea up to the stars that Finn had led them to safety.

My eyes stung, but I didn't have any tears to shed.

I tried to distract myself from the pounding in my head and the pain in my body as I kept walking down the chivving tunnel. I pictured Finn arriving at the camp, all the children safely with him. It was a happy image, a valiant success. Finn and I had not only protected four innocent sorcis. We'd also managed to keep powerful magic out of the hands of the Guilds.

Then I got to the bit of the fantasy where Liam found out Finn had returned without me, and the stinging in my eyes came back.

I banished the images from my mind and kept walking forward.

The blackness that lurked in my chest had always seemed an ally before. A place where I could hide hurts and memories that were too horrible for me to bear.

The blackness I journeyed through taunted me. I was the thing the world did not want to see. I was the pain the mountain could not stand. I had been tucked away and would stay hidden until I died.

I screamed at the high-arched ceiling. My rage tore at my throat and echoed down the corridor. There wasn't even the sound of a scurrying rodent to answer me.

"Keep walking. Even the eastern mountains cannot be endless."

I knew my own words weren't true. But my lie was enough to keep me moving for a while longer.

My throat ached, and my tongue felt as though it might crack with every dry breath I drew. The pain in my legs flared from a dull throb to terrible cramps that left me limping.

I'm not sure how long it took for the pounding in my head to develop a noise my ears could hear. Not long after the sound began, the tunnel started swaying before me. I staggered as I tried to make the walls and floor stay in place.

I wanted to lie down and sleep, but I was afraid if I allowed myself to rest, I wouldn't have the strength to stand back up again.

"If you want me dead, just kill me. If you want to torment me, then bring fire or knives. Do not make me wander down here."

I waited for the mountain to answer.

"Did you save me so you could have the pleasure of watching me die slowly?" I tucked my knife into the sheath in my boot and laid my palm on the smooth stone of the wall. "I am not a child of stone. I'm not a Black Blood. You shouldn't have let me in. Was it a mistake? Can you even make mistakes?"

The mountain stayed silent.

I took my hand from the wall and drew my pendant from the top of my bodice. The stone held a blissful and familiar warmth.

"Please. I just want to get back to camp. I want to help. I want to fight."

I pressed my forehead against the stone wall.

"I just want to get back to him."

I let my eyes drift shut as I waited for rocks to tumble down upon me, granting a bloody end to my captivity.

The pounding in my head amplified.

I pushed away from the wall and kept walking. I wished there were a branch in the tunnel, anything that might offer me the illusion of a choice besides following the mountain's will or lying down and waiting to die.

The pounding in my head developed a new texture. A strange and constant rumbling.

I wondered if it might be a sign that my body was giving out. I'd never seen a person die of thirst before. Through all the misery we'd suffered in Harane, we'd always had water to spare.

As I walked, the sound grew louder. The texture of the noise became familiar.

I moved as quickly as I could, limping as I ran toward the rumble. The ground beneath my feet lost its smooth perfection as the peak of the tunnel dropped to a less impressive height.

"Oh, please."

The end of the tunnel came into view. The walls disappeared, opening up into a vast blackness my lae stone was not large enough to light.

I ignored my fear of what could be lurking in the darkness and followed the sound.

A waist-high wall blocked my path.

I scrambled over the rocks, falling to my knees on the other side. I lost my grip on my lae stone. The light rolled away, stopping under a bench.

Cool moisture greeted my palms as I crawled toward my lae stone. The ground was not hard beneath me. As I lay on my stomach to reach for my light, something soft touched my cheek.

Moss.

The ground was covered in moss.

A plant with pale green leaves twined around the legs of the stone bench.

I wanted to touch the leaves, but the low rumbling called to me. I crawled toward the sound, not trusting my legs to carry my weight.

Another wall blocked my path. My hand slipped as I tried to pull myself onto the ledge.

The rocks were slick with water.

Gritting my teeth, I forced myself to stand.

The blue glow of my lae stone shimmered across the water cascading down from a fountain.

I dipped my hand into the pool and drank.

The coolness raced past my lungs as I drank and drank until I thought I would be sick from the wonder of water.

I was so desperate to quench my thirst, I didn't even have the sense to question how a statue of a woman had ended up in a fountain in the belly of the eastern mountains.

3

I slept beside the fountain once I had drunk my fill. Part of me was terrified I would wake to find the water gone, but I didn't have the strength to stay conscious any longer.

When I did wake up, darkness still surrounded me. I had slept with my lae stone clutched in one hand and my pendant in the other. The chill water of the fountain had soaked through the back of my coat. I didn't mind being soggy and cold as long as I had water.

I sat on the lip on the fountain and drank for a long time. The fullness in my stomach almost disguised my hunger.

The stone lady at the center of the fountain seemed to stare at me as I drank. She'd been carved wearing a beautiful dress with her hair woven into an intricate braid that draped over her shoulder. The fancy hair, long skirt, and drooping sleeves didn't look like they belonged hidden underground.

There was something about her—the severe angle of her chin, the slant of her shoulders—that made me quite certain the sculptor had known the woman, had wanted her in particular to be memorialized.

"Who were you?" I asked the stone. "You must have been very important to someone."

Neither the lady nor the mountain answered.

"How did you end up all the way down here?" I pushed myself to my feet. My body felt weak from lack of food, but the water had made it easier to think. "Why would anyone place a statue and a fountain beneath the mountains?"

I walked toward the rock wall I'd scrambled over before I slept. My lae stone barely shone bright enough for me to see a hint of the rock before I left the safety of the fountain.

Soft moss covered all the ground in view, but it wasn't the sort of moss I'd seen in the forest. The color was wrong, too pale, too silver.

I stopped at the rock wall, trailing my fingers along its surface. The barrier was not made of one solid slab as I'd assumed it would be. Stones had been piled together to form the wall, like a person had put a great amount of effort into creating it by hand.

The bench I'd crawled beneath had been built of three different stones, with no hint of magic in its making.

"Did you trap someone down here for so long they had to build a fancy garden to keep sane?"

I climbed up onto the bench and raised my lae stone above my head.

The angle of my light allowed me to see a bit farther.

There were two more benches on the far side of the fountain. A patch of plants grew clustered together against the wall as though reaching for some impossible light.

"Why?" I shouted to the mountain. "Who lives down here?"

I climbed off the bench and moved closer to the plants. Reason told me I was imagining them, but I'd already seen too many impossible things to be sure what couldn't be real.

Something that looked like sour grass grew in between wide-leafed greens. The coloring of all the plants was wrong. So were the sizes of the stalks and leaves.

I'm not sure if it was desperation or stupidity that made me rip a handful of leaves from the ground and start eating. I spent a long while shifting from the garden to the fountain and back again, eating, drinking, and waiting to see if I'd poisoned myself. I wasn't completely opposed to that end. A plant stealing my life would have been fitting.

But I ate my fill without consequence.

When my limbs stopped their constant trembling, I climbed up onto the lip of the fountain and held my light closer to the stone lady's face. Someone had taken the time to carve tiny worry lines around her eyes.

The longer I studied her face, the more absurd her presence became. She was a work of art, a beauty even the paun would have coveted.

"Does anyone know you're down here? Has the living world forgotten you?"

I turned away from her, toward the vast darkness.

"Is anyone out there?" I shouted. "What is this place?"

The darkness did not reply.

"Show me your secrets," I whispered.

I took another long drink of water and stuffed my pockets with leaves before climbing back up and over the rock wall.

I'm not sure what I expected to find in the belly of the black stone beast. Months later, I still had moments when I couldn't quite believe that everything I had seen was real.

There's a shadow in my mind that still whispers I imagined the entire place.

As I ventured through the darkness, I did not think the path the tunnel had spit me out onto, half-mad and desperate for water, would be a lane leading between houses. Real houses. Built of stone and two stories high. But the dark city was the place I was meant to see.

Decaying wooden shutters hung from the windows of the homes. Doors had been torn off their hinges.

I shoved away my horror as the thought of long forgotten bodies rotting in the homes quickened my pace. I couldn't allow myself to begin to count how many corpses might be hiding in the houses. That was a path I could not come back from.

I passed twenty-seven homes before I reached a crossroad. I couldn't see enough by the light of my lae stone to know what might wait in either direction.

"Do you want me to explore? Is that why you brought me down here? Is there something I'm supposed to find?"

A chill wind blew from my left.

I wanted to run from whatever waited in the darkness, but I had learned enough of magic to know I would not be able to escape, not unless the mountain wanted to set me free.

I walked into the breeze.

More houses stretched down that road, leading to a patch of wide buildings that seemed to have been shops. Pillars supported the roof of a pavilion. Chains dripped down where a sign had once hung. A cracked slat of wood lay on the ground beneath.

I knelt to pick up the slat. The wood crumbled at my touch before I could see if any trace of writing had been left behind.

I brushed my hands off on my skirt and kept walking.

The road I traveled down was longer than the entire village of Harane. Longer even than the streets I'd traveled in Nantic.

The farther I walked, the farther apart the homes were placed.

After a long while, I stopped beside a house where one of the walls had begun to collapse. Loose stones cascaded across the silver moss on the ground, but I didn't see any sign of violence or flames that might have destroyed the home.

I gripped my lae stone so hard, the odd angles of its crystal-like surface cut into my palm.

The road continued in front of me, but there was nothing within reach of my light.

I looked back in the direction I'd come. I didn't know the ways of the mountain. I didn't know if she would block me from retreating to the fountain and food that had saved my life.

You will not die here.

"I will find what you want me to find." I squared my shoulders and stepped beyond the reaches of the stone city.

A feeling of hopeless solitude tore at my chest as I walked through the barren blackness.

The path remained defined in front of me. One line of smooth stone reaching out into the distance. I kept promising myself that there couldn't be a trail leading to nowhere. I tried not to hate myself for my lies.

I walked and walked, munching on the leaves I'd tucked into my pocket like I'd become Finn.

Thinking of him sent a pang through my chest and quickened my step.

I hoped he'd reached the camp unharmed, but I knew that if he had, he wouldn't be grateful for my having led the dogs away. He'd be furious with me.

My brother's rage would be enough to burn through the mountains.

I didn't know if he'd blame me or Finn or the Guilds, but Emmet's wrath would fall on someone's head.

And Liam…

A hole punctured my chest, stealing the air from my lungs. I stopped and pressed a hand to my heart, trying to convince myself I knew how to breathe.

Liam would blame himself for letting me go to the Lir Valley. It had been my choice, but that wouldn't matter to him.

"I'm sorry. I'm so sorry."

I forced my lungs to accept air and continued on my dark path.

I don't know how long I walked before the black stone led me down another tunnel. The ceiling was low and lacked the fancy arch of the one I'd traveled before.

When I grew tired enough, I curled up against the wall again and slept.

I'm not sure how many times I slept under the mountain. I'd been trapped in a world of blackness with nothing to mark time. Without the sunlight, everything began to lose meaning.

I would walk until I was too tired to move. Then I would sleep until I woke up.

When I thought I was too thirsty or hungry to keep going, I would find food and water.

A tiny stream running through the rock, a pool gathered between two great columns of stone. I ate lichen that clung to the walls and mushrooms that grew in cracks in the tunnel. The mountain seemed determined to keep me alive, even if my life consisted only of darkness and walking through her endless realm of stone.

I did not allow myself to wonder if my wandering penance would last forever. I'd not seen much of magic, but the things I had witnessed left me terrified of curses and unwilling to contemplate spending a thousand years trapped in the belly of the mountains.

I did worry that I would go mad. That being alone in the darkness would steal my mind and twist me into a horrible creature that would torment innocents and spread nightmares. I felt my mouth for fangs and searched my hands for growing claws. I did not want to become the beast that had brought so much pain to our camp.

I didn't know if the beast was still alive. I didn't know if the camp still existed. I didn't know if the entire outside world had been a lie I'd created to entertain my own failing mind.

When I was afraid I would lose my sanity, I'd grip my stone pendant, foolishly promising that I would not allow myself to become a monster like the one who'd brought pain to those I cared for.

I'd been gripping the pendant for so long I couldn't move my fingers anymore by the time I reached the walled garden of the manor.

The stone wall had been built up ten feet high, and the metal gate still hung from its hinges.

"Hello?" I let go of my pendant. My fingers barely straightened enough for me to pull the gate open.

The squeak of the hinges sliced through the darkness.

I froze, waiting for monsters to come charging out of the black to devour me.

There was only silence.

"Hello?" I called again as I stepped into the courtyard.

A walkway had been built on top of the high wall, and a garden had been planted in the courtyard, reaching toward the back of the manor. A wide pond took up the center of the garden, and a stone chair sat next to the water, as though someone had once spent hours enjoying their walled-in sanctuary.

If I hadn't been thirsty I would have walked away from the walled garden and continued through the darkness. There was something about the space that felt too intimate to be disturbed.

"Is anyone here? I don't want to intrude. I've been traveling, and I need water and food."

I froze again, waiting for people or ghosts to swoop down upon me.

"Is this where you want me to be?" I looked up to the peak of the cavern far out of reach of my light. "Is this what you wanted me to find?"

I let out a shaky breath and headed for the back door of the house.

The plants in the garden had long since overrun their beds, leaving a knee-high sea of pale leaves and bright white flowers for me to wade through.

The back door of the home hadn't fared as well as the metal gate. The wood had crumbled, leaving a misshapen chunk hanging in the doorway.

"I am not afraid," I whispered so softly not even the mountain could hear as I ducked through the gap and into the house.

4

How did they get so much wood?

I'm not sure why the question seemed so important to me as I moved from room to room in the house.

The kitchen had a wide wooden table, and a set of wooden shelves sat across from the massive fireplace. The dining room had seats for twelve people. There were enough beds and bedrooms for that many as well.

Every time I reached a new doorway, I would take a breath, steeling myself to find some horror in the next room. But as I made my way through the home, there was no trace I could see of anything terrible having happened.

The only damage to the furniture I could find had been done by time. There were no dark stains of long ago bloodshed or bones of a person left unburied.

I stood in the bedroom tucked at the end of the upstairs hall for a long while, just staring at the bed.

It was small, as though built for a child, but there wasn't a toy to be seen. There wasn't anything at all besides the bed.

Months before, I'd spent a terrible night in the Blood Valley, listening to the screams of the long dead. I slowed my heart and tried to hear the pain of those who had once called the grand manor home.

There was nothing. It was as though the family had simply packed up, pushed the chairs in around the dining room table, and left.

"What drove you away?"

I kept silent as I climbed down the stone steps and went back out into the courtyard. I drank from the pond, then scoured the garden for things I could eat. I drank some more and curled up beside the stone chair to sleep.

My head felt muddy when I woke. I drank more and ate. I watched my lae stone gleam off the pond for a long while.

"How did people survive in this unending darkness?"

They were safe from the Guilds, Emmet's voice rattled through my mind. *Why would they have left?*

I dug my nails into my palms, fighting against my wish to have Emmet standing beside me. Not to save me, just to actually hear the voice of another person.

I pulled off my boots and dipped my feet into the pond. The chill water sent goose bumps prickling upon my skin.

A smile curved my lips for the first time in ages as I stripped away my clothing and slipped into the pond. The water wasn't deep, and I sorely missed soap, but scrubbing my skin seemed to tear away a bit of the fear that had seeped deep into my bones in the crushing darkness.

I scrubbed and scrubbed until the cold became too much. Even as my teeth chattered, I basked in the water for a few minutes more. When my feet had gone numb, I climbed out of the pond and got dressed.

Sense told me to stay in the garden a while longer, to rest with the bounty of food and drink, but people had left this home. Some desire or fear had driven them away.

A flicker of certainty sparked in my gut. This was what the mountain wanted me to see. This manor was the reason for my journey even if I had no idea why I needed to witness this deserted place.

I stopped with my hand on the metal gate.

"I am going to get out of here. I am going to find the camp. I'm going home. I…I hope wherever you went, you found a new home. I hope you were happy. I hope it was worth leaving the life you'd built here."

I stepped onto the path, but it only led me back the way I'd come. The mountain offered no new course for me to follow. Holding my lae stone high, I circled the stone wall, searching for any hint of a trail.

There was nothing but the wall and the black stone path I'd already traveled.

I made it all the way back to the metal gate before panic began creeping in around the certainty I'd found.

"I will not be trapped here!"

I strode away from the manor and into the darkness beyond.

"You took a child into your protection, and you let that child go. You saved me"—my steps faltered—"and I am grateful. But I have to tell Liam what I found here. I have to help him. I have to be sure the others are safe."

I tore through the darkness, though I could not name the terror that chased me.

I reached the edge of the vast cavern I'd been traveling for I didn't know how long. A smooth wall blocked my path. I headed right, trailing my fingers along the wall as I ran.

I searched the ground for any hint of a road and scanned the darkness for the shapes of more buildings lurking just beyond my light. My breath had begun to grate my throat before the wall vanished from beneath my fingers.

A gap, barely wide enough to slide into, sliced through the wall. There was no hint that the people who had lived below-ground had ever traveled through the crevice. No hint at all that a sane person should try to slip through the crack.

"You've given me worse than this." I held my light in the gap and peered into the shadows. There was nothing in view.

I turned sideways and sidled into the crevice. It was a slow path to travel, and the mountain had left loose stones to tangle my feet.

When I'd left the manor, my hair had been wet enough to leave a chill on my neck. The damp from my hair laying against my coat had dried long before the tunnel finally widened and began to slope up.

The path the mountain laid out for me curved and twisted, dove down deep and forced me to climb back up. But I kept going, charging forward even as my legs burned and reason told me I'd be trapped forever.

Just when a trickle of doubt dripped into my chest, coating the certainty that had kept me climbing, a wall blocked the tunnel.

"No! If you want me dead, so be it, but do not leave me down here alone." My breath hitched in my chest. "Please."

I pressed my forehead against the stone.

"The darkness down here is nothing compared to the outside world. I have to help them. I have to protect him. I need to be with them. Please let me out."

I shut my eyes.

"Please."

The wall trembled beneath my touch.

I opened my eyes to find blinding sunlight surrounding me.

I staggered forward, free of the rock and darkness, and into the wonderfully open forest.

The scent of trees filled my lungs. The wind lifted my hair. A bird soared overhead, twittering its everyday joy.

I sank to my knees as my entire body began to shake.

"Thank you," I whispered into the wind.

I knelt for a long time, watching the leaves twist on the trees.

A rabbit darted in front of me and dove into a patch of low bushes.

I had forgotten to be afraid of the monster that terrorized our camp until I saw the poor animal hide from me.

Pulling my knife from my boot, I forced myself to my feet.

I needed to keep moving. After the uncountable miles I'd wandered underground, I was chivving thrilled to be traveling in the sunlight, but I had no idea where I was or which direction might lead me toward the camp.

The eastern mountain range is massive. Large enough to swallow an entire civilization without leaving enough of a trace for anyone to notice. If I went the wrong way, I could end up roaming the mountains for as long as I'd been underground.

A horrible ache pulled at my chest, and a hunger burned inside me, a longing that tore at my soul until I thought I would crumble. Like a part of me had been ripped away and I was incomplete.

A bit of my soul was missing. I could feel the void the missing part had left behind. The pain of it pulsed through me like a deadly wound.

I shut my eyes and tried to press the ache away, but the longing would not be silenced.

I tucked my lae stone into my pocket and started walking.

There is no explanation I can give as to why I chose the direction I did, but I could not fight it.

Either I could keep following that path, or I could shatter into a thousand irreparable pieces. The stars did not allow any other option.

As the sun began to sink, I knew I was traveling northwest, which by all reason was the absolute wrong way to get to the camp from where I had been when the mountain had swallowed me.

But I couldn't stop. The fire that drove me burned bright. The flames fed the longing.

There was a way to repair the void inside me. I only had to find the bit of my soul I had lost. I could not rest until I had put my soul back together.

The sun set, and I pulled my lae stone from my pocket. I knew I should stop, find a tree, and hope for safety during the night. Even my fear of the monster's claws could not keep me from moving forward.

I cut along a tree-shrouded ridgeline and through a field of boulders that looked as though giants had tossed the great stones in a game. My boots were soaked as I slogged through a stream. The water ran swiftly, as though a storm had let loose in some higher part of the mountains. I searched the sky, but there was no hint of clouds masking the stars.

The moon shone bright across the woods. I scanned the shadows, reveling in the details beyond the reach of my lae stone.

A dark shape, larger than any man, appeared down the slope from me.

I froze, waiting for Death himself to catch me.

The shape did not move.

I crept closer to the hulking mass. A branch cracked beneath my foot.

Still, the shadow did not move.

It wasn't until I was twenty feet away that I recognized the shape of the great, dark boulder.

My breath hitched in my throat as I touched the stone.

The longing that had burned in my chest flared like a sun ready to explode as my fingers touched the cold surface.

Liam.

I stepped into the boundary his magic created, letting whatever spell allowed him to protect us surround me for a moment, before entering the camp.

5

"Ena?" a voice called. "Ena, is that you?"

"Yes." A giddy glee bubbled in my chest at the mere act of speaking to another person.

Patrick jumped out of a tree, an arrow still nocked in his bow. "By the gods, I didn't think I'd ever see you again." He smiled at me, like he was genuinely glad I hadn't died.

A knot pressed on my throat. "Finn. Did he make it back? I left him in the woods. He had—"

"Four demons with him?" Patrick slid his arrow into his quiver. "They're all here."

The trees swayed in front of me.

"Made it back two weeks ago. You've given everyone an awful scare."

"Two weeks?" I blinked, trying to make the trees hold still.

"Your brother charged out of here as soon as he found out you weren't with Finn. Then Finn went back out to search for you. Liam's been going half-mad trying to find out if you were taken to Ilara."

"Liam's gone to Ilara?"

"No, he's here." Patrick furrowed his brow. "Orders came all the way from Lygan Hall—"

I didn't wait to hear about the orders from Lygan Hall.

I cut through the trees and toward the center of camp. I'd come in from the southeast, opposite the clearing and kitchen tent. There wasn't even a hint I was traveling in the right direction until the line of lae stones that lit the paths between the rows of tents came into view.

I'd never appreciated the beauty of their blue glow. Not as I should have. Even if it hadn't been Liam's magic that made the stones, even if their light hadn't been a wonder that cast everything into gentle shadows, the presence of the stones meant people. My people.

The knot pressed on my throat so hard I could barely breathe.

My little tent was still there, sitting next to Liam's. No one had moved it in the weeks I'd been away.

A dim blue light glowed inside Liam's tent. I didn't even think about what I should be doing until I was standing right outside the canvas.

I raised my hand to knock on his tent pole and froze. I wasn't sure if I should wait until morning, or if I should shout that I was home, or maybe that I was sorry for having led Finn into such danger.

In the end, I just needed to see his face.

I knocked on the pole.

"What?" Liam's voice carried through the canvas.

I swallowed the knot in my throat but couldn't find the words to answer him.

"If you do not have news from Ilara, then do not dare to step into this tent." His voice came out gravelly and low, like he hadn't slept properly in weeks.

I brushed the canvas aside and stepped into his tent.

"I don't know anything about Ilara," I said. "But I have had quite the journey. Maybe that could distract you from your worries."

Liam looked up at me. His cheeks had sunken in, and new creases marred his brow. Dark stubble coated his chin. He stared at me but didn't move.

"I can come back in the morning," I said. "Though I'm tired enough I might sleep through—"

"Ena?" Liam still didn't move.

"I didn't mean to be gone for so long. The mountain swallowed me, and I didn't know if I'd ever make it out."

Liam stood and walked toward me.

"I'm sorry that Finn and Emmet went out to find me. I can go after them if you'd…"

He trembled as he took my face in his hands.

"Ena?" A wicked grief flashed through his eyes.

"It's me." I laid my hand over his heart. "I'm here."

"Ena." My name cracked in his throat as he drew me to his chest.

He smelled of fresh wind and reckless freedom. The scent swept through me, brushing away bits of the shadows that clung to my soul.

I buried my face on his shoulder and let his arms wrap around me, circling me like a suit of armor that could not be broken.

He let go of me enough to tip my chin up, as though he needed to look into my eyes. "You're alive?"

"I'm fine, Liam. I got a little lost, but I'm fine."

He kissed my forehead. "I thought they'd captured you. Gods, I thought they'd killed you."

A tear ran down his cheek.

I took his face in my hands and brushed the tear away.

"I took the long way round," I said. "That's all."

He held my gaze. I'd never seen so much grief and fear locked inside one person.

"I thought I'd lost—"

I pressed my fingers over his lips. "I promised I'd come home, didn't I?"

He kissed my fingers. He took my hand in his and kissed my palm.

Heat flooded my veins, racing through my body and destroying every hint of darkness that had festered within me.

I leaned close to him, and he kissed me.

Time stopped. All thoughts of the world disappeared.

His taste was all I knew until his hands trailed up my sides and a new, bright fire burst through my being.

I laced my fingers through his hair, clinging to him as though the world were trying to rip him away from me.

But he didn't back away.

He pulled me closer, like he needed to be near me as much as every fiber of my being longed for him.

I'm not sure when I took off my coat or which of us untied the knot at the top of my bodice. I don't remember our bodies separating until he dragged the fabric over my head. Then there was nothing but my thin shift and his shirt between us.

The heat of him surrounded me.

I deepened our kiss, tasting more of him as he unfastened the buttons of my skirt.

I pulled his shirt off, needing to be closer to him, wanting more of his skin to explore.

His muscles tensed as I trailed my fingers along his bare back. The strength of him sent shocks flying up my arms.

He kissed the side of my neck, and a pulsing fire blazed through me.

I pulled my shift off, letting my bare chest press against him. I needed to feel his skin against mine as I had never needed anything in my life.

I kissed him again, holding him close to me, desperate to feel every ridge of his body against mine before he came to his senses and shied away.

But he didn't back away.

He pressed his hips against mine, and I knew he wanted me as badly as I wanted him.

He lifted me and carried me to his bed.

I tumbled away in a blazing wanting and beautiful peace that I had never dreamt possible.

I lay in Liam's arms, our limbs tangled together so I wasn't sure where I ended and he began. Sweat coated the small of my back where he trailed his fingers along my spine.

I nestled my head on his shoulder and let myself drift into the most wonderful kind of exhaustion the gods have ever created.

Liam shifted beneath me, and fear demolished my peace.

"Don't." The word cracked through my chest.

Liam froze. "Did I hurt you?"

"Please don't." I fought the urge to wrap my arm around his chest and cling to him.

"Don't what?"

"Don't say this was a mistake. Don't say you care for me but I'm safer without you. Don't come up with some other chivving reason to kick me out of your bed."

"I thought I'd lost you."

"And now you've realized I'm alive and are going to protect me from you by refusing to look at me." I untangled my limbs from his.

He wrapped his arm around my waist, holding me closer. "I almost lost you. By all rights, you should be dead."

"I'm not."

He tipped my chin up and looked into my eyes. "I was wrong, Ena. From the very beginning, I've been wrong. You burn too bright, you're too vast, too bold for me to protect you by pushing you to the background." He brushed his lips against mine. "If I wanted to keep you perfectly safe, I'd have to lock you away."

"No. I will not be locked away."

"I know." He pulled me closer so my torso fit the curve of his. "You'd never survive captivity. It would break you. The only hope of protecting you I have is to keep you next to me. To stand beside you through whatever storm you choose to challenge. I can't stop you from running into danger. If I want to keep you alive, I'll have to charge after you with my sword raised, ready to fight every beast the shadows have to offer."

I studied his face. There was no hint of anger or jest behind his eyes.

"I'm yours, Ena. For as long as you'll have me, I'll stand by your side."

A pressure dug into my lungs, like something was carving away every broken part of me and replacing it with the undeniable armor of knowing Liam would stand with me.

"Don't say that unless you mean it," I whispered. "You might be stuck with me for the rest of your life."

"Then I will live the best life any Black Blood has ever dreamt of."

He kissed me and I wrapped my arms around him, and every sense of being two different people vanished as our bodies twined together. The terrible longing that had plagued my soul drifted away, and something new filled me and strengthened me.

I did not know I was drifting until I found the shore.
I did not know I was broken until I was whole.
I did not know what I had to lose until the thieves came.

Bright morning light peered in through the canvas of Liam's tent.

I knew I should get out of bed, but the comfort of his arm draped over me was too wonderful to cast away. I lay very still, memorizing the way his weight pressed against my side until he stirred.

For a split second, I worried that everything he had said the night before would be forgotten in the unforgiving sunlight.

He pulled me closer to him and kissed the back of my neck.

"Did you sleep?" he asked.

"Of course. I have a magic pendant to keep the nightmares away."

"Is it enough? You were gone for so long and—"

I rolled over to face him. A thrill shot up my spine as my chest grazed his. "I was fine. I was trapped beneath the mountains in a labyrinth I thought I'd never get out of, but no one hurt me."

"How did you get beneath the mountain?" Liam pushed himself up on his elbow.

"I was swallowed. The soldiers and the sorcerer had me cornered, and then I fell into darkness."

"What?"

"I don't know how it happened, but the mountain took me in and kept me below until yesterday."

"That's not possible." Liam laid his palm on my ribs, on the raven mark he had drawn on my flesh. "The mountain shouldn't have opened for you, and even if she did, how could you have survived for two weeks?"

"There are houses down there, Liam." My heart raced as the memory of the blackness surrounding me shocked through my body. "There was a fountain with a beautiful statue of a woman. There was a garden, and a fancy manor."

"There aren't any people living below the mountain."

"Not anymore, but there used to be. There is a whole abandoned city down there. I don't know who built it or why they left, but I know it's real. I was there. I saw it. I walked through the whole chivving thing for ages. I think the mountain wanted me to see it. I'm not sure why, but I know I didn't imagine it."

"The mountain's magic runs deeper than we want to believe." Liam kissed my forehead, sending a jolt of joy looping through my stomach. "She protected you, kept you safe underground away from monsters—"

"The monster. Is it still in the woods? I didn't see any hint of it on my way here." Reality beyond the warmth of Liam's bed trickled fear back into my veins. "And the traitor. Did Emmet tell you he thought someone had—"

"She's in there." A voice cut through the canvas.

A whispered reply came after.

"No." The voice got louder. "I'm telling you, Ena is in that tent."

"Evie." I dove toward my clothes, which lay scattered across the ground.

"You can't go in there," Gwen said. "Evie, don't you dare."

Liam leapt out of bed and raced for his cast-aside pants.

I swallowed my laugh as he hopped on one leg trying to yank them on.

"Ena will be happy to see me," Evie said.

"I'm sure she will." Gwen overenunciated each word. "But you know how grown folk are before they've had their breakfast."

I pulled on my shift and buttoned my skirt.

"Best to leave Ena alone until she's had something to eat and a chance to wake up!" Gwen shouted the last two words.

I yanked my bodice on as Liam pulled his shirt over his head and ducked out of the tent flap.

"Evie, Gwen," Liam said, "I have the most wonderful news to share. Ena arrived home last night."

"I know that," Evie said. "She's in your tent."

Heat burned in my cheeks.

I jammed my boots back onto my feet and slipped out the back flap of the tent.

"Let's go and see Neil about some breakfast," Gwen said. "I'm sure we'll meet Ena in the clearing."

I looked to the gap between Liam's tent and mine. It wasn't wide. Only two feet. Which was plenty of space for Evie to spot me.

"Let's all go to breakfast together," Liam said. "I'm very hungry this morning."

"I'm sure you are," Gwen said. "You should eat a hearty breakfast so you can feel recovered for the day."

I stayed frozen as their footsteps faded away. I peeked around the side of Liam's tent. There was no one in sight. Feeling like an utter fool, I leapt across the gap between our tents and dove into the back of my own canvas home.

Someone had come in to tidy my things. They'd rolled my blankets to fight off the damp and had laid everything I owned in a neat row on my cot. I couldn't picture Liam doing such a thing, and certainly not Emmet. Finn might have come in and protected my possessions before he left, but it didn't seem like him.

I sat down on the stump that was meant to be my chair.

Was it Marta or Cati?

It seemed strange that there were enough people who might've missed me that I didn't know who could've tidied my tent.

I dragged my fingers through my hair, wishing I had a comb. Digging into the bag that held the few extra bits of clothing I owned, I pulled out clean things to wear. I'd lost my pack in the Lir Valley. My comb, my powders and paints to give me a fitting set of armor to face the foul world of men—all of it was gone.

After I'd changed into my clean clothes, I stood staring at my cot for a long while.

I wanted to go out and greet all the people that filled the camp I called my home, but I wasn't sure what to say to them. I didn't know what they'd say to me.

"Don't be a chivving fool." I tied my hair back with a string and stepped out of my tent.

Nessa lurked on the path leading to the clearing. "You're back! How wonderful." She gave me a smile I couldn't trust as I passed her.

I forced my hands to relax as I strode into the clearing.

I passed Winnie, who gave me a wave from her seat at the side of the wide, open space.

"Nice to have you back." Kerry spoke through his mouthful of food and strode quickly away from me.

Others smiled and waved, but they didn't approach me. They didn't try to ask me questions or block my path.

I'd only ever seen them behave that way with two people. Liam and Emmet.

I stopped at the back of the line of people waiting for breakfast.

Sal offered me his place in line, but wouldn't look me in the eyes.

Do they hate me for sneaking away? Do they think I'm the one who betrayed them?

I shoved my hands into my pockets to hide their shaking.

"Ena!" I heard the shout the moment before Evie rammed into my torso. "I thought you'd died. Everyone thought you'd died. It's been plain awful around here what with everyone grieving for you."

I sucked air back into my lungs as Evie let go of me.

"We've missed you." Evie blinked up at me with her big brown eyes. "I don't blame you for sending us here without you, but it would've been better if you hadn't run away."

"She was protecting us." Gwen stepped up to her sister's side.

The other two Lir children followed close behind.

"That doesn't mean it was nice of her to leave," Evie said.

"At least we made it here alive," Dorran said. He alone seemed the worse for being in the camp.

Gwen and Evie had both gained more color in their cheeks.

Dorran seemed to have lost a bit off his skinny frame, and his brow looked to be stuck in a permanently furrowed position.

Cinni stepped around her siblings and stared up at me.

"Hello, Cinni." I bent down to be level with her eyes. "I'm sorry if you had a rough trip through the mountains, but I'm so glad you're here with my friends."

Cinni reached forward and brushed her finger across the back of my hand.

"I'm happy to be home as well," I said.

Cinni turned and walked straight up to Neil. He passed her a bowl and spoon without question or snipe. Then she sat by a tree to eat.

"Time for breakfast." Gwen shooed Dorran and Evie away.

I felt out of place as I reached the front of the line.

Neil examined me from my boots to the top of my head as he passed me my bowl and spoon.

"Thank you," I said.

"Of course," Neil said. "Of course. Good to have someone back who's slipped through the clutches of the Guilds."

"Right," I said. "Thanks."

I backed away from him and toward the clearing.

A glint of bright blond hair shone in the corner of my vision. I turned in time to see Marta stalk away through the trees.

"Right." I nodded to people, trying not to look like I was searching for Liam as I sat in the clearing. There wasn't a sign of him anywhere. "Right."

I took a bite of what could best be described as gruel. Despite not having eaten anything but scavenged plants in two weeks, the food turned my stomach.

"Not to your taste?"

I looked up to find Case standing over me.

"Not really," I said. "But I'm grateful for food."

"Did they not feed you where you were?" Case asked.

"There were no people," I said. "I ended up wandering on my own after slipping away from the soldiers."

I don't know what made me coat the truth.

Case shrugged and sat beside me. "Finn's been gone for a while now. I hope he has food."

"Have—" I swallowed the sour in my throat. "Is the monster still roaming?"

"Oh no," Case said. "As soon as you and Finn dodged out of camp, Liam went on a tear. The beast was destroyed before Finn got back. Then he, Liam, and Emmet went on a tear about your being missing."

"I'm sorry." I set my gruel aside. "I didn't mean for Finn to go out after me. If you know where he went, I can go and look for him."

"And you'll go one way and he'll go another and you'll end up missing each other in the woods? Best thing you can do is stay here and wait for him to come home."

"I'm sorry," I said again. "I'm sorry you have to wait for him because of me."

"He'll be all right." Case ran a hand through his dark hair, tousling his normally perfect locks. "Cati went with him. She'll make sure he hobbles home."

"But Cati isn't allowed to leave camp. Her job is to stay here and train the fighters."

"That all went out the chivving window when you went missing. All order went soaring into the wind when Finn showed up with four sorcis in tow and announced you'd sacrificed yourself to save him."

"But he made it home, right? That's got to count for something." I wished I had a mug of ale or something to grip in my hands besides a bowl of gruel.

"It counts for a lot that you set your life on the line to protect Finn. I just hope the gods care enough to bring him home safe."

I took Case's hand. "Finn is an impossible, chivving slitch, but if anyone can survive monsters and men, it's him."

"You're right." Case nodded and chewed his lips together. "Want to come and play with swords? My usual sparring partner is absent, and I have a horrible need for exercise."

"As long as you don't mind having to teach me." I shoved a few more bites of gruel into my mouth before following Case to the training field.

9

The rest of the day passed in a haze of flashing steel in the clearing and strained nods and smiles from my fellow Black Bloods. At first, I tried to convince myself they were just glad I was back and too confused about how I'd survived to say hello to me.

Then, I noticed how they whispered when they thought I couldn't see. How Nessa began making her way around the training field, stopping to chat with every person she could catch. How there was a spring in her step as though she were living the best day of her chivving life.

After Case had run me through enough training to leave a fresh set of bruises coating my body, and worn down my need to scream at every person who glanced in my direction, I slipped away for a bath in the cave. As I traveled to my tent, a rustle of whispers followed me like my own personal breeze.

I soaked and scrubbed with fresh-scented soap until my skin was raw. When I got back to my tent, someone had left a new wooden comb and a tiny glass bottle on the stump that served as my table.

I stared at the bottle as I combed my hair. Marta had given me one like it once before. I didn't know if she'd slipped into my tent to leave this one for me.

Maybe Liam had asked her to. Maybe Liam had brought me the comb and glass bottle himself.

When I'd combed my hair so thoroughly there wasn't a hint of stone or tangle left behind, I uncorked the little bottle and drank the foul liquid within.

The vile stuff sent bile into my throat, but I managed to keep it down.

As the sun began to fade, I stepped out of my tent, clean and groomed, and headed toward the clearing.

The whispers still followed me.

I passed by a pack of men.

They fell silent and stared at the ground, as though hoping I wouldn't notice them.

I wanted to shout at them but didn't know what I would say. Screaming that I was sorry didn't seem like it would help, and bellowing that I hadn't betrayed anyone didn't seem like a good way to prove my innocence.

Neil didn't meet my gaze as he passed me my bowl of stew and overly full mug of ale.

I took my dinner and sat on the side of the clearing.

The two fiddlers hopped up onto a bench once true night fell, taking turns drinking and playing as the lae stones became the only real light in the camp.

I wished Finn were in the clearing with me. Or Cati. Or even Emmet.

Marta strode up to the front of the supper line and took her bowl without even glancing my way.

I took a long drink of ale, dousing the bit of me that wanted to walk straight up to her, whether she wanted to greet me or not. Marta was my friend. She'd been a good friend. But I didn't regret journeying to the Lir Valley and couldn't bear the thought of asking her if she believed I'd betrayed the Black Bloods. I didn't want to even think about the other reason she might be angry with me.

Liam trusts you. He chose you. Let that be enough.

Dancers gradually filled the center of the clearing, but there wasn't the pack of them I'd grown used to during the height of the summer. The whole scene just looked wrong without Finn and Case frolicking through the heart of it all.

I tried not to notice the glances thrown my way.

I sipped my ale again. The taste sent me spiraling toward memories I didn't want to dwell upon. My hands shook as I set my mug aside. I ate my meat stew as the players switched from song to song and the few pairs of dancers spun through each other.

I didn't know where the children were. I didn't know where they slept or who had been taking care of them since they'd arrived in the camp. I was sure Marta knew, but I didn't fancy asking her.

The fiddlers began a new song, and a few more brave souls joined the dancers. They laughed and frolicked, but I wasn't tempted to join them.

Nessa appeared from the shadows and flashed a smirk my way before heading toward the men who had fallen silent in my presence earlier.

One of the men tipped his head back and laughed.

Heat soared into my face.

I stood to return my mug and bowl to Neil. But Marta still lingered beside him, and I didn't want to get close enough to look into her eyes and see what she really thought of me. I set my mug and bowl back down, ready to risk Neil's wrath sooner than Marta's judgment, and turned to walk back to my tent.

The dancers parted, and my heart twirled in my chest as I caught sight of Liam sitting in his chair.

I'd never actually seen him sit in the wide wooden chair with the great bird carved into the back. He looked as though he'd been watching the dancers, but a moment after I'd noticed him, he raised a hand, calling me toward him.

My heart hitched up into my throat.

Part of me wanted to flee from him, but he met my gaze and waved a hand toward me again.

A jolt of fear shot through me at the mere thought of walking toward him with everyone around me whispering, but the draw of being close to him was strong enough to lead me across the clearing.

The dancers stopped as I neared them, scattering to make a path for me. I'd have thought the whole world had stopped turning if the fiddlers hadn't kept playing. The walk from my bench to Liam's chair seemed to take hours, but he kept looking at me. And I wanted to be near enough to him to see the dashes of black in his dark eyes.

My heart banged against my ribs as I stopped in front of him. The gaze of every person in the clearing bored into my back. "Is there anything you need, Trueborn Duwead?"

"I'm quite content to sit and listen to the music." Liam's face remained placid.

"Do you enjoy music? I've never seen you sit in the clearing before."

"Honestly, I hate sitting here." He rubbed his hand along the arm of his chair. "This seat feels too much like a throne."

"It looks rather like a throne." I felt a smile curve my lips. "You could be King of the forest birds."

"I'm king of nothing."

"Then why has Your Grandness decided to join us on this fine night?"

Liam looked around the clearing before turning his gaze back to me. "I wanted to be sure you were all right."

"Why wouldn't I be?" My smile slipped into something less genuine. "The flutter of whispers following me is such a delight after spending so long alone."

"I'm sorry for that."

"I just wish I knew what they were all chivving chattering about. What Nessa is whispering to every person in camp about. I didn't mean to disappear for so long. I didn't mean for anyone to go out looking for me. I certainly didn't betray—"

"Ena"—a vague pink drifted up Liam's neck—"all the talk is about us."

My heart stumbled over a beat. "Who did you tell?"

"We live in tents, Ena." He gripped the arms of his chair. "There's never more than a bit of canvas between us and every other person in this camp."

Heat seared my cheeks.

"They all know," Liam said. "I would guess most of them knew before you snuck out of my tent this morning."

The heat turned into an inferno hot enough to melt a mountain.

"What do I do?" I asked. "Oh gods, what are they all saying?"

"I don't know. If they're all whispering that you spent the night in my tent, they're right. There's nothing we can do about that."

"So we should just stand here and wait for my brother to murder you?"

A new wrinkle appeared on Liam's brow. "Emmet is a problem for another day, but tonight we can take care of the rest of the camp."

"How?" The heat of all of them staring at me singed my bravery, threatening to send me running from the clearing like a wounded animal. "Does it involve fleeing across the Arion Sea? I've never sailed before, but I'm willing to learn."

"I can't run away, Ena. I can't stop them from whispering, but we can change what they say."

"Does it involve you making the entire camp swear oaths to you and slaying them all with tiny stones?"

"No." The wrinkles on Liam's brow vanished, and a tiny hint of a smile curved one side of his mouth. "Just sit with me."

"What?"

"Sit with me." Liam shifted in his wide seat, making a place for me by his side. "They want to whisper about you sharing my bed like it's something illicit or wrong, but it's not. I care for you, Ena. I nearly lost my chivving mind when I thought…"

"I'm fine." I wanted to reach out, to touch his cheek, but the stares of the other Black Bloods burning into the back of my neck kept me from moving. "I'm here, and I'm fine."

"I don't ever want to lose you again. I don't think I could survive it. Please, Ena, just sit beside me."

"With everyone staring?"

"Sit with me, and they'll all gape for a moment. But by morning, they'll see we've nothing to hide. I want to be with you, Ena. I don't see the point in pretending otherwise."

I froze, staring at the open place on his throne-like chair.

"Or," Liam said, "you can give me a nod like I've told you something I need you to do for me, and leave. I won't push you toward anything you don't want."

I wanted to sit beside him. I wanted to feel his arm around me. A pull buried deep in my chest screamed for me to close the few feet of space between us.

You are not a coward.

I let out a long breath and sat by Liam's side.

The chair was wide enough for both of us, but his arm still pressed against mine. The warmth of his touch dampened the flames that had plagued me.

I looked out over the clearing. Every single person stared at me. Even the fiddlers had their gazes locked on Liam and me as they played.

"I'm sorry the seat isn't more comfortable," Liam said.

"I hadn't noticed the wood. I'm too busy wilting from the glares I'm getting."

"They aren't glaring." Liam laid his hand palm up on his knee. "They're just a touch disappointed."

"Why's that?" I placed my hand in Liam's, lacing my fingers through his.

"They thought they'd just gotten a wonderful new piece of gossip they could chew on all the way to Lygan Hall." Liam squeezed my hand. "We've deprived them of that."

"So, they are glares then." I nudged my arm against his.

"Maybe," Liam said, "but not for anything worth glaring about."

A flicker of movement at the back of the clearing caught my eye. Marta strode up to the front of the barrel and poured herself a mug of ale.

Marta's movement seemed to have broken the trance that had kept the Black Bloods frozen.

Nessa left the people she'd been whispering to and sat on a bench, still openly glaring at me.

The line for ale shifted as Neil began filling mugs.

Case lured someone up from the benches to dance with him to the fiddlers' new song.

Marta cut across the clearing, looking up at the trees rather than at Liam and me.

"Is she going to hate me now?" I whispered. A sliver dug into my joy.

"It's not you she's angry with." Liam tucked my hair behind my ear.

Marta stormed past us and up the path to the tents.

I froze for a moment, trying to decide if I should run after her. I'd lost too many people I cared for. Most, there was no chance I could ever get back. I didn't want to ruin what I had with Marta if I had a chance of salvaging even an ounce of our friendship.

"I have to go." I brushed my lips against Liam's cheek.

"It's best to let her be," Liam said. "There's nothing you can say to—"

"I've at least got to try."

"Let me go." Liam held tight to my hand.

"Stay here. Be King of the birds. I'll be right back." I stood up and followed Marta, careful not to glance back to the Black Bloods who still stared at me.

10

I didn't allow myself to run after Marta until I'd gotten most of the way down the path to the tents.

Honestly, if her hair hadn't been so pale it seemed to reflect starlight, I wouldn't have been able to find her.

"Marta," I called softly once I was close enough I knew she could hear.

She didn't pause.

"Marta." I ran faster, sprinting to her side. "Could you just stop for a moment?"

She kept striding forward like I didn't exist.

"Marta, I'm sorry." I caught her arm and spun her around. "Please, let me explain."

Marta stepped away and took a drink from her mug.

"I never wanted to hurt you," I said. "You are my friend, and I hope you can forgive me—"

"Forgive you for what? For running out of camp and letting us all think you were dead? Did you even consider the people you were leaving behind when you went stomping off into Ilbrea trying to save the chivving world?"

"I had to help those children." I reached for Marta's hand. She backed farther away. "Have you seen what Cinni can do? What all four of them can do? Can you imagine what the Sorcerers Guild would have made of them?"

"Of course I know what they can do." Marta gave a cold laugh. "I, unlike some people, honor the oaths I have taken."

"I did honor my oath." My side stung as though my mark had come to life just by my thinking of it. "Liam gave me his blessing—"

"Don't you even mention that dishonorable slitch to me." Marta turned away, but I caught her arm again.

"Who are you talking about?"

"We're all here to help him in his chivving cause," Marta shouted. "People have died because they believed in him. People risk their lives for him every day. And he can't keep one chivving vow."

"What vow?" Everything around me went cold.

Marta stared over my shoulder.

I spun around to find Liam standing in the shadows.

"Marta," Liam said, "please don't do this."

"Is that an order, Trueborn?" Marta spat.

Liam didn't say anything.

"Gods, you're worthless." Marta turned and strode farther into the trees.

"Marta," I called after her.

"Ena—"

I didn't wait to listen to Liam. I tore through the darkness after Marta. I wished I had a lae stone. I wished I weren't chasing my friend through the woods. I wished I were still sitting by Liam in his uncomfortable, carved chair.

I slowed my steps as I reached Marta's side.

"Marta." My voice came out wrong, like grief and rage had already taken me. "What vow did he break?"

She didn't answer.

"Please." I dodged in front of her and blocked her path. "We're friends. At least I thought we were."

She stopped moving but didn't look at me.

"I knew…" Self-loathing curdled in my stomach. "I knew you were fond of Liam. But I didn't know you'd made any sort of promise to each other. I would've stayed away from him."

"I've heard enough lies without needing any from you," Marta said.

A pain stabbed at my chest right below where my stone pendant lay. "I'm sorry, I truly am, for whatever part I've had in his breaking whatever vow he gave you."

"The vow wasn't to me." A tear rolled down Marta's cheek. "That doesn't mean I have to forgive him."

She stepped around me and walked off into the shadows.

I couldn't follow her. I wanted to, but a horrible sickness rolled through my entire being, and I wasn't sure if I could breathe without being ill.

"Ena."

I'd felt many things at hearing Liam's voice before. Revulsion had never been one of them.

"I want the truth." I swallowed the sour in my throat. "All of it. Right now."

"Not all of it is mine to tell." Liam stopped right behind my shoulder. I could feel the heat coming off his body.

"All of it." The words tasted foul as I repeated them. "Right now."

"Your brother saved my life."

"I know that."

"I should have died in Nantic. I very nearly did. Emmet killed three men saving me, then hauled me up the mountain. I couldn't have asked that much from a member of my own clan. When I was finally able to do more than babble that we needed to keep climbing, I asked him to join us, and asked what I could offer in exchange for my life."

I dug my nails into my palms, trying to push down the pain that flared in my chest.

"He only wanted one thing in exchange for saving me. He wanted you kept safe. I vowed that I would protect you."

"But you have," I said. "You saved me in Harane."

"And led you through the mountains and brought you to Frason's Glenn and the Brien enclave, and let you go the Lir Valley. And now I've led you into a trueborn's bed. I've told you, you're safer far away from me."

"But it's my life." A tingle of feeling returned to my fingers. "I can make my own choices without my brother's interference. Whose bed I sleep in should definitely have nothing to do with his chivving opinion of where I'm safe."

"I know." Liam took a step closer to me. "And I mean to keep my vow to Emmet. I will protect you. I will keep you safe."

"But that doesn't make sense. If it's just Emmet thinking he knows what's best for me, why is Marta so fussed?" I looked through the trees to where she'd disappeared. "I'm sure he'll rage enough to scare the whole camp when he gets back, but what's that got to do with Marta?"

"She worries when he's gone," Liam said. "And from the way he tore out of camp, I'm not sure how much of Ilbrea he'll burn searching for you."

"Emmet." I said my brother's name like it would somehow make all the pieces of the shadowy mess fit together. "Marta's worried about Emmet. She's not angry because she's in love with you and I hopped into your bed." I clapped my hands over my mouth, muffling my gasp. "No."

Liam said nothing.

"You can't actually mean that Marta's in love with my brother? That sweet woman is in love with my demon of a brother?"

A wrinkle formed on Liam's brow. "Her secrets aren't for me to tell."

"Oh, chivving gods and stars." I took Liam's face in my hands. "They're actually together, aren't they? Is he in love with her? Does everyone in the chivving camp know but me?"

"I have no idea. I stay out of that sort of chatter."

"I thought she was in love with you. I've thought it from the beginning."

He placed his hands on my waist, as though testing to see if I'd want him near me.

I laid my cheek on his chest. "Does she blame you for Emmet going out to find me?"

"She blames me for letting you go to the Lir Valley. She nigh on murdered me when she found out you'd gone. But I am going to keep you safe." Liam pressed his lips to the top of my head. "I would never do anything to harm you, and that includes keeping secrets."

"My brother and Marta is a fairly big secret." I tipped my chin up to look into his eyes.

"It's not my secret."

"You could have told me you'd made some vow to Emmet." A horrible knot wrapped around my stomach. "I always thought you didn't want me. I thought I was a fool for fawning over you."

Liam leaned down and brushed his lips against mine. "You are the bravest, strongest, most incredible woman I've ever met." He kissed me, and his taste filled me. "You are everything I want. I would burn the sky to protect you, Ena Ryeland."

I laced my fingers through his hair and let my body meld against his.

His heartbeat pounded through my chest as I kissed him. Fear and worry drifted away, and there was nothing in the world but Liam and me.

I wished the stars would shine brighter so I could see the ridges of his bare chest. I wished time would stop and I could spend the rest of eternity with my body twined around his.

Embers seared my skin as he kissed every inch of me. Pulsing heat swallowed everything I was, until there could be nothing in existence but Liam. The wanting in my chest burned bright as I wrapped myself around him, and I knew I would crave him for the rest of my life.

We were a beautiful tangle. A mass of limbs and sweat and pleasure so brilliantly sweet I forgot we were in the middle of the forest until it was time to go back to his tent, and I had to spend ten minutes searching for my boot.

He held me close to his side as we crept back to camp, softly laughing as he picked moss and twigs out of my hair.

I slept in his arms again that night, feeling truly safe for the first time since I was a child and had been too naïve to know how cruel the world can be.

When I left his tent in the morning, a little glass bottle waited right outside.

I took my time combing my hair in my tent, making sure not a single trace of tree bark or moss had been left behind from the night before. Heat rushed to my cheeks as I remembered him touching me. I could hear him moving in his tent. I wondered how soon I would be able to convince him to sneak back into the woods with me.

When I was certain I looked as respectable as anyone who lived in a tent could, I stepped out into the morning light.

Liam stepped out of his tent a moment later. "Good morning, Ena." A twinkle of a smile lit his eyes. "Are you hoping for some breakfast from Neil?"

"I am, actually. I woke up very hungry this morning."

Liam's smile curved one side of his mouth. His lips were beautiful.

By the gods, I wanted nothing more than to kiss him.

"Shall we?" Liam placed a hand on the back of my waist.

The pressure of his hand against my back shot sparkling joy through my whole being. I tried not to grin like a fool as we joined the line waiting for gruel from Neil. The strange scent coming from the cook pot did not dampen my joy, though it did seem to leave the other breakfast seekers in a foul mood.

"Perhaps I should go foraging today," I whispered. "I might be able to find something to make the food a bit more palatable."

"You can't leave the boundary." Liam spoke so softly, I had to lean closer to him to hear. I didn't mind it. "If you can find something inside, then everyone will thank you for it, but don't go past the boulders."

"Why not?" I turned to face Liam, letting the back of my hand graze against his fingers. A thrill shot up my arm.

"It's not safe."

"The monster is dead," I said. "You killed it."

"That doesn't make us any safer."

The perfect warmth that had surrounded me drifted away.

"The traitor." It felt like the whole camp was staring at me again as I whispered the words. "Emmet told me someone had betrayed us. Did you find out who?"

Liam kissed my forehead. "Not now."

"Do you want food or not?" Neil banged his ladle against the side of the cook pot.

"Food, please." I pried myself away from Liam and gave a smile to Neil. "I was thinking I might prowl through the woods a bit today. See if I can find something interesting to bring to the kitchen tent. I can come and help fix dinner."

"No." Neil shoved a wooden bowl at me. "I'll take whatever you find foraging, but the last thing I need is one more bored Black Blood crowding into my kitchen tent like they think they're going to help me do my job. I've been feeding this camp since before Liam was allowed a sharpened sword, and I know chivving well how to chop a root. I don't need more warriors interfering like slicing vegetables is the same as cutting a man's throat."

"Right." I stepped away and let Liam claim his food. "I'll just drop some things off then."

"Thank you for working so hard to keep us all fed." Liam gave Neil a little bow.

"What's Neil so fussed over?" I asked once we'd retreated with our bowls of slop.

Liam glanced around, giving a few nods to people we passed before answering. "I've banned everyone but the hunting party from leaving camp."

"Why?"

"I don't know how else to keep everyone safe," Liam said. "Someone's betrayed us. I'd like to believe it's not someone in this camp, but I have no way to prove it. The monster's dead, but that doesn't make the forest any less dangerous."

"Why not?" I stopped. "Is the traitor lurking in the woods?"

"Keep walking." Liam led me into the trees, in the same direction we'd traveled the night before.

Heat rose to my cheeks just remembering the taste of his skin.

"You said you wanted the truth from me." Liam stopped once there were no other people in view.

"I do." I leaned against a tree and took a bite of my slop. The goo didn't taste much like food.

"Do you want me to tell you things even if knowing will do nothing but make you worry?" Wrinkles creased Liam's brow.

I set my bowl down and took his face in my hands, tipping his head so I could kiss the wrinkles on his forehead. "You shouldn't worry and stew alone. Besides, I have been known to help once in a while."

Liam stepped away from me and began pacing between two trees.

"The beast was a croilach," Liam said after his third pass.

"I don't have any idea what that is." I picked up my bowl and kept eating my slop, grateful to have something to occupy my hands.

"A stone monster," Liam said.

"It didn't look like stone when it tried to eat me."

"The flesh of the beast was real," Liam said. "Stolen from other animals and molded into one foul being."

"That's disgusting." My stomach rolled, threatening to toss up my breakfast.

"The croilach are animated by a stone heart."

"A what?"

"A stone is filled with magic and then placed in the creature's chest. The croilach then lives to do its master's bidding."

"Someone made that thing and sent it after our camp?" Rage burned through me. "That monster killed three of our people. Who sent it? The Sorcerers Guild? Do they know where our camp is?"

"Creating a croilach requires stone magic." Liam dug his fingers into his hair. "Only a trueborn could create such a creature."

The anger in my stomach turned from a raging fire to a deadly cold beast. The power of that awful hatred filled me.

"A Black Blood sent that monster to slaughter us?" My voice came out calm. "Was it Regan? Are the Brien that determined to stop us from helping the sorcis?"

"I don't know who it was," Liam said. "I sent word to Lygan Hall. Orla is on a war path, but she hasn't offered me any information beyond forbidding me from leaving the boundaries of the camp."

"Why would she do that?" I looked toward the eastern boundary of our sanctuary, waiting for an army of monsters to come charging up to attack.

"If I die, the boundary falls. The camp would be vulnerable."

My hands trembled too badly for me to hold my bowl. I set it back down before the urge to smash it broke through my reason.

"Is the trueborn who made the croilach the same chivving Black Blood who betrayed us?" My voice shook.

"I don't know."

"Could the trueborn send another beast?"

Liam reached into his pocket and pulled out a black stone.

The thing wasn't even as large as his fist. A crack split through the center, but other than that, there was no hint that the rock was anything other than an ordinary bit of the mountains' stone.

"Some parts of stone magic come easily to a trueborn. Others take something out of you, like they're tiring your soul. Creating a stone heart for a croilach is exhausting. I've heard stories of trueborn dying in the attempt. But if whoever made the monster wants to damage the Duweads badly enough to risk an unprovoked attack in our own territory—"

"Then who knows how far they would be willing to go to hurt us?" I reached out and touched the rock. "You'd think I would have noticed the beast had been magically made. It looked like a monster, but I never would have imagined that a person had created it. Even in the daylight—"

"You saw the croilach in the daylight?" Liam moved the stone heart away from me.

"The second time it came after Finn and me. The monster nearly clawed me in half when we left for the Lir Valley."

He slipped the stone back into his pocket and wrapped his arms around me, holding me close to his chest. His breath shook in his lungs.

"I'm fine." I kissed the side of his neck. "The mountain saved our lives. We ended up in a chivving awful tunnel and had to crawl for hours. I gained some nasty bruises, but that's all."

"I should have gone with you." Liam pressed his lips to the top of my head.

"You had a croilach to slay. Didn't Finn mention we'd seen the monster again when he brought the children here?"

"It was all chaos." Liam held me tighter. "He only stayed in camp for an hour. He probably didn't even think of it."

"He's still out there." I stepped away from Liam. "Finn and

Emmet and Cati are all out there looking for me. What if a new monster is sent after you and attacks them before they can reach the camp?"

"There are animals roaming near our boundary again. I don't think they'd be here if there was another monster in our woods."

"But you can't be sure." It was my turn to pace between the trees. "We have to find a way to tell them I'm back. We have to bring them home."

"I don't even know where they might be. Finn and Cati were going to retrace his steps to where you'd been lost, but if they'd stopped there, they should have been back by now."

"Then I'll go after them."

"And if they're not sitting in the woods waiting to be found? The mountains are too vast for us to hope to find them." Liam stepped into my path. "Emmet was going to head for Ilara, but there's no way to know where between here and there he might be."

"Then send one of your stone birds. Have the bird bring them a message."

"I can't. It doesn't work that way."

"Why not?"

"I've got to know where the person I'm sending the message to is." Liam looked toward the treetops. "If one of them were a trueborn, I could send a bird without telling the thing where to go. Even Orla's trackers in Ilbrea can send the stone birds she's given them straight to me. The birds can sense my magic wherever I am. But for me to send a bird to a normal person, even sending the bird straight to Ilara wouldn't work. I've got to know a clear destination I want the bird to reach."

I scrubbed my hands over my face. "So we're just supposed to sit here and hope they come back?"

"There's not much else we can do." He laid his hands on my shoulders. "Emmet, Finn, and Cati are some of the best fighters I've ever known. They can make it back."

I let my forehead rest against his chest. "How did you manage to kill the croilach?"

"I ripped the stone heart from the monster's chest."

I did not want Liam to keep any secrets from me. I was glad I knew an enemy had sent the monster to torment our camp. Being grateful for the knowledge did not diminish the ice-cold rage that filled me.

I wanted to kill the trueborn who had attacked the people I cared for. I wanted to drive a knife into their flesh. I wanted to watch them bleed.

I had killed before, but I had never felt the desire to murder.

After Liam and I spoke in the woods, he had to make his rounds of the camp, checking on all his people, making sure the villain who had tried to destroy us did not seize another from our pack.

I took my bag from my tent and foraged through the confines of camp, choosing the steepest slopes to scramble up and climbing a few trees to try and burn some of the raging energy out of my limbs.

It didn't work.

I dumped my bounty onto Neil's table and went straight to the training ground.

Case was there, fighting with the others. It didn't take much to convince him to give me another lesson.

Working with the sword didn't ease my anger, but it gave me a place to aim the rage, which was better than stomping through the woods trying not to scream my fury to the gods.

"Again." Case prowled around the ring, holding his sword in one hand as though its weight were nothing to him.

I nodded. My arms throbbed in protest as I hoisted my own sword. I tracked Case's movement, waiting for him to come charging at me.

He just kept sauntering around the chivving ring like he hadn't a care in the world.

I tightened my grip on the hilt of my weapon.

"Don't clutch your sword like that," Case said. "You'll wear your hands out before your enemy even gets a blow in."

I forced my hands to relax a bit as he kept circling.

His blade glinted in the morning light. Knowing the edges had been dulled did not diminish the deadly look of his weapon.

Case didn't seem to think there was anything treacherous or dangerous in the world. He barely had a hair out of place after he'd spent the whole morning fighting.

"Are you going to attack me?" I asked. "Or would you rather we go on a nice afternoon stroll?"

"You've got to learn patience." Case twirled his sword through the air.

I tensed at the sudden movement, but he didn't approach. He just kept moving in a slow circle around the ring.

"An anxious warrior will attack too soon," Case said, "go charging against their enemy before the time is right. If you want to win a battle, you've got to learn to wait for the right moment."

"Are you going to wait for me to fall asleep?" I lowered my weapon. "Should I just meet you back here in the morning?"

Case smiled. "You can come back and fight me again tomorrow if you like. Nothing else to do in the camp anyway."

Anger burned through me again. There was nothing for us to do in the camp. Nothing of use at any rate.

Out in Ilbrea, there were sorcis who needed our help. People I loved who could be in danger or even dead, and I couldn't get to them. The world needed us, and we were trapped inside a spell, waiting to see if another monster would come to terrorize us.

The sun flashing off Case's sword was the only warning I had.

I dodged to the side as I swung my sword up, parrying the blow.

Case brought his blade around in a wide arc, aiming for my neck.

I ducked low and sliced my own sword for the back of his legs as I dodged behind him.

The edge of my sword grazed the back of his calf.

"Good job, Ena!"

I glanced toward the high-pitched voice.

A blow to the shoulder sent me staggering forward.

I let the momentum knock me to the ground, using Case's own strength to send me rolling back up to my feet.

A round of cheers came after that.

I spun toward Case in time to parry a blow aimed for my other shoulder, but he used my own trick against me, and let the hit I'd given his blade carry his sword back around to knock me off my feet.

I landed on my back with a grunt.

"It was better before!" the high voice called.

"Thanks." I pushed myself up to my forearms, trying to ignore the throbbing ache in my spine.

Evie ran across the ring toward me. Gwen, Cinni, and Dorran followed close behind.

"I didn't know you could fight with a sword." Evie stood over me.

"I can't," I said.

"You're getting better all the time." Case lifted my sword out of the dirt.

"If that had been a real sword, you would be dead," Dorran said.

"That's why they used dulled swords," Gwen said, "so they can be safe while they practice. Isn't that right, Cinni?"

Cinni had two bundles of fabric tied over her ears, but she nodded at her sister's words just the same.

"I've asked to learn to fight with a sword." Evie took my hand, yanking on my arm for me to stand. "But every time I ask, Marta says no."

"With very good reason." Marta strode up behind the children. "All of you are too young."

"That's not what Neil said." Evie wrinkled her forehead. "Neil said the woman Cati learned to fight when she was even younger than I am now. I'm already behind. I should learn to use a sword."

"Not here, Evie." I brushed the dirt off my skirt.

"Why?" Evie asked.

"Because you are too special to be taught to fight here." I bent down to look straight into her eyes. "You see, Case and I don't have magic like you. You need to learn from someone as special as you are."

"She's trying to say we're frightening enough without teaching us to stab people." Dorran glared at me.

"You think we're frightening?" Evie bit her lips together.

All four of the children stared at me with their matching, dark brown eyes.

"Of course she doesn't," Marta said. "None of us do."

"That's a lie," Dorran said. "You're all afraid."

Cinni flinched.

"You're right," I said. "I am very afraid, but not of you. Not because of anything you've done."

Gwen stepped closer to Cinni.

"What I'm afraid of is failing you." I knelt in front of Dorran.

"I don't know how your magic is meant to work, let alone how to help you control it. Finn and I came to fetch you so you could be safe—and you are safe here in camp—but you've got to be patient and wait until we get to Lygan Hall where someone with magic of their own can teach you how to control yours. In the meantime, we'll just have to be grateful that you're all safe and together."

"That is a wonderful thing to be grateful for." Gwen squeezed Cinni's hand. "Aren't you glad we're all together, Cinni?"

I couldn't tell if Cinni had heard.

"We should let them get on with their practicing," Marta said. "We can't distract people from their work."

"It's all right," I said a bit too quickly. "I don't think I can do much more if I want to be able to walk tomorrow."

"Really, we shouldn't—"

"I'll go with you," I cut across Marta. "What are you up to this afternoon?"

Marta's jaw tensed for a moment before she managed to speak. "I was going to take the children to the clearing, let them play for a while before dinner."

"Perfect." I pressed my face into a careful smile. "I'd love to come with you. Hear how the children have been enjoying the camp."

"Well"—Evie took my hand and began leading me toward the clearing—"it was rather awful at first, what with everyone thinking you were dead. And it's still a bit boring since we're not allowed to go past the big stones, which is very sad since there's so much mountain we could explore."

"I would be happy to never see the mountains again," Dorran said.

"But there are some nice things about camp," Evie said. "Neil is very kind and very funny. Sometimes Marta is nice and tells us stories. But the best part is the bath. Have you taken a bath here?"

A much more genuine smile touched my lips. "I have taken a bath here."

"Isn't it the best thing you've ever seen?" Evie bounced as she walked. "In the miners' houses, a bath meant shivering in a tub of chilly water, but here the water is warm and deep enough to swim in."

"The bath is lovely," Gwen said.

"You are all going to be in for a real treat when we get to Lygan Hall," Marta said.

Evie stopped dead in her tracks and rounded on Marta. "That's not for forever. It's still summer, and you said we have to stay here until it snows."

"Well, yes," Marta said, "you are going to have to be patient. But once you get there, you'll see that Lygan Hall is worth all the waiting in the world."

"We can be patient, Evie," Gwen said. "We're very grateful to be here, and we'll be very happy to be there."

"Yes," Evie sighed. "Very, very grateful to be waiting for months."

She let go of my hand and charged through the trees toward the clearing as though the wind were carrying her.

"Evie, do not get so far ahead." Gwen ran after Evie, still firmly clutching Cinni's hand.

"I'm getting so tired of running," Dorran grumbled before taking off after them, leaving Marta and me alone.

We stood silently for a long moment.

"You should go back to the training field," Marta said. "I can manage the children on my own."

"I'm sure you can," I said. "Honestly, Gwen takes such good care of the others, they'd be fine without any of us."

"Gwen is practically a child herself. She shouldn't have the responsibility of raising three young sorcis tossed onto her shoulders."

"I didn't say she should."

I looked to Marta.

She didn't look back at me. Her gaze stayed fixed on the trees where the children had disappeared. I hadn't had the chance to properly look at her in the daylight since I'd been back in the camp.

Her face had lost a bit of its cheerful roundness, and her once porcelain complexion had been tinged with gray. Faint purple marked the skin under her eyes.

"Marta, if you need a break from watching them—"

"I can take care of four children."

"Right." I bit the insides of my cheeks. "Are..." I let out a long breath, trying to reason through what might make things better or worse. "Are you not sleeping with Emmet gone?"

A blaze of anger passed behind Marta's eyes.

"Liam didn't tell me," I said. "But there were only so many explanations for why you'd be so angry about Liam and me."

"He made a promise." Marta's jaw tensed. I missed the dimples I'd become so accustomed to.

"I know." I stepped in front of Marta.

She stared right through me.

"I'm the only relative Emmet has," I said. "It's just him and me in the world. I won't claim to know my brother. You've spent more time with him than I have if you don't count when we were children."

Marta shifted her gaze up to the sky.

"But I do know that no matter how many times I thought I might never see him again, he always came back." I took Marta's hand. "Even when I didn't want him to. Emmet's always come back."

"If you think I'm angry with Liam, it will be nothing compared to Emmet's wrath."

"I'm sure you're right." I squeezed Marta's hand. "But I'm not afraid of my brother, and I do have a right to live my own life."

"I don't think he could survive losing you. Wanting you to be safe is the only thing that's kept him going for so long. He'd be lost without that."

The knot came back, pressing against the front of my throat.

"I can't live in a cage. I won't let him stand between Liam and me. And when he decides to rage over my being a grown woman, I'll remind him that I was born with same blood as him. I am capable of wrath just as terrible as my brother's."

"Gods, the two of you together could burn the world." Marta gave a shaky laugh. "I'm not sure if it would be glorious or terrifying."

"I think that depends on who we Ryelands unleash our wrath upon. Get us riled enough, and maybe we'll march on the King."

"Just promise me you'll stay safe." Marta wrapped her arms around my neck, pulling me into a tight hug. "For Emmet's sake as well as mine. I was so afraid we'd lost you."

I held Marta close. I couldn't bring myself to lie and promise I would hide from danger.

13

Time does not always march along in a logical way. She surges forward, then slows and stops.

Being trapped in the camp was better than being locked under the mountain. Even if I had been all alone, having the sun to tell me the time of day would have been glorious enough to offer me a bit more sanity than the mountain ever granted.

Having Liam beside me was worth more than the sunlight. Sneaking to the far corners of the camp to revel in the wonders of his skin against mine gave me something other than worry and rage to fill my days. Spending my nights wrapped in his arms brought peace to my dreams that was better than pure blackness.

For three weeks, I woke up in Liam's arms every morning. There was a perfect beauty to huddling in the warmth of his bed for a few moments before the world demanded our presence. Even if the only bit of the world we had access to was contained within the boundary of the camp.

The Black Bloods became more restless. My worry and anger grew. But at least I could lose myself in Liam's arms. I should have been more grateful for the rest, for the quiet. For the hours spent hiding away with Liam.

I was not wise enough to understand that the peace was not a punishment.

Perhaps that's why time decided to speed up as though the gods themselves had declared we should be tested again. They pushed the boulder of our fate down the mountain, and none of us were strong enough to stop the fall.

14

I sat by Liam's side in his wooden chair, basking in the light of the midday sun. He'd taken to eating his meals in the clearing where the others could see him. I don't know if he wanted to keep an eye on the Black Bloods to be sure they were staying sane while trapped in the camp, or if he wanted them to see him eating Neil's slop without complaint.

His reasoning didn't matter much to me. At every meal, he'd place his hand on the back of my waist and offer me half of his seat. Taking my place beside him brought me enough joy that I didn't mind the foul food, and getting to be near him soothed the edges of my anxious anger enough to actually allow me to eat.

"I'm going to have to send the hunters out again soon." Liam took another bite of his root stew.

I stared down into my own bowl. I hadn't noticed the lack of meat. I'd been too busy enjoying the warmth of Liam's leg pressed against mine.

"We can survive without meat," I said.

"Marta's worried about our stores." Liam watched the Black Bloods in the food line. "If we go without meat, we'll run through everything else too quickly. Then we'd have to make a run into Ilbrea for supplies or risk having to go back to Lygan Hall early."

"I can spend some more time foraging. People may not like eating what I find, but the camp is large enough, we should be able to get by on the plants within the boundary. At least for a bit."

"It's not something they prepared me for." Liam set his bowl aside. "They trained me in combat. They trained me in stone magic. They taught enough about the evils of the paun to be sure I would fight them with everything I have. None of them ever bothered to tell me how hard leading a camp full of trapped people eating awful food would be."

"That's what you have Marta for." I laid my hand on Liam's leg. A burst of joy shook my chest at being allowed to give such a gesture of affection in full view of everyone.

"We'd be doomed without her." Liam placed his hand on top of mine.

"Liam!" A shout carried through the trees. "Liam!"

He was on his feet before his name had been called the second time.

I followed him as he raced east.

"Liam!"

Dread slithered through my veins.

"Ena!"

As the voice shouted my name, fear locked around my heart. My steps faltered as I looked over my shoulder toward the tents hidden behind the trees. If my name was being shouted, it had to be because someone was hurt.

But Liam was still running forward, and whatever disaster had come, I needed to be by his side to greet it.

"Liam!" Sal raced through the trees. He stopped in front of us, gasping for breath.

"What?" Liam took Sal's shoulders. "What's wrong?"

Sal brushed his sandy blond hair away from his face. "They're back." He gasped for air between phrases. "Looking fit to murder. I'm not dealing with it."

I took off running up the path Sal had traveled down, not slowing my pace as two people stepped into view.

Filthy and worn, there was no mistaking Finn and Cati as they strode through the trees.

A bit of my horrible worry drifted away as Finn smiled through the red beard that had taken over his chin.

"All that, and she's already here," Cati said.

I reached Finn first and dove at him, nearly tackling him to the ground as I hugged him.

"Thank the gods you're safe," I said.

"You were worried I wasn't safe?" Finn held me tight. "You ran off toward a pack of chivving soldiers."

"I had to get them—"

"And then you chivving well disappear!" Finn stepped away as he began shouting. "Do you have any idea the mess you left me in? No? Well, how could you since you went charging away without me?"

"You had to stay with the children. You had to bring them—"

"You don't get to make decisions like that," Finn said. "You don't get to decide to sacrifice your chivving life and leave me standing in the shadows without you. What under the godsforsaken stars did you expect me to do?"

"Get the children here safely, which you—"

"I've spent a month looking for you!" Birds scattered as Finn's voice pounded through the treetops. "We massacred a chivving soldiers' unit trying to find out if you'd been captured. All they would say is that you'd slipped away from them. But did you know there are soldiers along the western edge of the woods now? Whole units scouring the forest. Do you know how far south we had to lead them to make sure they didn't catch wind of our camp?"

"Finn, I'm sorry."

He gathered me back into his arms like he was afraid I might disappear again. "If you ever pull a stunt like that again, I'll chivving well kill you myself."

"That sounds fair." I held Finn tight. "Thank you for looking for me."

"Thanks for saving me, I suppose." Finn kissed my forehead. "But that doesn't mean I forgive you. I'm going to have a chivving chip on my shoulder for quite a while over this."

"I don't blame you," Cati said.

I stepped away from Finn and took both of Cati's hands in mine. "Thank you for searching for me."

"It wasn't all bad, aside from worrying that you were being tortured for information by the Guilds, of course. I finally got to stab some paun soldiers." Cati winked at me. "That made for a nice change."

The sound of running footsteps carried through the trees behind us.

Marta sprinted into view. She stopped for a moment, looking at our little group, before smiling. The expression was not large enough to display her dimples.

"I'm so glad the two of you are back," Marta said. "You were gone so long, we were worried something had happened."

"A flock of soldiers roaming through the woods happened." Cati let go of my hands and looked to Liam. "And not just the usual few prowling the outskirts. They weren't searching for tilk daring enough to brave the mountains for a hope of escaping the Guilds. They're looking for something, and I'm willing to bet, whether they know it or not, we're what they're after."

Liam scrubbed his hands over his face.

"We left a trail for them leading south," Finn said. "Might've led them straight into Brien territory. By accident, of course. It's so hard to tell when it's all just trees and mountains."

"What sort of a trail did you leave?" I asked, foolishly picturing a path of shining black stone.

"That kind that involves lots of dead bodies," Cati said. "Unfortunately, none of the soldiers I had time to chat with knew why they'd gotten orders to search the mountains."

"Best we could get out of any of the sniveling messes was that bandits were roaming the woods," Finn said. "Evil types who kidnap children."

Sour rose in my throat. "Those monsters are the ones who lock children away. We help them. We protect the sorcis from the Sorcerers Guild."

"That's not a very good line to feed soldiers who are terrified of the forest," Finn said. "But saving sweet littlelings from kidnapping bandits—that'll steel a man's nerves."

"How?" Liam said. "How did they find out where we've been taking the children?"

"I don't know," Cati said. "But I've come up with a few new knife tricks I'm eager to show the bastard who's feeding the paun information about us."

"We need to start questioning the people in camp." Marta held up a finger to stop Liam from interrupting. "I hate the idea of doubting our own people as much as you do, but we've got to rule out the possibility of it being one of our own before we start tearing through Orla's trackers or accusing the Brien."

"And how do you suggest we accuse our own people of betrayal and murder?" Cati said. "I'm pretty good at questioning, but I don't think anyone would forgive me afterwards."

"You might have to live with people not liking you," Finn said.

"We send for a sorcerer of our own," Liam said.

Cati, Finn, and Marta all froze.

"Would that be a bad thing?" I asked.

"Asking for Orla's aid is never the best idea," Finn said. "Asking for one of Orla's sorcerers to travel this far west—"

"If the traitor is in this camp, we can't risk them doing more damage than they've already managed," Liam said. "I lost three people because I didn't act decisively when the croilach came. I won't make that mistake again. I don't care what Orla wants in return for her aid."

I took Liam's hand, lacing my fingers through his as though Orla might swoop down from the sky to snatch him away from me.

Cati looked from me to Liam. "At least that got settled while we were gone. I don't think I could have stood you two dancing around each other much longer."

Heat burned from my neck up into my cheeks.

"Can we eat?" Finn said. "I've been half-starved for five weeks."

"Sure." I slipped my hand out of Liam's, still a little convinced my face had actually caught fire. "I won't lie and tell you it'll be decent food, but at least your stomach will be full."

"Good." Finn started down the path. "It's nice to know some things haven't changed while I was gone."

"My adoration of you hasn't changed." I looped my arm through Finn's. "Though I will warn you, Case has been training me with a sword, and I am improving."

"I'll be the judge of that," Cati said.

"He's all right then?" Finn's shoulders relaxed.

"Going a bit mad without you," I said. "But other than that, he's just fine. We're only waiting on Emmet to get back from raiding Ilara, and we'll all be safe and hiding in camp together."

"About Emmet." Finn glanced to Cati.

"What?" Marta said. "Did you see him?"

"No." Cati studied the hilt of the knife tucked into her belt.

"We did hear a rumor of a demon from the mountains who'd set fire to a caravan of soldiers," Finn said. "And another about a scribe's shop catching fire. Seems a beast of a man is working his way north toward Ilara, just sensibly burning his way through every paun he can find."

I was amazed my feet were still carrying me forward when my mind seemed to have shuddered to a stop.

"How far north did the demon get in the rumors?" Liam asked.

"Last I heard," Finn said, "they'd added guards to the gates of Ilara to keep the demon out."

"So he's not late in returning then," Marta said, "just got a bit distracted by vengeance."

"One of the soldiers we caught begged me not to burn him," Finn said. "Emmet is definitely leaving an impression."

"Should I feel guilty?" I asked. "He's on a rampage because of me."

"No." Finn kissed the back of my hand. His beard tickled my fingers. "I only wish I could have caught up with him to join in on the fun."

The kitchen tent came into view.

Neil caught sight of Finn and sighed.

Patrick shouted a greeting, and then it seemed like the entire camp had surged toward us to greet Finn and Cati.

Finn didn't let go of me until Case shoved his way through the crowd to reach him. Tears streamed down Case's cheeks as he held Finn in his arms.

I backed out of the pack of people, letting the Black Bloods greet their fellows, wondering if they would ever really consider me to be one of their own.

"We should celebrate tonight." Marta stood at the outskirts of the crowd. A line creased her forehead even as she smiled at the Black Bloods' joy.

"You don't have to pretend you're not worried," I said.

"I'm not worried."

"Liar."

"At least not the way you mean." Marta let out a shaky breath. "I love him, you know. I have for two years now. I know he's got to fight. I know he could never be happy stepping back from the battle while the Guilds are still hurting people."

"But?"

"I worry he'll enjoy fighting so much, he'll forget to come home. But that's just me being silly." Marta flapped a hand through the air. "He'll have to come back here in order to find out if you're safe. He'll come back to make sure you're safe."

"Marta—"

"I think we should pull out the ale early tonight. A bit of fun will do everyone some good." She strode away before I could say anything else.

15

By the time the sun had set, the camp had already spent a few good hours in the clearing. The fiddlers had moved from dancing tunes to tavern songs and back again, while Neil produced a new barrel of ale from wherever he and Marta stashed the stuff. No one seemed to care how foul dinner was as they chatted and laughed and sang.

Even the children got in on the fun. Evie pranced through the couples, making up a dance all her own. Dorran seemed keen to speak to the men who frequented the training ground, though I couldn't imagine the child having much interest in going through the pain required to learn to fight.

Cinni stood on a bench opposite the fiddlers, staring at them as they played. She had the two bundles of fabric tied over her ears, but she looked as close to happy as I'd ever seen her. Gwen sat at Cinni's feet, beaming as she watched her sister enjoying the music.

I stayed close to Liam's side as he made his way through the crowd, chatting with each of his people as I'd never seen him do before. He didn't ask them anything important. Still, I couldn't help but wonder if he was searching for the traitor.

I watched the eyes of the people he spoke to, trying to spot a murderer lurking behind the faces of the people I'd known for months. I didn't want to distrust any of the Black Bloods. Even wondering if someone as dreadful as gossipy Nessa had been the one responsible for all the pain we'd been through made me ill. I hated the girl, but I couldn't think that she'd had a hand in Pierce's death, even if she had whispered to the entire camp about him and me running into the woods together.

"Ena will enjoy it." Winnie's high voice broke through my thoughts.

I looked down to where Winnie sat on a bench, trying to reason through what I could be meant to enjoy.

The healer smiled, deepening the wrinkles on her face.

"I think the healers' garden in Lygan Hall is beautiful," Liam said. "And I've never known what most of the plants are meant to do."

"I'm very excited to see it," I said.

"You could do with some more training," Winnie said. "You've the makings of a fine healer, but you've some things yet to learn."

"Right," I said. "I'm sure I do."

"We should check on Neil," Liam said. "Make sure he's not being stampeded at the barrel."

"Some folks get too eager when they celebrate." Winnie held up her own mug and winked. "We should start taking bets on how many come crawling to me in the morning."

I laughed as Liam led me away.

"She means well." Liam spoke as softly as he could over the music and chatter.

"I know," I said. "But I never asked to be a healer. I've never wanted anyone's life in my hands."

"Then don't let Winnie train you." Liam touched the back of my waist, guiding me toward Neil.

"But what if I don't let her train me and then something horrible happens and I don't know enough to help?"

Liam stepped in front of me and took my face in his hands. "It is not your duty to save everyone in the world."

"That's a bit rich coming from you."

Liam smiled and kissed me. I swear the trees began to spin around us as his thumb grazed the side of my neck.

A flutter of murmurs changed the tone of the chatter as the fiddlers stopped playing.

I blushed and stepped away from Liam, but the people in the clearing weren't staring at us. They were looking to the upper edge of the lae stone light where a black bird glimmered in the blue glow.

The bird made a full circle around the clearing before Liam held his palm up in the air. The bird dove straight toward him, landed on his hand, and froze.

The murmurs didn't stop as Liam tucked the bird into his pocket. He didn't acknowledge all of his people watching him as he walked up to Neil and accepted a mug of ale. He passed by me as he strode toward the tents. He'd made it twenty feet before he stopped and turned back.

I held my breath, waiting for him to say something. I think everyone in the clearing did the same.

Liam reached for me.

I ignored the fluttering in my chest as I walked to him and placed my hand in his.

Whispers surged behind us as we walked out of the clearing.

"You didn't have to bring me with you," I said as we hurried down the path to his tent.

"I want you with me." Liam held the flap of his tent open.

I ducked inside the canvas, wishing we had entered for a chance to enjoy each other's bodies rather than because of a stone bird.

Liam sat at the table before pulling the bird out of his pocket. He stroked the back of the bird's neck and the stone came to life, hopping onto his palm before tipping its chin up. A little scroll of paper came out of the bird's throat.

Liam unrolled the paper. Wrinkles appeared on his brow before he'd even begun to read the note. As his eyes passed down the page, his expression shifted from worried to furious.

"What's happened?" I stepped closer to him, but he didn't reach for me. "Liam?"

He stood and stormed out of the tent without answering. I stepped outside to follow him, but he didn't head back to the clearing where the rest of the camp waited. He strode alone into the shadows of the trees—not toward someone who had caused his rage, but away from me.

I stood in the darkness, staring after him for a moment. The music started back up in the clearing. I took two steps toward the glow of the lae stones and the sounds of the crowd. But the people I'd want to speak to had worries of their own and joys to be celebrated. It would be wrong to bother them with my petty woes.

I went back into Liam's tent and sat at the table. The stone bird did not move.

My fingers trembled as I reached out and stroked the back of the bird's neck.

The bird fluttered its wings as it came back to life. I watched it hop around the table as the noise in the clearing regained it joyous uproar.

I touched the bird's neck again, and it turned back into a statue of itself.

"He'll come back." I rubbed my hands over my face, but the motion didn't soothe me. The minutes ticking past only made me more anxious.

I slipped out the back of Liam's tent and into my own, gathering a fresh set of clothes before walking to the bath.

The music from the clearing didn't penetrate the cave. The

trickle of the water streaming out of a crack in the stone wall was the only sound.

The scent of my soap didn't soothe me. Neither did the warmth of the bath.

"Do not be a chivving fool, Ena Ryeland."

I slid beneath the water, but all the silence did was make me think how much better the bath would have been if Liam were with me.

The world does not need another lovesick fool.

I scrubbed myself until my skin was raw, then lingered in the bath like a coward. When I couldn't bear the shame of hiding in a cave any longer, I dried off, got dressed, and headed back toward my tent. I stopped in front of Liam's tent for a moment, listening for any hint of movement inside.

"You're ridiculous." I went into my own tent and lay down on my cot, trying not to worry at what the note in the stone bird might have said, trying not to spin myself in circles wondering what I might have done to make Liam walk away from me.

The music in the clearing had turned entirely to drunken singing before I managed to drift to sleep.

When my eyes snapped open, there was nothing but darkness and silence surrounding me. I lay very still, trying to reason through what had startled me awake and how quickly I could pull my knife from under my pillow.

"It's only me."

I turned toward Liam's voice.

He stood near the flap of my tent, the tiny trace of lae stone light from outside silhouetting his form.

"Are you all right?" I started to sit up.

"Go back to sleep. I didn't mean to wake you, I just wanted to hold you."

I lifted the edge of my blankets. "No boots in the bed."

He gave a quiet laugh.

I turned over as he climbed into my cot.

His clothes were chill against my skin. He kissed the back of my neck and wrapped his arm around my waist, pulling me close to him.

"Your cot is tiny," Liam whispered.

"Not all of us are given big tents and wide beds."

"You could have slept in my bed."

"You weren't there."

He was silent for so long, I thought he'd fallen asleep.

"My bed is yours, Ena. Whether I'm there or not, my home is yours."

I closed my eyes, willing my heart to still. "Where did you go?"

"To beg the stars for mercy."

"Why?" I nestled as close to his body as I could.

"It doesn't matter tonight. Sleep for now. This trouble can wait for morning."

"But—"

"Please, Ena. I just want to hold you."

I lifted his hand and kissed his palm. "Just promise that whatever it is, I won't be separated from you."

"I promise."

I tried to find comfort in his words but couldn't rid myself of the tinge of fear that had flown in with the stone bird.

"Try not to fall off the cot." I laid my arm over his, as though I could somehow bind him to me.

"Wait until we get to Lygan Hall. I have a proper bed there."

I laughed a bit, and we both fell silent. I'm not sure how long it took for either of us to drift into sleep.

16

The gray of dawn peering through the side of the tent woke me in the morning. I lay very still, too afraid of waking Liam to take a proper breath.

I wanted to know what news the stone bird had brought, but I didn't want to face another disaster. The weeks I had spent trapped in the camp had left me feeling caged but had also granted me time with Liam. I didn't want to lose that time to whatever new enemy threatened us. I didn't want to mourn another friend, or almost worse, wonder if they'd betrayed us.

"It wasn't about any of our people." Liam's voice came out low and raspy.

"What is it then?" I laced my fingers through his. "Does another sorci need us? Is there a new croilach come to attack?"

Liam held me closer, as though he were afraid I might be stolen from him.

"The Blood Leader of the Healy Clan was murdered," Liam said.

"By a croilach?" I wiggled enough to turn over. I needed to look into Liam's eyes to be sure that another monster hadn't been sent for his blood.

"I don't know." Liam brushed my hair away from my face. "The letter from Orla didn't say."

"Then what did it say?" Cold began at my fingertips and started drifting farther up my hands. "You seemed awfully upset for having gotten news that the blood leader of another clan had been killed."

"She's calling me back to Lygan Hall."

"Tell her no."

"I can't."

"No, you can't leave the boundary." I sat up and scrambled over Liam to pace the tiny space of my tent. The cold of the ground stung my feet. "You've got to stay in here where you're safe. If a blood leader's been murdered, it could have been by the same traitorous bastard who sent a croilach after this camp."

"I don't have a choice. I have to go."

"I'm coming with you. I have to. If there's a monster out there—"

"All of us have to go."

"All of us? She wants all of us to go to Lygan Hall?" I froze, stuck between gratitude and fear. "Can Orla do that?"

"Orla is the Elder of the Duwead Clan. As far as we're concerned, she can do whatever she likes. The whole camp is packing up this morning. I spoke to Marta last night. We're leaving before midday."

"But why? Why would she want you to come back?"

"The letter said nothing but to pack up for the winter and return to Lygan Hall immediately."

I started pacing again. "If there is a beast lurking in the woods waiting to kill us, the worst thing we could do is tramp a hundred people through the mountains. And what about the children? It won't be safe for them."

"We aren't farmers, Ena." Liam stood and took my hands in his. "The people in the camp are prepared to fight. If a croilach comes, we'll kill it."

"We could be marching straight into the traitor's trap. There could be monsters out there, just waiting for us to be vulnerable. This is a chivving terrible idea."

"It doesn't matter. Orla has sent her orders."

"But"—I pulled my hands from Liam to try and pace, but there wasn't any room in the tent to move—"winter hasn't come. There is still work to be done. We cannot leave without my brother."

"Emmet knows the path to Lygan Hall. He can find us."

"What if there are sorcis who need us?"

"We can't help anyone trapped in the camp. In a way, it's good we're leaving. Getting back to Lygan Hall will only help us figure out who's betrayed our clan."

"By going farther from Ilbrea?"

"By getting closer to Orla. By rooting out the traitor before they have time to hurt us again."

"Unless the traitor planned all this to get you out in the open. If they knew Orla would call you back to Lygan Hall, they might have killed the blood leader just to get to you."

"We're going to be all right." Liam kissed my forehead. "I will keep us safe. I will make sure Emmet finds us."

"I believe you." I tried to promise myself I wasn't lying.

"I've got to make sure everything gets packed up properly." He pulled on his boots. "We can't afford to let our hurrying now lose us supplies we'll need for next year."

"Right. I'll pack my bag and find Marta to see how I can help."

Liam gave me a smile that didn't reach his eyes.

"Liam," I said when he'd started to open the flap of my tent, "will I still share your bed in Lygan Hall?"

He stepped back into the tent and kissed me. "I've told you. My bed is yours as long as you will have me."

I tried to remember the feel of his arms around me as I laid out everything I owned on my cot. It wasn't much. I'd lost most of my possessions in the Lir Valley. All I had was two spare sets of clothes, a wooden comb, and the black cloak Mave had given me in Frason's Glenn.

The bag I'd brought with me from Harane still wasn't large enough to fit everything.

When I stepped outside, I expected to be greeted by the usual early morning stupor, but tents along the path to the clearing were already being lowered. Like it was normal, routine even, to pack up our home and leave.

I stuffed my hands into my pockets to hide their shaking as I walked toward the clearing.

Neil stood by his cook pot, but half of the wooden seats were gone.

Case and Tirra carried a bench past me, heading toward the tents.

"Ena," Marta called softly as she hurried toward me.

I kept my gaze fixed on her, not wanting to see if they'd already carried away Liam's wide chair.

"Do you know where Liam is?" Marta whispered.

"He was coming to make sure everyone was packing up."

"Hmm." Marta chewed on her thumb.

"Do you need help?"

"Not with packing. But I want him to send a stone bird. To Frason's Glenn, you know, to Mave. In case Emmet is there."

"Aren't there other places Emmet might go?"

"If he needed help, he'd go to Mave and her girls." Marta gnawed on her thumb. "I just want to be sure he knows that we've gone. That you're here and safe. That he should come back."

"I'll let Liam know when I see him."

"I left a pack for you in front of his tent. Yours should be taken down soon. I hope the children stay asleep until we're done. I don't want to begin to imagine how upsetting this might be for Cinni. I think she was really starting to feel safe here."

Marta turned and strode off through the trees toward the bath cave.

I wanted to call after her. I had no idea what I wanted to say, but postponing the walk back to my tent seemed important. I stood with my mouth open, trying to think of some reason to stop the camp from moving, until Marta had disappeared.

"Just pack your bag," I whispered. "That's all you have to do."

I walked back toward the tents. The patches of earth where the benches had sat were darker than the ground around them. The rectangles looked like freshly dug graves. I closed my eyes when I passed the dark swatch where Liam's chair had been.

Most of the tents were down by the time I'd snatched up my new pack and dodged into my tent to shove my belongings into the bag. When I stepped outside, Liam's tent had been taken down. There was a barren patch of dirt where the canvas that had made his home had kept the plants from growing, and four gouges marked the ground where the legs of his cot had dug into the earth.

But that was all.

The place where I had slept in Liam's arms had been shoved away, as though the bed we'd shared meant nothing. I watched the line of Black Bloods walking toward the bath cave. Each of them carried a tent, or cot, or cook pot with them.

I crept beside them until I could peek into the cave. The water had vanished from the bath. The crack in the cave wall had disappeared like a wound that had been healed.

Marta supervised the men laying out the fabric of the tents in the dry basin that had been the bath. One side had been nearly filled with tent poles, while the canvas on the other side had been stacked higher than the lip of the basin.

Neil fussed over the cook pots and stacks of plates and mugs in one corner while Cati stood on the far side of the cave, lovingly packing the practice swords into wooden crates.

I didn't know my feet had carried me into the cave until Marta spoke to me.

"We should be ready to leave within the hour." Marta snatched a bundle of canvas from a gray-faced man. "Could you wake the children? I'd do it myself, but"—she lifted a canvas bundle from Case's hands and shot him a glare—"our Trueborn has charged me with making sure people who are regretting the ale they drank last night don't make us regret losing supplies next year."

Case gave Marta a pained smile. "I regret absolutely nothing."

"You will when the sun comes up all the way and the light pounds through your eyes," Marta said.

"I'll get the children up." I ducked back out of the cave.

I took a deep breath, savoring the scent of the forest. I knew what the high, barren peaks of the mountains smelled like, but I wasn't sure what scents would fill Lygan Hall. I sent a foolish wish up to the stars that Lygan Hall might seem a bit like home.

My tent had been swept away in the few minutes I'd been inside the cave. I knew I should be happy for the efficiency—we needed to leave—but I still clung to the straps of my pack as though someone might steal it as I walked toward the sole remaining tent.

The tent was tucked into the back corner of the rows of canvas that had been standing the previous night. It was the only sleeping tent that had been nearly as large as Liam's. I'd seen the children going in and out of their canvas home, but I'd avoided the place.

I didn't know why. I was too tired and hollow to know if I should feel guilty.

I stood in front of the tent flap, watching two gray-faced women carry a wide bench, trying to decide if knocking or calling out would be less frightening to the children.

"Someone's waiting right outside," a voice whispered from inside the canvas. "Does that mean we're allowed to leave now?"

"Are you awake in there?" My voice stayed steady and calm.

Evie dove out of the tent and lay on the ground at my feet. "I've been awake for hours. Hours and hours."

"That's an exaggeration." Gwen pushed the tent flap aside. "We woke up when the camp started packing."

"I'm sorry about that. We were hoping you'd…" The inside of the tent made my speaking useless.

The children's blankets had been rolled up, and their things had been stuffed into one pack.

"Evie heard people packing," Dorran said. "She woke all of us up."

"We're going to Lygan Hall." Evie lay on the ground, beaming up at me. "We're finally going to learn how to fight with magic."

"We're going someplace nice and safe." Gwen took Cinni's hand and led her sister out of the tent. "We're going somewhere we won't have to fight anyone."

"Absolutely." I made myself smile.

Cinni looked up at me, staring into my eyes with an odd intensity.

"If you're all done in there." Patrick appeared next to the tent. He'd started reaching for the tent pole before I could say the children were ready to be moved.

"Come on then," I said.

Evie bounced by my side as I led the children across the barren patch where the tents had been and cut west, beyond the bath cave, and then up the slope toward the stone boundary.

I didn't really know where the camp was supposed to leave from, but before the ground leveled out, Evie took off in front of me, sprinting through the trees. I followed behind her, not wanting to say I didn't know where to lead the children.

Evie led us straight to Tirra, who waited next to one of the great black boulders.

Tirra watched the five horses she minded as though waiting for one of them to shout that they didn't want to carry the burden they'd been loaded with. The horses huffed and twitched their tails but didn't seem afraid of straying beyond the boundary.

"I suppose this means we'll be walking the whole way." Dorran's shoulders rounded as though he'd already walked a hundred miles that morning.

"Walking is healthy," I said.

"It's only right that you should walk," Tirra said. "The mountains are meant to be traveled by foot."

"Then why do you have horses?" Dorran said.

"Ena."

I turned as Finn called my name.

He'd shaved off his beard and looked positively blissful. "You're ready then?"

"Sure." I made myself smile again. It felt as though my cheeks might crack. "A bit quick, but here we go."

Finn pulled me into a tight hug. "It's for the best. Tromping all the way to Lygan Hall will give Emmet time to cool down."

"Right. I'm sure you're right."

"Everything will be fine now." Finn kissed my cheek before stepping back and tipping his face up to the early morning sun. "You have no idea the wonders that are waiting for us."

"Does it involve a proper house and decent food?" Dorran asked.

"Most definitely." Finn grinned.

"I'll believe it when I see it," Dorran muttered.

"I'm sure we'll be very happy." Gwen stepped on Dorran's toe.

"Will we be leaving soon?" Evie asked.

"Very soon," Finn said.

Evie peppered Finn with questions about our journey and about Lygan Hall.

I wanted to have something useful to say, but I didn't know anything. I just stood next to the boundary, watching as the line of Black Bloods grew longer.

The sun had properly lit the sky by the time Liam strode up the slope to stand beside me.

"Do you have everything?" Liam whispered.

"I've no chivving clue," I whispered back.

Liam touched my cheek and kissed my forehead. "We're going to be fine." He looked out over the people behind us. "Guards, to your posts."

Men and women bearing swords, spears, and bows stepped out on either side of the group.

"We're fine," Gwen murmured to Cinni. "It's good to have people protecting us while we go for a nice walk."

Finn stood on one side of the children, his sword drawn even though he wore a full pack.

Case stepped up to flank our other side. He kept his sword in its sheath, choosing to hold a knife in each hand instead.

A whistle came from the end of the line.

Liam kissed the back of my hand before turning to the black boulder in front of us.

Evie giggled.

"Hush," Dorran whispered, "he's doing magic."

Both children fell silent as Liam laid his hands on the black boulder.

I'd felt the magic that protected our camp a hundred times before. I'd felt the pull of it long before I knew it was Liam who'd created the spell.

Liam closed his eyes and lowered his head.

I wanted to reach for him, but there was something in the way he pressed his palms against the stone that kept me still.

As much as I cherished the magic that surrounded our mountain home, it had always seemed a quiet thing, an invisible cocoon that was not meant to be seen by the world.

I gasped as bright light enveloped the camp.

A brilliantly blue bubble flashed around us, reaching from

boulder to boulder and arcing high overhead to surround us completely.

In an instant, the blue shifted, funneling into the boulder in front of Liam. The blue moved faster and faster, ripping out of the sky and racing into the rock.

A light began to glow around Liam, illuminating his face, and making him seem more than human.

The light terrified me, like somehow the magic would swallow the man, and the mountain would claim the one I cared for.

Liam took a deep breath, and the light around him began to fade.

In another breath, the blue glow had vanished.

Liam balled his hands into fists, as though trying to keep them from shaking as he stepped away from the boulder to look out into the forest beyond.

I studied the trees, waiting for a monster to come charging through the woods to slaughter us. There was nothing but quiet.

Liam nodded, pulled his sword from its sheath, and led us east, away from our sanctuary and into the wilds of the mountains where magic roamed free.

When I was little, I thought I knew the difference between a lie and a story.

A lie was a thing that had terrible consequences. Whether it was being walloped when the truth came out, or something far worse. Even as a tiny girl, I knew a lie could end a life.

But stories—they were beautiful things. Stories of fairies Emmet would whisper to me when I refused to sleep. Stories of love to give a lonely girl hope. Stories of freedom to make living another wretched day possible.

I knew the stories weren't true. I knew at the heart of the tales there was nothing but lies. Still, I never counted the stories as dangerous.

Never dreamt a story could cost someone their life.

My feet throbbed, my shoulders ached from the weight of my pack, and I wanted nothing more than to curl up beside a boulder and sleep. But I kept a smile on my face as we marched through the mountains.

It had been two days of nothing but walking. I wanted to run or climb, but the great caravan of Black Bloods plodded along at a steady pace that drove me mad.

"I never dreamt there could be so many mountains," Gwen said. "Can you believe how many mountains there are, Cinni?"

"My feet can certainly believe it," Dorran said.

"The peaks are so beautiful." Gwen shot Dorran a glare. "I never dreamt I'd see snow on mountains when I wasn't cold."

Cinni didn't seem to care that Gwen had spoken. She was too busy staring at the case lashed across the fiddle player's back. Cinni stared at that stained leather like the case were a magical thing created by the gods. She grinned as she followed the case across ridgelines and alongside riverbeds. I think she would have walked into fire if the fiddle case had led in that direction.

Cinni's perpetual grin didn't stop the rhythm of the chatter between her three siblings. The children kept the pace of their words as the people of the camp kept the pace of their steps.

By the gods, I wanted to sprint in front of everyone and climb something. But Liam had asked me to help mind the children. I wanted to rage at him and shout that I could fight, but Cinni had the ability to wreak havoc on our journey as easily as any monster. If having Marta and me walking beside the children kept Cinni calm, then Liam was right to make me mind the little ones, even if I would rather have been marching on the perimeter of our group, weapon in hand as I scanned the horizon in search of Death himself come to torment us.

"What sort of magic are we going to learn?" Evie bounced on her toes as she walked. "I want to learn all about fire."

"Evie!" Gwen caught her sister by the wrist. "We do not light things on fire."

"Yes, I do," Evie said. "Sometimes by accident, but sometimes on purpose and it saves us."

"Light me on fire," Dorran muttered.

"You'll be able to learn all sorts of magic," Marta said. "There are many people who will be able to help you."

Evie twisted out of Gwen's grip. "What sort of people?"

"There are plenty of people with magic in their blood born into the Duwead Clan," Marta said.

"Then why weren't there any in camp?" Evie asked.

"Why didn't you send a sorcerer to take us away from the Lir Valley?" Dorran said.

I gritted my teeth, swallowing my urge to shout that Finn and I had been the only ones willing to make the journey to the chivving Lir Valley.

"If you were honey, would you go prancing about near a bear's den?" Marta asked.

Cinni glanced away from the fiddle case.

"If I were honey, I wouldn't be walking," Dorran said.

"The Sorcerers Guild searches for people with magic in their blood," Marta said. "They will do whatever it takes to hoard magic. If we brought a pack of sorcerers to the camp and had them run out into Ilbrea to find children like you, the Guilds would catch their scent and steal them away. It's harder for normal people to help sorcis like you, but it's safer for all the Black Bloods if the Guilds don't know what sort of magic we have hidden in the mountains."

A prickle sprang up on the back of my neck.

The Guilds do know. A traitor has risked all our lives.

A whistle sounded from the back of the line. The group stopped.

The sound of weapons being slid from their sheaths surrounded us, followed by the rasp of swords being tucked away a moment later.

I hated that vulnerable noise.

The outermost people came closer to the center of our group as a new batch moved to the edges to replace them. Less than a minute later, a second whistle came from the back, and we started moving forward again.

"How much longer until we reach Lygan Hall?" Dorran said with the air of someone who was quite sure they wouldn't survive the ordeal laid out before them.

"Not too long," Marta said. "But you're lucky we left camp so early this year. The weather is nice and warm."

"It is warm," Gwen said. "We're lucky to have such wonderful weather to travel."

"You don't know how lucky you are." Finn filed into step beside me. "Last time we made this trek, we had snow up to our knees. I'm honestly amazed I made it back to my mother's hearth with all my toes still attached. To be honest, not everyone was so fortunate."

"Who's missing toes?" Evie stared wide-eyed at Finn.

"That is not my secret to tell." Finn winked.

Evie pursed her lips together and began scanning the feet of everyone around her as though searching for signs of missing pieces.

Finn massaged the palm of his right hand.

"I could take your next turn on the edge," I said.

"If he were a sorcerer, he wouldn't need a sword," Dorran said.

"I'm happy to take my turn guarding," Finn said. "What's a sore hand when compared to the honor of protecting one's clan?"

"Well put," Marta said.

"I could be of use protecting the clan," I said.

"You've already been of use," Finn said.

"You're still of use." Marta raised an eyebrow toward Cinni's back.

I took a deep breath. "You know what I'm most excited to see in Lygan Hall? How all the houses are built. I've been told the houses are made of stone, but I wonder how it's done. Are the walls made of lots of rock packed together with masonry, or grown from the ground in one big piece?"

We prattled on and marched along until the sun began to set. As darkness shrouded the mountains, Liam circled the sad pack of Black Bloods, laying small stones all around us while Cati organized the night watch.

Cati took a moment, staring at each of the guards before assigning which watch they were to take. It was as though she were reading a clock set into each of the Black Bloods and judging how much time they had left before the darkness began playing tricks on them.

I was not deemed fit to stand with the other guards, so I dropped my pack onto a spare bit of ground beside a wide rock and pulled my bedroll free.

I wished we had an overhang to offer a hint of protection or even a tent so I could pretend I had a bit of privacy. Neither wish came true and I was stuck unrolling my blankets alongside the children in full view of the rest of Liam's people.

Gwen gave a huge sigh as she dropped her pack to the ground.

"I'm not tired enough to sleep," Evie said.

"I'm tired enough for both of us," Dorran said. "Just sit still and be quiet. I'll manage a double share of sleeping."

"Both of you will sleep." Gwen pulled the blankets out of her pack. "We've got another long day ahead of us, and we all need our rest."

Gwen kept her face calm as she laid out the bottom blanket the children were to share, but there was a tightness in the corners of her eyes I couldn't ignore.

I had made that same face before, when my body and soul were beaten down but my heart was not ready to surrender.

"I think we should find a place for your pack on one of the horses tomorrow." I took extra care smoothing out the edges of my blankets. "A bit more weight shouldn't bother the animals at all, and it will be better for you to move freely, Gwen."

"I'm fine." Gwen sat Cinni down and began unlacing her sister's boots. "I don't mind the pack."

"Gwen is very good at carrying things," Evie said. "She likes it."

"Very true." Finn dropped his pack next to mine. "When you left us in the woods, Gwen carried your sack of goodies all the way back to camp."

"I don't mind being of use." Gwen sat Cinni in front of her and began braiding Cinni's hair.

"There's a difference between being of use and carrying too heavy a burden," Finn said.

Gwen's face went ridged, like she'd somehow become the stone statue hidden beneath the mountain. "There is no such thing as too heavy a burden. There are only people too weak to survive."

I opened my mouth, ready to argue with the child.

But Gwen was only a few years younger than me, and she'd

been bearing the weight of caring for her siblings for so long, perhaps I had no right to call her a child.

"I think everyone should have a bite of food," Marta said. "A quick dinner and then off to bed will be best for everyone."

Gwen looked down at the boots she'd already taken off her sister's feet.

"I'll bring food over." Marta gave a quick smile before disappearing into the crowd.

"It's not even real food," Dorran said.

"I've been making that same argument for years," Finn said. "No point in fussing. It doesn't make the stuff taste any better."

I elbowed Finn but couldn't completely hide my smile.

The next hour was lost in everyone trying to claim a spot to sleep and rotating the guards so everyone would greet the night well-fed. Hardtack and dried meat didn't seem like a fitting meal for more than a hundred hungry people, but I was in awe that we had enough of the horrible stuff to feed all of us. I don't know how Marta had managed to prepare for so many people to travel so quickly. Maybe she'd left the supplies for the return journey packed since they'd arrived at the camp in the spring.

When the signal came for the first watch to properly begin, I sat on top of my blankets, trying to convince myself I was actually going to sleep. I'd claimed a decent spot near a wide rock that gave me something to lean on as I watched Gwen shoo her siblings under the blankets.

The fiddler had set up close to us. Cinni lay down, still staring at the fiddle case.

I looked up through the glow of a hundred lae stones, trying to see the sky high above. I could only make out a faint hint of the stars. I knew I would be able to see more soon. The Black Bloods not chosen as the first watch would pocket their lights as they fell asleep, and the growing darkness would welcome more and more stars until the whole sky became a wash of tiny, glowing specks.

Finn clicked his tongue, calling my attention his way.

I glanced over to find him holding out a waterskin. I could smell the frie before I got the skin anywhere near my mouth.

"Not on watch then?" I whispered.

"I'm third shift." Finn sat against the rock beside me.

I took a sip of the frie, letting the strong liquor burn a path down my throat. "How much longer until we reach Lygan Hall?"

"Two days if we make good time." Finn took the skin back and had another sip.

"I don't think I ever really understood the need for the camp, but Lygan Hall really is too far from Ilbrea to be able to do much good during the warm months." I leaned against Finn's shoulder.

"The Black Bloods and the Ilbreans are meant to be two separate people," Finn whispered. "Maybe there's a reason the land tried so hard to keep us apart."

"Wishing you'd never met me?"

Finn shifted away from me.

Hurt flared in my stomach. For a moment, I thought he really did want to be rid of me, but he didn't look angry as he fished in his pocket and pulled out a worn cloth.

"When I was little, I was always taught that Ilbrea was a completely different realm than the mountains, and the people in that distant country were not like us," Finn said. "I was a descendant of the child the mountain had shielded from the gods' storm. I had stone in my blood and a connection to this land no Ilbrean could match. I had a home, an obligation to protect the mountains."

"We do have to protect the mountains from the Guilds," I said. "We can't let those murderers invade the Black Bloods' home."

"It's not just about the Guilds," Finn said. "It's about us and them. The stone in my blood should run deeper than the Guilds' control over Ilbrea."

He looked to the children. They'd all gone still.

"But what if the stone in my blood means nothing?" Finn

leaned close to my ear. "What if there is no extraordinary magic in the mountains."

"There is magic in the mountains. It's saved both our lives."

"But what if it's not just in the eastern mountains." Finn unfolded the bit of cloth. A shard of dark stone glinted in the blue light.

It was only a sliver, a fragment of dark rock that should have been nothing but a tiny bit of earth to be crunched under our feet. But I recognized that bit of stone. I remembered the fear on Finn's face when he'd found the shard in the mine beneath the Lir Valley.

"This is mountain stone." Finn held the cloth close enough that I could see the lae stone light glinting off the fragment's dark surface. "This should not have been in the Lir Valley."

I took a deep breath. "Maybe it's not mountain stone. There are other sorts of rock that black. It could be obsidian."

"I can feel it." Finn bundled up the dark stone and tucked it into his pocket. "It holds the same fire as the stone in the mountains."

"But you said you weren't a trueborn."

"I'm not, thank the gods, but that doesn't mean I can't feel the stone that is supposed to course through my veins."

I took Finn's hand, lacing my fingers through his. "The mountain does run in your veins. You were born into the Duwead Clan."

"I know that. I know my family has been in the mountains since anyone bothered to keep track of where people were from."

"But?" I asked, leaning into the question he'd left hovering in the air.

"What if there was no child sheltered by the mountain?" Finn spoke so softly I could barely hear. "What if there is no special magic deep beneath the eastern mountains? What if the stone is just stone?"

"It can't be. The mountains do hold amazing magic. We've both seen it. Liam can use stone magic."

"I know that, I do. But…" Finn looked up to the stars glaring at us through the lae stone light. "What if it's all just chance? What if the magic, or whatever it is that allows the mountain to open to us, has nothing to do with a woman pouring her own magic into the stone? What if the magic was here first, and the Black Bloods just stumbled into something chivving wonderful and made up a story so it would seem like they had a right to claim this land? What if it's magic that Lir is mining in his valley?"

"Is it even possible to mine magic?"

"It's mountain stone Liam uses for the rocks that protect us and to make our lae stones. The clans used to forge the stone for other, darker magic before the treaty. If the Black Bloods could come up with foul uses for the material granted them by the mountain they adore, what horrors could beasts as evil as the Guilds achieve?"

"I…" My mind raced as I tried to come up with an argument to calm Finn. "Have you shown the stone to Liam?"

"No." Finn gripped my hand tighter.

"He's a trueborn. If anyone would be able to tell you if that really is the same stone as in the mountains, it's him. And you can't deny that stone magic doesn't exist in Ilbrea, right?"

"I don't know."

"Then ask Liam."

"I can't." Finn kissed the back of my hand. "There are some questions not worth asking."

"Why?" A hint of dread swooped through my stomach.

"Everything the Black Bloods believe comes from the story of the child beloved by the mountain. Our laws, our clans, our borders. We live and die because a mother poured her magic into the cold, dead stone inside the mountain. If that isn't true, if we're just a pack of wanderers who happened on a magical place and decided to claim it, everything we are has been built on a lie. The clans are barely maintaining peace as it is. We'd be lost. We'd all be lost."

"There's a city under the mountains," I said. "When the mountain swallowed me, I found it. People lived down there once. A whole mess of them. There was a fountain and gardens. It would have taken a long time to build."

"Were there still people down there?"

"It'd been abandoned. A long time ago from the looks of it. I told Liam."

"What did he say?"

"That he was glad the mountain had protected me."

Finn kissed my temple. "Have you told anyone else?"

"No. I almost told Case, but—"

"Don't," Finn said. "Don't tell anyone."

"Why not?"

"Because whether it's the mountain, the gods, or the stars, something has kept me alive this long. And whatever that force might be, it's screaming in my gut that fire and death are lurking in the shadows."

I tried to think of something comforting to stay as the lights kept dimming around us, but the dread in my stomach had turned into a prickle on the back of my neck, as though Death lurked behind me and his own chill breath tickled my skin.

19

Liam's arm weighed heavy on my side when I woke in the morning, assuring me that I was someplace safe and hadn't drifted into a foul and terrible dream.

"You can rest a little longer," Liam whispered in my ear.

"Have you slept at all?" I twisted to face him, finding a new rock to dig into my side.

"Of course." He kissed my forehead.

"You need at least a bit of rest. If you drop from exhaustion, who will keep the stones going to protect us?"

"It's only a bit farther, and we'll be safe in Lygan Hall."

We lay still for a while. I hoped he was drifting to sleep, though from the pace of his breathing, he was still awake.

I didn't want to try to picture Lygan Hall—I knew I could never do the place justice—but a childish part of me couldn't help but imagine grand stone hallways filled with magic.

I drifted back to sleep with images of Liam riding on a stone horse flitting through my mind.

When he woke me for the day, half the bedrolls had been packed up. A string of little cook fires had been lit, and Neil lorded over them, making sure no person or horse disrupted his work.

"What does Neil do in Lygan Hall?" I asked as I rolled up my bedding.

"His family tend sheep in the outskirts of the settlement." A hint of a smile curved one corner of Liam's mouth.

I stopped working on my pack to watch him, not wanting to miss a moment of that beautiful expression.

"Neil's got a flock of children to match his sheep," Liam said. "They tend the animals for him in the warm months."

"But if he's got a family, why is he running off to cook in camp?"

"Almost everyone in the camp has some sort of family in Lygan Hall. They sacrifice their time at home to help protect all Black Bloods against the Guilds. It is a great honor to journey west and work to stop the paun from invading the eastern mountains." Liam leaned close to me. "If you want the honest truth, though, Neil's wife volunteered him to come and cook in the camp."

I bit back my laugh. "I'm not sure if she's brilliant or evil for having dropped him on us."

"We're not starving." Liam tied his blankets to his own pack. "And she's got a bit of peace. Seems like a fair enough trade."

"I wonder what she'll think of him coming home early."

Liam finished tying his pack closed before he answered. "I don't know what any of them will think of us returning so early. We can only have faith in Orla's judgment."

I took Liam's hand and pressed his palm to my cheek. "I'm glad I'll still be with you."

"I don't think I could breathe if you weren't." He kissed my forehead, shouldered his pack, and walked to the eastern-most part of our group.

The morning passed like the others had, with everyone

speaking in hushed voices as we all packed up and snagged a bit of slop to eat.

Cati would whistle from the western-most tip of the group, and the first guards would head to the edge of Liam's stones. Once their weapons were drawn, Liam would walk the perimeter of the place we'd slept, collecting the rocks. The children would watch in awe as the stones flew up from the ground and into his leather pouch one by one, stacking in more weight for Liam to carry.

I pressed my pendant to my chest as he tucked the pouch of stones into his pack and started leading us east.

I still wore the pendant hidden beneath my bodice. I didn't have a real reason for not wanting people to see it—all of them knew I'd been sharing his bed—but the stone felt too intimate to be displayed. I'd let the pendant be seen in Ilbrea without worry, but the Black Bloods would know that Liam had made it for me. I didn't know how many might guess why.

I studied the peaks of the mountains around us as the children kept up their patter of words. I'd started to find it soothing, even when I didn't listen to exactly what they were saying. I wondered if Cinni felt the same. If the rhythm of her siblings' speech was nothing more than a gentle rain against the canvas of a tent, hushing the world and lulling her into a steady calm.

The noise stilled my nerves as I squinted against the sun to see the summits around us.

Liam had led us into a valley that cut between two massive mountains, but even the peaks that loomed over us were nothing to the mammoths towering above them. The snow-covered summits stood out against the sky, glittering white in the morning sun.

Even though I wasn't cold, I pulled my coat tighter around me, as though I could somehow stop winter from coming by carefully keeping myself warm.

"Right, Ena?"

I turned toward Evie, scrambling to think what I was supposed to be agreeing to.

"I don't think so," Marta said. "You'll have a nice place to live, but I don't think it will be with Ena."

"Why not?" Evie asked.

Gwen's face turned pink, and she carefully studied her shoes.

"I…" I swallowed, feeling like my throat had suddenly started to close as heat rose up into my cheeks.

"Ena will have to go back to camp to help other sorcis when the weather warms up again," Marta said. "We're going to find you four a nice place to live with someone who will be with you all the time."

"Oh." Evie furrowed her brow. "Can we live with you, then?"

Marta's face paled a shade. "I don't think so."

"Marta's got work to do in camp, too," I said. "She's got the most important job of all."

"What's that?" Evie said.

"Keeping everyone fed and in line," Dorran said. "I can't think of a tougher job."

"Thank you, Dorran," Marta said.

"I would have thought you'd be too smart to say yes to it," Dorran said.

"Then don't go next year." Evie seized Marta's hand. "Stay with us and take care of us. I promise, we'll be just as difficult as caring for the camp."

"I don't think that's how to—"

Cinni's gasp silenced Gwen.

The other three children froze, staring at Cinni.

I tensed, waiting for the ground to writhe to life and trap me.

"You'll be all right." Marta stepped in front of Cinni. "I promise there will be someone to take care of you."

Cinni clapped her hands over her ears and looked to Evie.

Evie wrinkled her brow and tipped her head to the side. "I don't hear anything."

"What is there to hear?" the fiddler turned around to ask.

People looked toward us in a wave as more of the group realized we'd stopped moving.

"There's nothing," Evie said. "Just the thumping of all of us walking."

Cinni's breath came in quick gasps as her gaze darted around as though she were desperately hunting for something.

"You're all right, Cinni." Gwen pressed her own hands on top of Cinni's, adding an extra layer over the child's ears. "We're all together, and we're going someplace wonderful."

Cinni started shaking, like she longed to run or might catch fire and burn us all.

"Just breathe, Cinni," Gwen said. "You've got to breathe."

"Oh no," Evie whispered.

The world seemed to fall silent as I looked toward her.

"Something's coming." Evie met my gaze. "They're so big."

"Liam!" I pulled my knife from my boot. "Which way, Evie?"

"Everywhere." Evie grabbed Gwen's arm. "They're everywhere."

Liam raced toward me, his sword already drawn.

"Something's coming," I shouted. "There's something—"

"To the north!" a man bellowed.

I looked to see what the man had spotted, but a scream from the southern edge of our pack came before I could find what the man had seen.

Liam looked south before he reached my side. He froze, his sword raised. For an instant, it looked as though he were balancing on the edge of the world, trying to reason through which direction led to an endless doom and which to salvation.

Another scream came from the south.

"Stay with the children! Stay at the center." Liam charged south, shouting as he raised his blade.

This time, I did catch sight of the terror that had descended upon us.

The beast had white fur, which had been matted with deep red blood. The creature's claws flashed in the morning light as it slashed through the stomach of one of the Black Bloods. A spray of red flew through the air.

Liam kept running toward the blood.

I wanted to shout his name, wanted to call him back to me, but I was terrified that distracting him might cost him his life.

The fiddler dropped her case and pulled her short sword from its sheath.

A horrible cry came from the eastern edge of our pack.

"Stay right here, children," the fiddler said. "A nice tight group, that's how we do this."

Marta held a knife in her hand. I didn't know where she'd pulled it from.

"Cinni, you've got to breathe." Gwen hadn't looked away from her sister.

A visceral cry of rage and grief came from the south.

Cinni groaned.

"Please, Cinni," Gwen begged. "Breathe. You've got to breathe."

I scanned the chaos around me, searching for an impossible remedy to the bloodshed and fear.

Two beasts attacked us on every side.

Blood and screams swept around me like the raging wind of a storm.

"We can't let them do this. They've all got to stop." Evie charged north, racing toward the monsters.

"Evie, no!" I sprinted after her, gripping my knife.

Evie pulled her hands back before she even reached the edge of our people.

I held my breath as she shoved her palms forward.

A hiss and a crack split the air. The monster did not stagger or sink to the ground.

"Just die!" Evie screamed.

The beast turned its awful pale eyes toward Evie. Its dark fur didn't betray any hint of the blood the monster had spilt as it charged toward us.

Evie lashed her hand through the air as the beast drew near her. I raced to her side, gripping my knife, knowing there was nothing I could do to defend the child against the monster's terrible claws.

But the monster staggered and stopped as flames erupted from its fur. The beast let out a horrible keening snarl and stumbled back.

"Evie, we need to get back to the others," I said.

I don't know whether she heard me or not.

She raced toward the next monster. This one had patchy fur that didn't match in length or color. Its legs were all different sizes, like someone had gotten confused in its creation.

Croilach.

The misshapen beast caught fire as well but didn't slow its attack. The croilach swiped its flaming claws, slashing through Patrick's stomach.

"Stop!" Evie shouted, but a louder cry drowned out her voice as Cati charged the flaming croilach.

My heart leapt up into my throat as Cati plunged her blade into the monster's chest.

"Cut out its heart!" I shouted as I raced toward Cati.

Black coated her sword as she pulled it from the croilach's chest and swung for the beast's neck.

The monster batted Cati's blade aside.

She dove to the ground, rolling beneath the monster's claws, and leapt back up to her feet. The monster lunged toward her, and she drove her blade back into the croilach's chest. The monster growled but showed no signs of dropping.

Cati twisted her blade in the beast's chest with one hand while yanking her knife from her boot with the other.

The monster gnashed its teeth at Cati's neck.

"Stop it!" Evie slammed her fist through the air, and the beast's flaming head jerked to the side as though the child had actually struck the monster.

That moment was all Cati needed. She drove her knife between the monster's ribs and leveraged the blade against her sword, ripping the stone heart from the beast's chest.

20

It seemed like the battle should have stopped. Cati had killed a croilach. But there were seven more monsters attacking our people.

Cati left the bloody stone heart on the ground and charged the other monster Evie had set on fire.

"We need to get back to the others." I reached for Evie, but she dodged away from me, racing toward the fight on the eastern edge.

One of the beasts on that side had been surrounded by a dozen fighters. The other had broken through the ranks of the Black Bloods, leaving its victims screaming on the ground. Both croilach burst into flames as Evie sprinted toward them.

A wail came from the southern edge where Liam had gone to fight.

I spun toward the sound.

A new noise cut over all the clamor of the battle, a scream that pierced my mind and shook the world.

"Cinni." Sour rolled into my mouth as I said her name. I forced my feet to move and ran toward her.

The ground split beneath me, forming cracks that grew with

each heartbeat. I leapt over a fissure in the earth, stumbling as I landed on the trembling ground.

Gwen had wrapped her arms around her sister and spoke into Cinni's ear, though what she said I had no hope of hearing over that terrible scream.

The ground shook again. The fiddler's case tipped into a crack in the earth and tumbled into the darkness.

I watched Gwen's mouth move, forming words that looked horribly like *I'm sorry.*

Bright light poured from her skin as she stepped away from Cinni.

"Stop!" I tried to shout the word, but all the air had vanished from my lungs.

Cinni's scream fell silent as the glow around Gwen grew, pulsing and flashing, until a bright burst of radiant light soared from her body, covering the battlefield with its brilliance.

The world went quiet for a moment as Gwen swayed and fell.

I leapt forward, catching her before she could slip into one of the cracks in the earth.

Sound came back into being as I clutched Gwen in my arms.

The screaming only carried from one side. The east.

I looked up to see Liam leaping across the shattered ground, racing toward the battle.

Red flew through the air as another Black Blood met a horrible end.

"Gwen." I laid her flat on the ground, but I couldn't tear my gaze from Liam.

He held out his hand, and a storm of stone rose from the earth and plunged into the monster.

The beast reared back, exposing its chest.

A horrible black misted through the air as the croilach's stone heart burst from its chest and soared into Liam's hand.

Then the din of the battle ended, and the sounds of grief and pain took over.

Liam looked back across the battlefield toward me. Gore coated him, but he was on his feet without any sign of life-threatening injury.

"Gwen, I need you to look at me." I tore my gaze from Liam.

Gwen seemed younger as she lay unconscious on the ground, like the child she wasn't allowed to be.

"She won't wake up." Dorran clung to Marta's arm. "There's nothing you can do for her."

"Has this happened before?" I asked.

"Not this bad," Dorran said.

"Then we can't just leave her like this." I pressed my fingers to the side of Gwen's throat. The faint thump of her pulse still carried through her skin. I laid a hand on her chest. Her ribs still rose and fell with each breath.

I couldn't see anything wrong with her that should have left her unconscious.

"I need to find Winnie." I stood to search for her, and the whole world came crashing down.

The cracks in the earth had spread out like a giant spiderweb, leaving chunks of solid ground standing in towers that looked as though they might tip and fall into the darkness from one ill-timed breath. Our safe havens were nothing more than columns reaching to depths reason declared impossible. The little island the children, Marta, and I stood on was the largest patch of solid ground left, with a gap more than six feet wide separating us from the next bits of land.

The rest was all tatters and blood.

Around the edges lay dead and wounded Black Bloods. Cati was already leaping over cracks, trying to reach the ones too wounded to move on their own. Others were trying to help as well, but some of the gaps were too large to cross and some of the people too far gone for help to make any difference.

"Cinni." I knelt in front of her. Tears streamed from her fear-filled eyes. "Cinni, I know you were trying to help. I know you wanted to keep the monsters away, and you did a wonderful job, but I need you to help me again. I need you to put the ground back together."

Cinni looked toward the crack in the earth where the fiddle player's case had tumbled into darkness.

A horrible pained scream came from the east.

"There are people who need my help," I whispered. "There are people who are hurt, and I need to get to them. I need to get to Winnie so she can help Gwen."

"I can try to do it." Dorran let go of Marta and stepped toward me. "But Cinni's magic is bigger than mine. I don't know if I can move that much at once."

"Cinni can do it." Terror clenched my chest as someone called my name from the west. "Cinni, I know you're scared, but that doesn't mean you aren't brave. Being afraid doesn't make you any less strong. I need you to do this for me. I need you to be strong and help me so I can help them."

Cinni reached forward and touched my cheek, running her fingers across my skin as though brushing away tears I was too afraid to cry.

"Please," I whispered.

Cinni balled her hands into white-knuckled fists and screwed up her forehead as though she wanted nothing more than to scream at the top of her lungs.

Crack.

The noise shook the ground, and a fresh wave of cries filled the air.

Crack.

The earth shuddered as rocks flew up from far below, filling the web of gaps with shining black stone that glimmered in the sunlight.

"Thank you." I stood, searching for any hint of Winnie.

The pattern of the black against the mountain dirt should have been beautiful, but as I sprinted across the dark stone, it seemed like a giant spiderweb trying to trap us all, or worse, a dark stain on the land that would become a monument to the horror of the croilach's attack.

"Winnie!" I shouted as I ran west. "Winnie."

"Ena!"

I turned toward the sound of my name.

Nessa knelt on the ground beside a man so covered in blood I couldn't properly see his face.

"Are you hurt?" I sprinted toward Nessa.

The man beside her screamed in pain.

"I'm fine." Nessa's voice trembled. "Shane was bitten by that monster. I don't know what to do."

I knelt next to Shane.

The croilach had bitten his shoulder, shredding both flesh and coat.

I wiped the blood from the wound with my own sleeve. Indigo blue lines trailed through Shane's skin.

"I'm sorry," I said. "There's nothing to be done for him."

"No," Nessa said.

"I have to find Winnie."

"No!" Nessa shouted after me as I sprinted away. "You can't just leave us. You have to help him!"

I passed three more already screaming in pain from the venom in the croilach's bite. Others were luckier.

Patrick lay still on the ground, his blank eyes open to the sky, his stomach torn by terrible claws. His death had at least been quick.

I raced past Tirra, who stood between four horses, trying to calm them.

Winnie's dark blue bag was still tied to one of the horse's backs.

I turned around and sprinted back toward the horse.

The bay stomped her foot.

"Don't charge the horses," Tirra snapped.

"I need Winnie's bag."

I don't know if the bay recognized the desperation in my voice or remembered me from the time she'd spent carrying me through the mountains, but she stood still as I untied the dark blue bag.

"Ena!" Liam's voice cut above the rest of the chaos.

I turned to find him racing toward me.

"Are you hurt?" I tried to search him for wounds, but he was too covered in black and red gore for me to be able to see if he had been injured. "Were you bitten?"

"I'm fine." Liam reached for me but stopped before touching me with his bloody hands. "So many people are hurt. I don't know how to help them."

"Where's Winnie?"

"She didn't make it." There was no grief in Liam's voice. He just sounded hollow.

I let myself have one breath—just one moment where panic raced through my veins.

"If the injured can be moved, take them all to the eastern edge," I said. "Put pressure on the wounds of everyone who hasn't been bitten. Try to keep them from losing too much blood."

"What about the ones that can't be moved?"

"Have someone stay with them," I said. "I don't want anyone to die alone."

21

Two Black Bloods were missing. I think they fell into the cracks in the ground with one of the horses and three of the monsters.

Twelve Black Bloods were dead before the battle had ended. Dorran used his magic to dig graves for them before the wounded had been gathered.

Six Black Bloods had been bitten. Their screams will haunt me for the rest of my life. I still don't know if it would have been kinder to cut their throats and relieve them of their agony.

Seven Black Bloods were too badly wounded for me to be of any help. I don't think Lily or Winnie would have been able to save any of them either. The croilach's claws had sliced too deep.

Dorran dug that set of graves before I had finished seeing to the people I could help.

Fourteen Black Bloods were wounded in the end. I stitched up the ones I could, stealing the frie from everyone's secret supplies to clean the wounds. I set a broken leg and wrapped cracked ribs with sliced strips of blanket.

By the time I'd patched up everyone well enough for us to start moving again, the ones who'd been bitten had fallen silent.

Dorran dug twenty-five graves before we'd loaded the worst

off onto the horses and paired the other wounded with someone strong enough to help them keep moving forward.

I wanted to tell Liam we needed to stop, to set up the little stone boundary and let the wounded rest. But the scent of blood clung to all of us and wafted away from us on the wind like a siren's call luring in other beasts who wanted to slay us.

The whistle came from the back. Cati hadn't been hurt, not badly at least. She'd only needed a bandage and some salve on her burned arm.

None of the people I cared for most had been terribly wounded. I was lucky. My relief made me ill.

I stayed close to Liam at the front of the pack, with the children just behind me.

Neil carried Gwen in his arms.

She looked like a sleeping doll. I still hadn't thought of anything that might help wake her.

Marta had taken Gwen's place, holding tight to Cinni's hand and whispering comforting words.

Case walked with one arm around Finn's waist. Finn had gotten a slice on the arm that cut through to the muscle. Case kept glancing to Finn as we walked, terror creasing the corners of his eyes as though Finn might drop at any moment.

I didn't blame Case for his fear. Finn had lost enough blood that his pale face looked like a death mask.

"This shouldn't have happened." Case's voice was hoarse. I don't know if it was from screaming or from horror at what the monsters had stolen from us. "This should never have happened."

"This is what happens when there's vermin hiding in your home." Finn's voice came out worse than Case's had.

"Don't," I said. "Save your strength to keep moving."

Finn looked at me and opened his mouth to speak.

"We can talk once you've rested." I shot a glance to the children. "For now, we need to keep moving."

"We're not stopping until we reach the gates of Lygan Hall," Liam said. "We march through the night."

I took two quick steps forward so I could see his face.

Blood had smeared and spattered across his skin and clothes. The sword he carried in one hand still had a streak of black on the hilt. In his other hand, he held a fistful of stones, which, in a trueborn's grasp, were more deadly than any blade.

I had seen many sides of Liam before. Protector, friend, confidant, leader, lover. I had never seen the warrior. Not really. I'd seen him fight, but I'd never seen him hungry for blood.

"You're going to love the gates of Lygan Hall," Marta said. "The inside is beautiful, and then you'll get to have a nice meal and sleep in a warm bed. Won't you like that, Cinni? Then all four of you will get to learn from the sorcerers. I can't wait to see what wonderful things they teach you."

Neither Evie nor Dorran added to the patter.

I took a deep breath and forced my rage behind the shroud of fire that crackled in my chest. "I think you're going to learn lots of nice things. And I hear there's a lovely garden packed with all sorts of herbs and flowers. We'll have a long walk, then a nice sleep, and then you'll get to learn and see the garden. Won't that be a wonder, Cinni?"

My throat went raw as the hours passed, but I was too afraid to ask Marta for silence. One of the wounded died. Dorran had a grave dug before anyone asked for his aid. Then the horse was free to carry Gwen.

She lay draped across the animal's back. Still breathing, but with no other sign of life.

Neil stayed close to her even after the horse had taken over the task of carrying her weight.

Cati gave the whistle to rotate the guard, and even though different people took the edge of our group, not a single Black Blood sheathed their weapon.

When the sun began to sink in the sky, no one pulled out their lae stone. We traveled in darkness with only the stars to light our path until we reached the lip of a rise.

Liam stopped and looked down the slope in front of us. Even in the darkness, I could tell the path ahead was too narrow for us to continue in our wide formation.

"We could stop here for the night," Marta whispered. "Lay out the stones and wait for sunrise."

"We aren't stopping," Liam said. "We are not sitting down and waiting for the next disaster to strike."

He pulled his lae stone from his pocket. The magic in the sphere glowed more brightly than normal, as though it recognized the magic in Liam's blood. Or maybe the light fed off his rage.

He stepped onto the winding path that led down the slope.

It was the first proper path I'd seen while traveling in the eastern mountains. I didn't like taking such an obvious route, but as I followed Finn and Case, I understood why enough people had walked this trail to wear down the ground.

The dirt on the trail was loose and shifted with each step, but if I'd strayed from the path, the ground would've given way, leaving me to tumble down the side of the slope.

To the north and south of the trail, rocky cliffs overtook the terrain. I might have been able to make that climb in the daylight but not in the dark. And most of the Black Bloods couldn't have scaled those rock walls, even if a pack of monsters hadn't decided to attack us.

Liam pocketed his lae stone and slowed his pace as he reached the bottom of the rise, giving the rest of the group time to catch up. But he didn't stop. He kept pushing forward through the wide valley that seemed to have been scooped out by a giant's hand. I wanted to ask if there was some sort of legend as to how the valley had been formed, but I didn't want to hear another story. Wondering how much truth hid in legends was more than my mind could bear.

I tried to distract myself by examining the plants in the valley instead. Everyone had put away their lights, so I couldn't see much more than shadows. There were scrub bushes and a few hardy-looking wildflowers, but nothing that gave me any hope of a large group of people being able to forage and survive.

I tried studying the stars above me as I kept up the endless chatter for the children.

None of it could drown out the word banging in my head.

Traitor. Traitor. Traitor.

I wanted to scream the word into the night. Keep screaming it over and over until whoever had brought this hell down upon us confessed their crimes. I would see them cower in fear and then watch them die.

I didn't know the face of the person I hated so badly, but I knew what their fate would be and looked forward to their terrible end.

My legs and feet moved beyond sore to throbbing and then went numb as the cold of the night surrounded us.

Still, Liam led us onward.

When Finn's steps started to falter, I gently looped his injured arm over my shoulder, bearing some of his weight as he sagged closer to the ground.

How much farther?

I wanted to ask but wasn't sure the children could survive the answer.

A great string of mountains rose up in front of us, soaring so high I wasn't sure I had the strength left to climb them.

Liam quickened his pace, and everyone else in the line followed without complaint.

As we traveled through the shadows, the summits never seemed to grow any nearer.

We will be trapped in the dark forever.

I would have thought I'd be more grateful for the stars.

The base of the mountains rose up in front of us.

I gritted my teeth, determined not to be the one who endangered our group by slowing my pace.

"A warm bed and good food, that's what's waiting for you," Marta said. "I need you to be ready for lots of people and bright lights first, but after that, I promise I'll find you a nice, warm place to rest."

Liam stopped. So did Case and Finn. My knees almost buckled as I tried to remember how to stand still.

"I am Liam, Trueborn Duwead, returning to his home in Lygan Hall on the orders of Orla, Elder of the Duwead Clan. We have been attacked on our journey. Many were killed, and we have wounded desperately in need of care. We ask for safe passage and need your help."

I strained my eyes, trying to see who lurked in the darkness. There was nothing but stone.

"Open the gates for your Trueborn." Liam's voice rang through the night.

I leaned down, trying to reach the knife tucked in my boot without letting go of Finn.

My breath caught in my throat, and my body tensed, preparing for an attack, as a bright slice of light cut through the night.

22

I shielded my eyes and blinked against the growing glow.

A crack had appeared in the side of the mountain. The light that shone out of the stone wasn't the blue I'd become accustomed to, but instead glowed a warm, dazzling orange, as though a thousand torches lit whatever wonders waited beyond.

Liam led us forward but didn't sheath his sword or toss aside his handful of stones.

The light of the cavern streamed out into the night, casting him in a striking silhouette, like something out of a story. A warrior venturing into a world of magic.

I wanted to run after him to be sure no magic could separate us, but I couldn't let go of Finn.

"We're nearly there," Case said. "Just a bit farther and you won't have to walk anymore."

"I'll keep walking if you promise a proper chivving meal," Finn murmured.

More silhouettes joined Liam's as we neared the gate of Lygan Hall. Men and women all bearing swords, all flocking toward Liam while keeping their weapons raised to fight off whatever beast waited in the shadows.

"I need to go to Orla," Liam said as soon as he stepped into the mouth of the cavern.

"I'll let her know to expect you." A young man with dark skin and no hair at all on his head ran down the long tunnel.

But it wasn't a tunnel. Not really. That word can't describe the outer chamber.

The space was wide enough to fit three houses. The opening to the outside spanned the entire width, as did the line of armed guards. The ceiling was twenty feet high and set with dazzling orange orbs that cast their shimmering glow on everything in sight.

Real torches burned along the walls, reaching to the back of the wide space where the room narrowed into a tunnel blocked by metal gates.

"Wes," Liam said, "we need healers, everyone you've got available. Now."

A man with black hair sprinted away.

I helped Finn past the line of guards and into the center of the chamber.

A woman with gray streaks in her hair stepped in front of us. "Let's get him down." She took my place under Finn's arm. "Your mother is going to have a chivving fit, Finn, coming home a bloody mess like this."

"She'll be glad of it." Finn smiled as he sank to the ground. "You know how she likes to fuss."

"Ailis," Liam called. "Ailis!"

"I'm here, Liam." A girl with flaming red, curly hair ran toward him.

"Take her to the crag." Liam pointed to me. "See her cared for, and keep her guarded."

"Good to have you back." Ailis started toward me.

"Ailis," Liam said, "do not leave her."

"I won't." She reached for my arm.

"Liam, I should stay with you." I backed away from the girl.

"Go with her." Liam didn't look at me. "Get the outer gate closed!"

Men ran toward the far corner.

I wanted to stay and see what people could possibly do to make the mountain move, but Ailis gripped my arm, dragging me forward.

"I should stay here," I said. "I can help with the others. There are children who need to get settled."

"Someone else will do that," Ailis said.

"How do you know?"

"Because Liam told me to take you to the crag." She strode down the chamber so quickly, my numb feet could barely keep up.

"I can help here," I said.

She squeezed my arm tighter. "I've been told to take you to the crag, and you're going." Ailis stopped at the metal gate.

A man peered through the bars before swinging it open. A second metal gate waited just beyond.

"If you have a problem with Liam's orders, take it up with him." Ailis led me through the second gate.

I wanted to argue, but my mind had gotten stuck on the racks of weapons lining the sides of the room. There were hundreds of swords, bows, spears, and knives all along the walls, as though an entire army hid behind the stone, ready to march at a moment's notice.

A line of people tore past us, heading back toward the outer chamber. Each of them had a heavy pack on their back. I hoped they were the healers.

We reached another gate that another man had to peer through before letting us pass.

On the far side, the tunnel split in five directions. One path led straight forward, two branched up to the right and left, and two sloped downward just beside them. Ailis steered me toward the upper left corridor.

"Stop." I wrenched my arm away from her.

"We should keep moving." Ailis reached toward me.

"No." I held up my hand. The orange light cast a horrible glow on the blood staining my skin. "I don't know you. I don't know where you're leading me. I don't trust you, and I have to know how to find Liam."

Ailis pursed her lips for a moment before speaking. "I'm taking you to the crag."

"How do I know that?"

"Because Liam told me to."

"That doesn't mean anything. You could be leading me anywhere, and I wouldn't know the difference."

"Look." Ailis gave a false smile. "I don't know who under the chivving stars you are. I don't know why you're here. But Liam, my Trueborn, has given me orders to take you to the crag, see that you're cared for, and guard you. I can drag you up this tunnel by your hair, or you can walk nicely. Either way is fine with me, but you are going to the crag."

"Unless you decide to slit my throat." Pain pressed against my chest. "I need to go back there. I have to make sure they're safe. We lost so many today. I can't—We can't lose any more."

A crack appeared in Ailis's armor. "Who did you lose?"

"Winnie, Patrick. Twenty-eight today."

Ailis's neck tightened. I wasn't sure if she wanted to scream or cry. "Do you trust Liam?"

"Absolutely." I pressed my blood-covered hand to my chest, needing to feel the shape of the stone pendant against my skin.

"He ordered me to take care of you. Would he have done that if he didn't trust me?"

"Never."

"All right then, let's go." She started toward the tunnel.

"What about the others?" I took a step back, toward the outer chamber. "I can't abandon them."

"Chivving just—" Ailis laid her tongue over her teeth. "You

can't trust a trueborn and think they can't care for their own people. So move. Now."

My breath rattled in my chest.

You have nothing if you can't trust him.

I nodded and tucked my hands into my pockets, as though hiding the awful stains could somehow separate me from the horrors of the day.

"What happened to all of you anyway?" Ailis led me into the tunnel.

The gentle slope of it curved and wound up in a spiral.

"We were attacked," I said.

"By who?" Ailis tightened her grip on her sword.

"Does it matter?"

"If I'm supposed to protect you, then yes."

"Why you?"

"I thought you said you trusted our Trueborn." Ailis looked at me, raising one red eyebrow.

"Good people can still be wrong about evil men."

Corridors branched off the still-spiraling tunnel, but Ailis kept leading me up.

"I've known Liam since before either of us could talk." Ailis cut right, down a wide corridor that led to a staircase.

Two guards waited at the bottom of the stairs. Both nodded and let her pass without asking why the girl with her was covered in blood.

"Liam and I are about as close as two people can get," Ailis said. "I have no idea why he wants you in the crag, but I trust him. So I'll fight and risk my chivving life to protect you."

Six guards with swords drawn waited in front of the intricately carved metal door that blocked the path ahead of us. The guards stepped aside and opened the door before Ailis and I had to slow our steps. A wide hall with walls polished to gleaming black perfection greeted us beyond the fancy door.

"Is Liam safe here?" I asked. "Will there be guards to protect him?"

Ailis glanced over her shoulder, looking at me with a puckered brow. "We are the Duwead Clan. We would do anything to protect Liam."

She stopped at a wooden door. She didn't knock or anything before shoving it open.

"Wash up in the back. I'll see that you have something clean to wear."

I stepped through the door, and Ailis closed me into the darkness.

23

I'd often been grateful for the light of my lae stone, but the gleam of it meant more to me as I stood in that dark room.

A wardrobe sat against one wall, while a vanity and chair sat along the other. A bed, wide enough to fit three people, took up the entire middle of the room. White blankets lay on top of the bed. They looked sickly in the light of my lae stone, like they'd been contaminated by a croilach's venom.

Sour rose in my throat, and my stomach trembled.

A door stood open at the back of the room.

I ran toward it, trying to convince my stomach to be as strong as my heart.

A metal cylinder waited in the corner. I dropped to my knees and emptied the sparse contents of my stomach. My hands trembled as I leaned against the cold stone of the wall.

I wanted to be angry at the world and the traitor. I wanted to rage and fight. I wanted to bolt past Ailis and find Liam.

"He knows her." I gripped my light in my hand and forced myself to stand. My legs wobbled as I walked to the stone tub and turned on the silver taps. "He would not have sent you with her if he didn't trust her." I set my light on the ground and let my pack fall from my shoulders. "Liam would not place you in danger."

My fingers protested being asked to work enough to undress myself.

Steam rose from the tub by the time I'd finally managed to shed my blood-caked clothes.

"He would not have sent you away if he were in danger." I could not stomach my own lie. I raced to empty my belly again.

The hot water of the bath could not convince me he was safe. The soft cloth I dried myself on did not mean he hadn't been killed. The fine feathers of the bed did not mean I would ever be able to sleep in his arms again. But exhaustion still stole the world from me, and I drifted into blackness, unsure of what I would find should I ever wake up.

24

Bright light beamed into my eyes, making me quite sure I was back outside the gates of Lygan Hall, left in the open with a herd of monsters eager to kill me.

I reached for the knife under my pillow before I'd even opened my eyes.

But the bright strip of light streaming into my room wasn't from the outer chamber, and I wasn't outside.

I wrapped a white sheet around me as I crawled off the feather mattress, searching the corners of the room for any hint of a person waiting to attack. I crept toward the bathroom, still gripping my knife, but there was no one in there either.

I didn't move toward the strip of light until I was sure I was alone.

Shame weighed on my shoulders as I realized I hadn't noticed the shutters in the stone wall the night before. With the light streaming between them, it seemed a horrible danger to have missed.

The shutters were only made of wood, nothing that could be considered battle worthy, and the window was nearly as big as a door, more than large enough for a person, or monster, to slip through.

I tightened the sheet around my chest before pushing the shutters open.

A vast valley stretched out before me. The bright morning light bathed the houses, fields, and patches of dense trees in a beautiful glow.

Snowcapped mountains surrounded the valley like soldiers standing guard, protecting Lygan Hall.

A cliff face stretched out on either side of me, with other windows scattered in all directions. High above, a balcony poked out of the rock, and far below, a raised garden had stairs that reached down to the valley floor.

People already roamed through the paths of the garden. None of them moved like a monster might come for their blood.

A dark bird soared across the bright blue sky, looping and swirling in blissful freedom.

"How do they convince anyone to leave?"

I had pictured Lygan Hall as a sturdy place made of stone with surviving the mountain winters the only concern in its building. I had never pictured a valley paradise.

A click sounded from the other side of the room.

I spun around, gripping my knife as the door swung open.

Ailis stepped into the room. Her gaze slid from the knife in my hand to the sheet wrapped around my body.

"At least you're clean," Ailis said. "I assume you're hungry as well."

"Where's Liam?" I didn't lower my knife.

"I've no idea." Ailis beckoned in two women. One carried a tray of food, the other pushed in a long, rolling trunk. "Last I heard, he went to see Orla."

"I have to find him," I said.

"If Liam wanted to see you, he would be here," Ailis said.

"Since he's not here, you're going to eat and put on a decent set of clothes."

"I'm not hungry."

"I didn't ask if you were hungry," Ailis said. "I told you you were going to eat."

The woman with the tray set the food on the vanity table and left. The woman with the rolling trunk hovered awkwardly for a moment.

"Yes?" Ailis turned to the woman.

"I don't know what size boots?" the woman said. "Liam said to be sure she was cared for—"

"You've seen Liam?" I started toward the woman.

Ailis stepped into my path.

"I will walk through this place naked," I said. "Do not test me."

"Take her boots and work from there," Ailis said.

"Where did you see Liam?" I asked as the woman scampered to my pile of blood-crusted clothes.

"I was called to Orla's council room." The woman gingerly lifted my boots.

"When? Is he still there?" I asked.

"Out," Ailis said. "Now."

The woman curtsied and hurried through the door.

"Where is the council room?" I headed toward my pack.

"It doesn't matter, because you're not going."

"I have to find Liam." I rounded on Ailis. "We were attacked. People were killed. I don't know if he's safe."

"He's in Lygan Hall."

"That doesn't mean anything!" My voice bounced off the stone walls of the room. "If Liam trusts you enough to protect me, I would have thought you'd be smart enough to know that."

Ailis looked up to the ceiling, as though searching for guidance from the gods. "I can't take you to the council room. I can't let you leave this room. If I have to set a pack of guards on you, I will, but it would be safer for everyone if you'd just agree to stay put. If Liam wanted you brought to the crag and protected by me, then it's clear he's worried about your safety.

"So, instead of running around trying to see if you can get into trouble, can't you just stay here and trust that Liam's doing what's best? Or at the very least stay safely in here so he doesn't get hurt running around trying to save you?"

"I thought you said Liam was safe." I looked to the window. "What would he have to save me from?"

"Whatever had him so fussed he ordered your protection and comfort before he bothered to close the chivving outer gate." Ailis sighed. "Please just eat some food. Then we'll get you into some proper clothes. If Liam still hasn't come by then, I'll send a runner to the council room to tell him you're looking for him."

I eyed the door to the hall.

"You won't make it out of this corridor without a flock of guards stopping you," Ailis said.

"Fine." I sat at the vanity, staring at the tray of food.

I'd been brought fruit, cheese, and rolls that still radiated heat. After days of trudging through the mountains, I should have been grateful for the bounty.

"Who are you anyway?" Ailis stepped up beside me and snagged a bit of cheese from the plate.

I opened my mouth to speak but couldn't find the right words.

The one Liam promised to share a bed with sounded absurd even in my head. Petal whore would have been the most common description. Lover might have worked if I'd been able to say the word aloud without feeling like a chivving fool.

"I'm Emmet's sister."

"Emmet?" Ailis said. "I didn't see him last night. He wasn't killed in the attack was he?"

"No." I took a bite of a roll. The gentle sweetness soothed the awful feeling in my stomach. "He's still in Ilbrea. On Liam's orders."

"Good." Ailis stole another piece of cheese. "I've always liked Emmet. He's such a nice man."

I coughed, choking on my roll. I took a sip of berry-sweetened water from a finely etched glass. "You're thinking of the wrong Emmet. No one has ever called my brother nice."

"Emmet Ryeland," Ailis said. "You look so much alike, I might've guessed you're related last night. Of course you were fairly caked in blood."

"How well do you know my brother?"

"Well enough." Ailis perched on the edge of the vanity. "We've trained together the last two winters. Been in some of the same hunting parties as well."

"Don't tell me"—I leaned back in my chair—"you have a wonderful story about Emmet doing something daring, but you can't tell me."

She laughed.

I liked the sound. It was easy, confident, like she wasn't afraid of the stars knowing she was happy.

"I don't have a daring story about Emmet. I was, however, there when he got tossed off the back of his dog sled and left behind."

"What?" I coughed on my berry water.

"Dog sleds are the fastest way to travel once the snow hits. Emmet does well enough hunting, but he learned to hold on tight to the sled the hard way. The dogs just kept racing on without him."

I started laughing along with her.

"He was just stuck standing in rib-high snow, watching his sled race away from him." Ailis spoke through her laughter.

"What happened?"

"I caught up to his dogs and turned them back. The lead dog hadn't even noticed they'd left him behind."

"I would love to have seen that."

"I can try to have him tossed off another sled this winter." She ate one of the berries. "I'd honestly love to see it again."

"He'll be here," I said. "Emmet will join us soon."

"I'm sure he will." Ailis's laughter faded from her eyes. "If you're not going to do more than pick at your food, we should get you dressed. The biddies downstairs banded together when they got word that Liam himself had said to look after you."

"I'll have to thank them." I stared at the trunk but couldn't convince myself to stand.

Ailis walked over and tossed the top open. Three different stacks of clothes waited inside. One of only shifts, one of skirts, and one of bodices.

At least the clothes you recognize.

"I can sort through them on my own," I said.

"Nonsense." Ailis pulled the stack of shifts from the trunk and began laying them out on the bed. "I was told to take proper care of you. You can't be in the crag looking like a little forest rabbit."

"Should I be dressed as a wolf instead?"

"You should be dressed to fit the station of someone in the crag."

"What does that even mean? What is the crag?"

"Right." Ailis stopped fussing with the shifts and pursed her lips as she studied me. "I'd have thought Liam would have told you more. Emmet knew all about Lygan Hall before he arrived. Seemed like he'd memorized a map of the Hall. Did you only just join up with Liam?"

I watched as she laid out a second full line of shifts.

"I've been in the camp since the spring." I picked up another roll just to have something to busy my hands.

"Huh." She moved on to laying out bodices. "Liam's busy during the summer months. It's not surprising he didn't have time to tell you about the Hall."

I stood and walked over to the bed.

I don't know what made me do it. Maybe it was jealousy, or

pride. Maybe I wanted to stake my claim, and maybe I was just sick of sitting around wrapped in bedding.

I stopped beside Ailis and dropped the sheet, letting the white fabric fall to the floor. I reached for a lavender-dyed shift, giving a full display of the raven mark Liam had drawn on my side. I turned to Ailis holding the shift low enough that she could not miss the black stone pendant lying against my pale skin.

"This is a pretty color." I ran my fingers over the soft fabric. "I suppose, now that I'm in Lygan Hall, I won't have to worry so much about blood stains on my clothes."

"No," Ailis said, "you won't."

I held her gaze as I unfolded the shift. "I hope not. But standing beside Liam comes with its dangers. I suppose that's the price I have to pay."

Ailis didn't say anything as I slipped the shift over my head. The luxurious texture of the fabric caressed my skin, offering a foreign kind of comfort.

I chose a deep blue bodice and a dark gray skirt with black stitching forming a design of mountains along the bottom. They were the finest clothes I'd ever worn.

I hated them.

I wished I had the skirt I'd worn when I fled from Harane. None of my clothes had been fancy, but I'd been able to run and climb in them.

The weight of the gray skirt would only have been an obstacle if I'd had to escape.

I looked at myself in the mirror once I was fully dressed. I'd hidden my pendant beneath my bodice, covering any hint that Liam and I were connected. Still, I couldn't look at my reflection and claim I was the girl who'd followed Liam away from the flames of Harane.

My face had lost its last traces of childish roundness. My eyes didn't hold fear anymore, only vicious courage. I was not one to wait for the Guilds to slaughter her. I was a demon who would chase the monsters into the flames.

"Where is Cati?" I asked. "Where are Finn and Marta? And the children, where are they?"

"Below, I suppose."

"Where is below?" I turned to Ailis.

"Where the healers live. The children were either taken there or, from what I hear, straight to the sorcerers' compound."

"I should go see them."

"No." She stepped in front of the door.

"I can't just wait here. You say I can't go to Liam, fine. At least let me check on the people who may need my help."

"There is one of me," Ailis said. "Liam put your safety under my care. Defending you in the open is far different than keeping you safe in the crag. Believe it or not, I can't watch all directions at once."

"Then I'm not safe here at all."

We'd sorted through all the clothes to find what actually fit me before the midday meal came. Then I sat on the bed and stared out the window for a while. Three more birds had joined the dark shape soaring through the sky.

I hated being powerless. Hated sitting in a fancy room, waiting for Liam to come for me.

Do not be a fool, Ena.

There was no way I could make it past six armed guards. Even if I did, I'd never find Liam or the others.

Knowing I was powerless only made the waiting worse.

Ailis stayed with me, though we didn't speak much. I wondered what she thought of the mark on my side. If she thought Liam was a fool for allowing someone who knew so little of Lygan Hall to swear an oath to him. I wondered what she thought of my pendant. If she thought me weak for needing his protection.

I could bear her thinking me useless as long she knew I was not a stranger to Liam.

Knock. Knock. Knock.

The sound carried through my room. I gripped the white

blankets beneath me, trying to decide if I should be ready to fight.

"Ena?"

"Liam." I leapt to my feet and raced to the door before Ailis had time to sheath her sword.

He stood in the hall, alive and whole.

Seeing his face brought me more comfort than I knew a person could feel.

He trailed his fingers along my cheek and down my neck. He kissed my forehead, as though wanting to be sure I was actually real.

His scent filled my lungs and wiped away the hours of worry.

"You're all right?" I whispered.

He kissed me. Heat surged through every fiber of my being. Then he held me tight in his arms, and the stone room no longer felt like a prison.

"I'm sorry." He pressed his lips to the top of my head. "I'm sorry it took so long. I had to be sure Lygan Hall could be defended against croilach."

"Against what?" Ailis asked.

"The beasts that attacked us." Liam stepped away from me and pulled her into a tight hug. "Nine croilach have been sent after us."

"What?" Ailis broke free of Liam and gripped the hilt of her sword.

"Orla is sending messages out to each of the clans," Liam said. "All the perimeters have been warned."

"Will it matter?" I laid a hand on Liam's chest, needing to feel his heartbeat beneath my palm.

"She called us back to protect me from assassins," Liam said. "Orla will not allow an attack on Lygan Hall."

"What about the others?" I asked. "Cati and Finn. Are they safe? Did the healers help them?"

Liam wrapped his arm around my waist, holding me close to

his side. "They're up in the keep. The healers have tended to them."

"And the children?" I asked. "Is Gwen awake?"

"Marta is with them," Liam said. "She would have sent word if anything bad had happened."

"I need to go to them," I said. "You need to rest. We have to find out who sent the beasts after you."

"We will," Liam said. "We can see Cati and Finn now. We'll go to the children once the sorcerers send word that we're welcome."

"What?"

"We can't just walk into the sorcerers' compound," Liam said. "But Wyman will send word when it's time."

I closed my eyes, pressing down all the questions rattling through my mind.

"Let's go to Cati and Finn," I said.

I think Liam must have sensed my urge to flee, my absolute hatred of being told I wasn't allowed to see the children I'd taken from their home.

He laced his fingers through mine and kissed my cheek. "Trust me," he whispered so softly I would have thought I'd imagined the words if I hadn't felt his breath caress my neck.

"Shall I escort you?" Ailis asked.

"To the keep, if you will," Liam said. "Then you should sleep."

"Have you slept?" Ailis asked.

"No," Liam said. "But that doesn't give you an excuse not to."

"I'll set a new guard around the base of the keep and then rest." Ailis led us out the door. "The Healy Blood Leader has been murdered, and there've been two attacks on the Duwead Trueborn. I won't trust a gnat as safe until we find whatever vermin is responsible for all this."

Is it the same rat who's killed so many?

I hadn't considered it before. For some reason, I'd thought the beast that had tormented the camp had been created solely to harm the Duwead Clan. In my mind, the beast had been made to hurt Liam and stop our work in Ilbrea. It had never occurred to me that the terror we'd suffered at the camp hadn't been aimed solely at the people I cared for.

The idea that the attack hadn't been so specific, that there was some vile person sitting in a cave, sending death and horror after people they didn't even know, who'd never done anything to offend, just for the joy of spreading bloodshed like so much sheep shit, brought a familiar helpless hatred to my gut.

The Guilds killed without care. That was their world, their unforgivable flaw. I could not believe I had escaped one hell to walk willingly into another.

I kept Liam's hand tightly in mine as the guards bowed us past the carved metal door. We walked down one hallway and up another, passing through a gate and another door before entering a wide hall.

Even though the sun shone outside, orange spheres and torches glowed brightly in the corridor. A fountain shaped like a mountain peak spat water in the middle of it all. Women in well made skirts sat around the fountain like Death himself hadn't chased us to their gates only hours before. Men in perfectly clean clothes chatted in groups like none of their fellows could possibly be plotting murder.

Liam led me through a wide entryway where more guards waited, then up a sweeping set of spiral stairs that seemed as though they'd go on forever.

I wanted to stop Liam and ask him what under the chivving stars was happening and how a place like this had been built in the side of a mountain. But I didn't know Ailis well enough to speak with her walking behind us.

As we climbed higher, windows began appearing along the stairs. The shutters had been left open, and every window we passed offered a vaster view of the valley below.

When I thought my legs would give out in protest at being

asked to work so hard after the distance we'd traveled the day before, the stairs opened into another wide chamber.

More guards stood along the edges of the room, and more corridors branched off in different directions.

A person could spend a lifetime lost in this labyrinth.

Two guards nodded to Liam and followed behind us as we walked down a side hall. One of the walls was made almost entirely of windows, with places to step through onto a narrow balcony beyond. I wondered when we had climbed past the wide balcony I'd seen from below.

Liam stopped in front of a wooden door and knocked.

He let go of my hand and slipped his arm around my waist while we waited.

The door opened, and a woman with gray-streaked, red hair peeked into the hall.

"Liam." The woman smiled for a moment before a scowl took over her face. "Finn needs rest. He's been tramping through the wilderness and attacked. I mean no disrespect, but he is not ready to be running about."

"Let it be, Mother," Finn called from inside. "If they want me to march into battle, I'm going to go, so there's no use in fussing."

"I'm your mother." The woman rounded on Finn. "It is my job to fuss. And you will not be fighting anyone or running anywhere until your arm is healed up. I absolutely refuse to let my sweet little boy lose an arm because he's too foolish to realize flesh needs time to heal."

"Mother"—Finn appeared behind her shoulder, wearing a long, purple dressing gown—"can you just go steal a bit of pie from Granny's and let me be?"

"The moment I leave, you'll be running off and ripping your stitches." Finn's mother jammed a finger into his chest.

"I'm stuck here till spring," Finn sighed. "Can't you fuss over me when there aren't people watching?"

His mother's lips turned into one thin line as she looked from Liam, to me, to Ailis, and finally to Finn.

"If I hear one whisper of you doing something foolish, gods help you I'll break your legs and tie you to my hearth."

"Yes, yes." Finn shooed her out the door. "I love you too, Mother. Don't forget about the pie."

Finn's mother kept shaking her head until she turned out of the corridor and disappeared from view.

"We really should find a way to stay closer to Ilbrea year-round," Finn said. "I don't know if I can survive a whole winter of her fussing."

"I thought you said she cried tears of joy when you decided to travel outside Lygan Hall." I stepped closer to Finn.

"Ah, but I live in the keep now," Finn said. "She's not the one to feed me."

"Are you all right?" I asked.

Finn wrapped his good arm around me and pulled me into a tight hug. "We live to fight another day. That's what matters."

"What about the people who didn't make it?" A horrible pain swiped at my throat.

"We find comfort in vengeance." Finn bowed us into his room. It looked much like the place I'd slept—there was a fancy bed and a wardrobe—only Finn had a desk in place of a vanity, and hints of permanent occupation lay scattered across the room.

A worn bow and quiver of arrows had been tucked into one corner. A small painting of a red-haired man sat on the desk. A stack of books waited beside a stuffed chair.

"I'll send new guards," Ailis said before she closed the door behind us.

26

Finn's face drooped into exhaustion as he sank down onto his bed.

"Tell me we know something." He rubbed his good hand over his face.

"I wish I could," Liam said. "I spent the night going through everything that's happened with Orla. She sent messages out and posted more guards, but I've no chivving clue who attacked us."

"It has to be a trueborn." I wished I had my knife in my boot, or even had any chivving shoes at all, so I'd be ready to run from whatever horror lurked in the shadows.

"It wasn't a Duwead trueborn who made the croilach." Liam paced beside Finn's bed.

"I think we can all be sure of that."

"How?" I asked.

"Orla is the only other trueborn the Duweads have," Liam said. "If she wanted me dead, she wouldn't bother exhausting herself making monsters."

"Regan then." I sat on the stuffed chair. The comfort of the seat set my nerves on edge, like the blue fabric were some sort of deadly trap. I stood back up.

"Maybe," Finn said.

"Not alone," Liam said. "To make nine croilach, to know when we were leaving the camp… If it was Regan, she had help."

"Is there any way she could have done it without the help of someone from the camp?" I dug my fingers through my hair, trying to pull through the tangles of this awful mess.

"I can't see how," Liam said. "I wanted it to be one of Orla's people in Ilbrea who'd helped a trueborn send the monster to camp and let the soldiers know where we'd been ferrying the children."

"But someone in Ilbrea wouldn't have known the camp was packing up." I froze for a moment, then started weaving my hair into a tight braid. "It was someone from the camp then."

"Who would bring eight croilach down on their own head?" Finn said.

"I don't know." Liam dug his knuckles into his temples. "I told Orla about the attacks and the soldiers on the western edge of the forest. She agrees that someone has betrayed the Black Bloods."

"But she doesn't have a chivving clue as to who?" Finn said.

"She's allowed me to ask for the sorcerers' aid," Liam said. "I don't think we have any other choice."

A deep cold rattled my spine.

"What do we do now?" I asked. "Sit by and wait for magic to fix the problem?"

"We can ride for the Brien safe haven," Finn said. "Visit their elder and demand answers."

"You're not riding anywhere until your arm is healed," I said.

"None of us can leave," Liam said. "Orla's banned all travel outside the valley. She takes the attack on our caravan as an attempt on my life and an act of war."

"Chivving gods and stars, Liam." Finn shook his head. "We can't leap into a clan war right now. We can't just walk away from the good we've finally managed to do in Ilbrea."

"I know," Liam said. "But we've got to make sure everyone here is safe, convince Orla that what we've accomplished in Ilbrea matters, and avoid destroying the peace that's kept the Black Bloods alive for more than a century."

I wrapped my arms around Liam and laid my cheek against his chest.

"We'll do it." My voice sounded strong, like someone who was capable of challenging a war. "We'll sort all this out."

Liam held me close and kissed the top of my head. I held him tighter. The world could have burned us and I still would have been grateful to be wrapped in his arms.

"Where do we start?" I asked.

"We root out the traitor," Finn said. "Find them, find who they've been feeding information to, kill that whole lot. Then we worry about the clan war. We don't even know who the enemy is right now. We've got to do that before anything else."

"I'll speak to Wyman," Liam said. "Give him a list of everyone from the camp."

"You'll lose a lot of followers if the sorcerers offend loyal people," Finn said.

"I lost twenty-eight yesterday," Liam said. "I'd rather have my people hate me than put any more of them underground."

"Can you send a bird to Mave?" I asked. "In case Emmet turns up in Frason's Glenn. Warn him that there could be more croilach in the mountains."

"I pray to the gods there aren't more of those beasts lurking on our land," Finn said.

"I can't send word to Frason's Glenn." Liam stepped away from me but kept both his hands tightly around my waist.

"Is there news? Is Emmet hurt? Was he captured by the Guilds?"

"Orla thinks Emmet is the one who betrayed us."

The room swayed, and he gripped my waist tighter.

"That is utterly ridiculous." Finn stood and placed his hand on my back.

"Emmet would never betray you," I said. "And he couldn't have known we were leaving the camp. He's out in Ilbrea right now burning his way through the paun."

"I know that," Liam said.

"You told me Orla liked him." I broke away from both men. "You said he'd saved your life so she liked him."

"She does," Liam said.

"Then how could she accuse him of causing the deaths of so many people?" My words echoed around the room. I was sure they'd carried into the hall. "Emmet wouldn't betray you. He'd never risk monsters like the croilach coming anywhere near me. And what about Marta? Does he treat her so casually he'd risk her life?"

"I believe you," Liam said. "I believe in him."

"Did you tell Orla that?" I asked.

"Of course I did," Liam said. "But it's easier for her to believe that Emmet is a traitor than to consider that one of the people who grew up in her halls betrayed their clan."

"This is chivving ridiculous," I said. "My brother isn't even here to defend himself."

"So we'll do it for him," Finn said. "We'll use the sorcerers to find the traitor and clear Emmet's name well before he gets back to Lygan Hall."

"I'll go now," Liam said. "We'll start sorting through people from camp before the end of the day."

"Good." Finn reached for me. "Ena and I will stay here and try to work out how we can slog through this chivving mess faster."

Liam kissed the back of my hand. "I will make sure we find the scum who started this. I promise we'll be safe again."

I nodded. I couldn't think of anything bracing to say.

Liam left. The door clicked shut behind him, and I was alone with Finn.

"We'll need to rally the people from camp," Finn said. "As soon as they're cleared by the sorcerers, we'll need to make sure they spread the word of all the work we're doing in Ilbrea to the rest of Lygan Hall."

"How will the sorcerers know who betrayed us?" I dragged my fingers through my hair again and began weaving the strands into an even tighter braid.

"They have their ways," Finn said. "I can't say I understand the magic they use, and the process isn't pleasant. But if they question the murdering slitch, they'll know."

"Does it count as murder if the traitor never even held a blade against any of our people?" My hands shook as I finished my braid.

"Yes. They worked to kill our people. That makes them a murderer in my book."

"That means I murdered Drason, you know. If that's how you count it."

"It does." Finn went to his wardrobe and fished around the bottom for a moment. "But Drason was a monster who stole women and children from their homes. He was responsible for a lot of death and horror. There's a difference between slaying a beast and murdering people you counted as friends."

"Whoever betrayed us drank with us in the clearing." Sour rolled into my throat. "They grieved with us when Pierce and Dillon were killed."

"And they'll pay for all of it."

"What will Orla do to them when they're found?"

"The treaty lays out the method of their punishment." Finn handed me a short leather cord. "Honestly, if I was the cacting slitch, I hop off the high summit and plunge to a much quicker death than the end Orla will offer."

"What if she won't believe it wasn't Emmet?" I tied the cord around the end of my braid.

"She will."

"But what if she won't?"

Finn rubbed his hand over the red scruff on his chin. "We'll ask the gods for aid and hope they bring an answer that won't make us traitors to the clan."

Knock. Knock. Knock.

My shoulders tensed at the sound, like somehow my body knew it wasn't Liam outside the door.

"Who's there?" Finn called.

Knock. Knock. Knock.

The sound came again.

Finn slipped a dagger with a carved wooden handle out from under his pillow. He held the weapon behind his back, wincing as he opened the door with his wounded arm.

"Hello there," Finn said.

I inched to the side to peer around him.

Four men in blue jackets waited in the hall.

"Can I help you gentlemen?" Finn asked after another moment.

"We're here for the girl," the man in front said.

"I'm sorry," Finn said, "I had an awful day yesterday, so my mind is running a bit slow. You're here for who?"

"Ena Ryeland." The man looked straight into my eyes.

"Ah." Finn nodded. "I see. Unfortunately, Liam told her to stay here with me. Perhaps you might be able to come back for her later, once Liam is here to give—"

"We are to collect the girl by order of Orla," the man said. "Move out of the way before we make you."

The sides of Finn's neck tensed as he gripped the weapon behind his back.

"It's all right, Finn." I laid my hand on his shoulder. "No point in making a fuss over going to see someone, right?"

"Of course not," Finn said.

"You need to rest anyway. Get some sleep, and we'll talk later."

"Right." Finn tucked the dagger into the back of his purple robe's sash. "A bit of sleep is exactly what I need."

I gave him a smile before slipping past him into the hall.

The four men in blue coats surrounded me. They didn't reach for me or brandish any weapons, but the feel of them, the way my heart thundered in my chest like it was shouting a terrible warning, felt like I'd been penned in by Guilded soldiers.

They all started walking without asking me to move along with them. I had no choice but to follow or try and fight.

For one foolish moment, I wished I'd taken Finn's dagger. Then the swords on the guards' hips caught my eye. I'd been training to fight, but I was not Cati. I could not battle four swords and hope to come out alive.

I moved down the corridor with them, keeping step within my cage of men.

I wanted to ask questions, if only to bother the guards, but a whisper in my mind told me to stay quiet. To wear my armor well even if I was barefoot and the only shield I had was silence.

We went into the wide corridor. There were more people in the space than when I'd passed through with Liam. The fancily dressed men and women stared as the guards escorted me past.

We cut down one hall, along another, and out into the grandest chivving place I'd ever seen.

The black stone of the walls had all been polished to perfection and carved into an intricate pattern of swirls that somehow formed a picture of a mountain range. White, gray, red, and blue stone had been set into the black, making the whole room look like we'd stepped into an artisan's masterpiece.

Wide windows granted light to a sweeping staircase that spanned the whole width of the room. The steps cut down and twisted out of sight. A polished set of massive metal doors stood opposite the stairs, but the door the guards had led me through was a normal size, like we'd cut into the grand space through a side passage.

There were more men in blue jackets lining the walls of this hall. Each of them held a sword. Each of them looked ready to kill me.

Maybe all the world is actually the same. Maybe the colors of the uniforms are the only difference from one place to another.

I lifted my hand to press my stone pendant to my skin.

The rasp of swords being drawn from their sheaths stopped my movement.

"Are you really this afraid?" I said, not asking anyone in particular. "You're in a place guarded by the magic of the mountain. You've got dozens of passages between here and the entrance to Lygan Hall. You have sorcerers of your own. What could have made you this afraid? What leader is this terrified of her own people?"

None of the guards bothered to answer.

We stopped in front of the giant metal door. I studied the images carved onto the surface.

At first, it seemed like a simple design of mountains, but the longer I looked at the picture, the more defined the scene became.

Streaks of lightning cut along the top, reaching toward the highest of the peaks. A woman stood on the summit of the mountain, her shawl blowing from her shoulders as she clutched a baby in her arms. At the very bottom of the door, an orb hid beneath the mountains.

I wondered if the person who'd carved the picture had meant the circle to look as though an evil lurked beneath the woman's feet, waiting to devour her.

We stood silently for a long while.

I wanted to ask the guards if they were going to knock, but I kept staring at the orb, wondering what malice would spring up from below to swallow the mother and child.

Without a word or a sound, the doors swung open, allowing us into Orla's council chamber.

27

She sat on her throne at the end of the dark stone room. Tiny orange glowing orbs hung from the ceiling like a king's chandelier. The light should have been enough to give the place a cheerful glow, but the magic within the orbs was not strong enough to banish the darkness.

There was no design in the walls of the black stone room. Nothing at all to suggest the space might offer peace or contentment. A round table and set of chairs took up one half of the room. They had been carved of richly hued wood, but the effect brought no cheer.

Orla's throne was made of black rock molded into swirls and curves that should have been beautiful. But the stone only looked like the tendrils of a great shadow beast ready to taste my blood.

Even the woman herself offered no hint of light.

Her dark hair and eyes were accented by the deep sapphire of her dress. She might have been beautiful if her face weren't filled with quiet loathing.

Orla studied me, starting with my face, moving down to my feet, and coming back up again, as though wanting to be sure she had thoroughly observed the horror of me.

"I should have known you'd be pretty," Orla said.

A bit of rage sliced through my reason.

"Thank you." I met her gaze as I curtsied. "I'd like to know who pays me such a compliment."

I waited for her to rage or laugh, but she only stared.

"Orla, Elder of the Duwead Clan." Her voice stayed calm as she spoke. "And you are Ena Ryeland, sister of Emmet Ryeland."

"Yes ma'am. I'm sorry my brother isn't here to greet you. Last I heard, he was out torching paun as he searched for me. Knowing Emmet, it might be a while before he lets his anger at the Guilds go long enough to realize I'm not being held captive in Ilara."

"Right to it then," Orla said. "How refreshing not to dodge around the conversation."

"Sorry to disappoint you"—I gave another curtsy, not bothering to try and hide my bare feet—"but I've no idea what conversation we're meant to be having."

"Your brother betrayed the Duwead Clan." Orla laid her hands on her lap. "He has been feeding information to one of our enemies. His betrayal has resulted in the deaths of more than thirty of my people."

"Ah." I nodded. "I see. Your people are dead, and you want to blame my brother. Emmet's not perfect, I'll be the first to admit that, but he would never betray Liam. My brother would do anything to destroy the Guilds."

"Perhaps Emmet believes that sending the clans into a war would somehow make them strike out against the Guilds."

"What?" I pushed out a laugh. "I don't know how you think that would work. The clans fighting amongst themselves wouldn't do anything to help the common folk in Ilbrea. It would only leave more dead scattered in the mountains."

"A man who sets off in a blaze of fury to conquer one enemy can easily be turned to believe others are his foe."

"Emmet did not betray Liam." I laid my palms flat against the sides of my legs, refusing to let them display any hint of my anger. "He couldn't be responsible for the croilach attacks. He was in Ilbrea on Liam's orders the first time—"

"How convenient."

"—and he's been in Ilbrea searching for me for the last month," I pressed on. "He's been terrorizing paun soldiers, which you should chivving well thank him for."

"Are you always so foul-mouthed when faced with authority?"

"Only when the authority warrants it." I stepped closer to her dark throne, ignoring the rasps of swords clearing their sheaths all around me. "Three times, croilach came close to killing me. My brother would never, ever place me in such danger. He'd never place anyone from the camp in that kind of danger."

"I'm not naïve enough to believe he genuinely cares for anyone in the camp."

"They really don't tell you much, do they?" I smiled, relishing the deepening of the wrinkles around Orla's eyes. "Emmet would die before allowing a monster anywhere near me. He'd die before he let a beast threaten the camp. I'm sorry one of your own people has betrayed you, but your problem has nothing to do with my brother. He wasn't even in camp when Liam got the orders for us to pack up. He couldn't have sent word that we'd be vulnerable. It's just not possible."

"Then perhaps the two of you are working together," Orla said. "Perhaps you sent word that Liam would be in the open."

"Me?"

"You were in camp when Liam received my orders." Orla stood. "You were missing for weeks. You had plenty of time to run to the fiend who created the croilach."

"I had nothing to do with any of this." I pressed my hands against my legs, trying to squeeze away my urge to run. "I've only met two trueborn—Liam and Regan. Liam was with me when I met Regan, so I certainly couldn't have tossed together some plan to help her. If you don't believe me, ask him."

"Oh, I'm sure Liam would tell me you couldn't possibly have done this terrible thing." A tiny smile curved one side of Orla's mouth.

"He trusts me."

"I'm sure he does. Men with hungry snakes have lost their senses for much less pretty faces. My son may be an excellent leader, but that doesn't make him immune to a beautiful liar."

Her words rang through the room. I searched each syllable, trying to find where my mind had lost its reason.

"He really doesn't tell you anything." I spoke softly, barely loud enough for Orla to hear.

"I know everything I need to." Orla's skirt swished as she walked closer to me.

I hated that starched sound. She might as well have been a growling beast.

"There are two outsiders in Liam's camp." She stopped three feet in front of me. "There were no problems in the camp until the Ryelands inserted themselves into Liam's cause."

"I didn't insert myself into anything." My laugh grated my throat. "Liam came to me as my home burned. He saved me. He brought me through the mountains to the camp. So unless you think I have the chivving power to stage an attack by Guilded soldiers on my own village, then you've lost your mind and are just searching for anyone to blame."

"How dare—"

"I'm sorry you're grieving."

The guards stepped closer to me.

I ignored them and pressed on. "I'm sorry you're hurt and scared, but it's got nothing to do with me. If you want something to blame me for, I'd be happy to give you a list of all the ways I have failed. But I would never hurt Liam."

"You will regret the day you met my son," Orla said.

"Never. Nothing could ever make me regret meeting Liam."

Sounds of shouting carried through the metal door.

"Wanting someone to blame doesn't make me guilty," I said. "It only gives the murderer more time to plot against you."

The shouting grew louder.

I waited for a monster to burst through the door and slash me to shreds with its claws, or for Orla to begin executing me in some horrible and painful manner, but she didn't move. Neither of us did. We just stood glaring at each other until the metal doors banged open.

"Ena."

I turned at the sound of Liam's voice.

Sweat glistened on his brow, and he gripped the hilt of the blade on his hip.

"What is she doing in here?" Liam looked to his mother.

"Being accused of treachery and murder," I said.

Liam stopped beside me, his stance wide as though ready to defend me from an army of beasts.

"Ena had nothing to do with this," Liam said. "She is completely innocent."

"It is so easy to believe the beautiful are innocent," Orla said. "That doesn't make it true. She and her brother betrayed the Duwead Clan. She will pay the price, and I will hunt for Emmet. Justice will be done."

"Then kill me." Liam let go of his sword and spread his arms wide. "If you think Ena is guilty of murder, then run me through right now."

"This is not the time," Orla said.

"Of course it is," Liam said. "There is no punishing her without hurting me. Ena took the oath. Her deeds are bound to my fate. If she is guilty, then I die, too."

Orla froze.

"Even if she hadn't given me her vow, I would not let you harm her." Liam took my hand in his. "She is mine as I am hers. Find someone else to accuse, Mother."

He began leading me away, but I couldn't tear my gaze from

Orla's face. There were hints of Liam in the cut of her cheeks. I'd seen the quiet anger that raged behind her eyes in Liam's as well.

"You're a fool," Orla said. "You trust Ilbreans as though the Guilds have not contaminated them all."

"And you trust your people as though one of them has not tried to murder your only child." Liam kept walking.

I looked away from Orla as we neared the door.

"I will find the one who betrayed our clan," Liam said. "Either help me or stay out of my way."

I waited for the guards to leap in front of the door and bar our path, but they did not move as Liam led me out into the grand room with the fancy stone walls. We passed by more and more guards wearing blue, enough to fend off a proper attack.

Who does Orla fear so deeply?

My heart raced too fast for me to form the words.

Liam didn't lead me back the way I'd come. We walked down the wide, stone stairs.

Statues flanked the hall that waited at the bottom—life-sized monuments to men and women who all seemed to look a bit like Liam. Guards waited between the statues, but still, no one stopped us.

We reached another metal door, and two men sprang forward to wrench it open before Liam could touch the handle.

A hall with six doors, all on the same wall, waited within.

Liam led me through the second door on the left, then slammed the door shut behind us and slid the metal bolt into place.

The room was beautiful, by far the fanciest quarters I'd ever set foot in.

A massive bed sat on a low stone pedestal. Curtains of gauzy, pale blue fabric surrounded the bed, though I had no idea what purpose such delicate material might serve.

A set of windows covered the front wall, displaying the view of the valley like a work of art. A stone fireplace, carved to look like the profile of a massive bird, took up one side wall. To the other side, an open door led into a room with a table, chairs, and two massive wardrobes.

Liam let go of my hand as he stormed through the door into that room and bolted the entrance from the hall.

I walked toward the bed. A rug woven of blue, red, and silver surrounded the bed's pedestal. The dense softness beneath my feet didn't bring any comfort.

I stepped back onto the stone floor.

Where I belong.

Liam came back from the second room and paced in front of the door.

I watched him go back and forth. Back and forth.

"Did she hurt you?" He didn't stop his pacing as he spoke.

"No." I took a deep breath. The room smelled of fresh flowers, though I didn't see any blooms. "She sent her guards to collect me. Told me Emmet was a traitor, said I was a traitor, then you came in."

"She will not hurt you." Liam shook his head. "I will see to it that she leaves you out of this."

"How could she accuse me again? I've given my oath to her son."

Liam stopped. He stared at the bird carved around the fireplace for a moment before looking at me.

"You could've told me," I said. "You could have mentioned once that Orla was your mother."

"I didn't think you'd be meeting her the day you stepped into Lygan Hall." Liam ran his hands over his hair. "I thought I'd have time—"

"Time to what? Warn me that the man I'm rolling around with is the son of the woman who leads the Duwead Clan? I should have been told before I stripped my clothes off for you."

"Would it have changed your mind?"

There was hurt in his eyes. Actual worry and fear.

I took his face in my hands and pressed my forehead to his. "You could be the son of the King and I would still want you."

He wrapped his arms around me.

"But in all the times I heard her name, in all the plans for Marten, and helping the sorcis, how did no one ever mention that Orla is your mother?"

"It's not important."

"Chivving gods and stars, Liam, yes it is." I stepped away from him and swept a hand around the room. "Clearly it is. I thought Lygan Hall was a cozy cave, not a chivving palace."

"I never said the Hall was a cave."

"You never mentioned the few hundred guards or the giant chivving valley, either."

"I forget what other people don't know."

"You told Emmet." It was my turn to pace. I hated the stone floor beneath my bare feet. I felt too vulnerable without my shoes. "You told him about the Hall and the layout of the whole place. Ailis told me. Ailis was very confused as to why I didn't know a chivving thing about your home."

"Emmet needed to hear," Liam said. "He needed to know there was something in the mountains besides a camp full of people willing to fight. Do you think he would have gone so far away from you if he didn't know he was fighting alongside people with more than five horses and some tents?"

"How many horses do you have here?" I went to the window. A wide balcony waited beyond. I stepped outside and looked down to the valley below. "There must be thousands of people in Lygan Hall. You have sorcerers here. Why can't the Duweads march on the Guilds?"

"We have twelve hundred guards." Liam stepped out beside me. "We have tanners, cobblers, farmers, healers, and sorcerers. There are even Duweads outside the valley. Brave folks who homestead beyond the protection of Lygan Hall. But there are about as many people in Frason's Glenn as in the whole Duwead Clan. We could launch an attack on Ilara, but even if every man and woman in the valley fought, we'd never win. We might make it through a day, but we'd never break the walls or hold the city."

"And Orla knows it, doesn't she?"

"She does." Liam laid a hand on my shoulder.

I leaned into his touch. "Yet she sends her only child to the woods to work against the Guilds."

"I have to go. There has to be a trueborn to protect the camp. The last trueborn to lead the camp died six years ago. Now it's only Orla and me. She can't go, so it became my duty."

I stepped closer to him, resting my head against his shoulder.

"I knew it was coming," Liam said. "I'd been trained to assume the responsibilities of a trueborn since I was too young to understand what that meant. Orla hoped someone in the valley would give birth to another trueborn baby, but there hasn't been one since me."

"She's your mother. All those stone birds have been coming from your mother."

"Orla's never been much of a mother." Liam laid his cheek against the top of my head. "She gave birth to an heir. That's more important to her than a son. To me, she's always been the Elder of the clan. *Mother* is just a title I use when I want to annoy her."

"I'm sorry."

"Don't be. An excellent woman raised me. She's just not the one who carried me in her womb."

I twisted to look into Liam's eyes, searching for some hidden wound I'd never managed to see.

"I will not let Orla hurt you. She can't risk hurting me. I'm the only one who can take her place." Liam gave a tired smile.

"You need to sleep."

"I can't."

"If you don't rest now, it won't be Orla's wrath that ends you."

"There's a traitor. There is work—"

I kissed Liam, cutting off his list of everything that had to be done to protect us all.

"How do I get to the sorcerers?" I asked.

"I'll go."

"No." I stepped around him, making sure he didn't try to head for the door.

"You can't. It's too dangerous to send you out into the open while Orla's angry."

"Fine. You're Orla's son, heir of the Duwead Clan. Send a message and make the sorcerers come to you. Then you sleep."

He stayed silent for a moment before nodding. He stepped in and kissed me.

He tasted the same as he had when we'd been living in tents in the woods. He had the same scent of fresh wind and reckless freedom. His body felt the same as I leaned against him. I tried to find comfort in all those familiar things.

Liam tipped my chin up and looked into my eyes.

"Even if you hadn't sworn an oath to me, I would not have let Orla take you. I need you to believe that. I would fight the entire world to protect you."

I did not know how soon that battle would begin.

29

I stayed on the stone balcony as Liam spoke to the sorcerer in the sitting room beside his bedroom. I sat gazing out over the valley, trying not to be grateful that I couldn't hear what they were saying.

The two spoke for a long time. I watched the clouds race across the sky and looked at the tiny people far below. I tried to picture Liam living in this room, the Liam I cared so much for growing up in a fancy hall, surrounded by guards and catered to by servants.

The door to the side room opened, and a woman stepped through. She watched me sitting on the balcony with an air of modest interest on her angled face.

The woman didn't look magical. She wore her plain brown hair in a simple bun. Her dress was pretty enough but didn't seem to have a special color or any other marking of being a uniform. But there was something about her that screamed she was dangerous and powerful.

She walked closer to the balcony.

I pressed my hands against the stone beneath me, preparing to spring to my feet to fight.

"I'll be sure the groundskeepers know to let her in," the woman said.

"Thank you." Liam stepped out of the sitting room door to stand behind the woman.

She bowed to Liam and started toward his bedroom door.

"Deirdre," Liam said.

She stopped with her hand on the lock.

"Ask Wyman to be gentle," Liam said. "There is a traitor among us, but there are far more innocent people who don't deserve to be in pain."

"He will only be as intrusive as he must." Deirdre nodded, slid the bolt aside, and stepped out into the hall. The door closed behind her, and the bolt slid back into place without Liam reaching for it.

"Makes locks seem a bit pointless." I stood up, trying to convince myself I had no enemy to flee from.

"Locks only work on people who are willing to be kept out." Liam climbed the stone step and sat on the bed. "Gwen still isn't awake."

"Why?" Panic clenched around my heart. "Can the healers help her if the sorcerers can't?"

"She's not ill." Liam rested his head in his hands. "She burned out."

"What does that mean?" I stepped up onto the stone platform and sat beside Liam.

"She pushed more magic through her body than she should have. Her body didn't know what to do, so it shut down. She'll sleep until she's recovered."

"But she will recover?"

"She will. It may take hours or weeks, but she'll wake up when she's ready."

"And the other children?" I did not want to think of the children without Gwen to guide them. I didn't know if Cinni would be able to survive without her older sister.

"Deirdre didn't seem happy about having Ilbrean children in the compound, but she'll learn to enjoy their presence. Marta is still with them. She'll make sure they behave."

"Then that's all you can do for now." I rested my hand on Liam's leg.

"I should go stand guard at the outer gate or send more messages. I should find a way to do more good."

"You will, when you wake up." I took Liam's hand and dragged him to his feet. He didn't argue as I pulled back the blankets, whose thickness and soft texture didn't seem to match.

"Promise you'll stay with me."

"Sleep." I pointed toward the row of pillows along the top of the bed.

"Only if you'll stay with me." He took my hand and kissed the inside of my wrist. "I've lost too many people since the last time I slept. I need to feel you beside me if I'm going to slip into darkness."

I brushed my lips against his. "I will stay right here. My place is with you."

I had only had new boots once in my life before Lygan Hall.

When I was little, Lily had bartered for used boots other children of Harane had outgrown.

When I was finally old enough to keep a pair of shoes for a bit, Lily bought me brand new boots. They were plain brown and belonged only to me. I'd destroyed those boots on my way to the camp in the mountains.

When Liam finally woke up the day after we arrived in Lygan Hall, a woman was waiting outside his door. She had a pair of boots with her. They were made of fine black leather and had been built just for me. The cobbler had torn apart the second-hand boots I'd worn since I'd joined Liam and made a brand new pair from the marks my feet had left in the tatters of my old shoes.

The new boots were soft on my ankles and made with a hardy sole. They fit me perfectly.

Those chivving boots were nicer than any shoes anyone in Harane had ever owned.

The woman curtsied to me as she left Liam's rooms.

"What exactly do you propose we do about it?" Cati stormed back and forth across Liam's sitting room. "I'm not going to be able to entertain them with blunted swords for long."

"I don't want you to," Liam said.

"Then come up with another plan." Cati smacked her hands against the table. "Yesterday, I had a sorcerer show up at my room. They want me to go to the compound. Fine. Wyman himself wants to be sure I'm not the traitor who got our people killed. Fine. I let him use his magic on me. Why?"

"To set an example for the rest," Liam said.

"Exactly." Cati pointed at Liam's chest. "I let that man question me so the others couldn't be angry. I hop onto the training field to get rid of my will to slaughter everything that moves, and you know what? So does the next one Wyman messes with, and the next. Now I've got a field of raging mad people."

"And I am grateful to you for taking care of them." Liam pushed his chair away from the table and stood.

I didn't move. I stayed in my seat, staring at the remains of my lunch.

"What would really help them is having something to do," Cati said. "Get Orla to open the gates."

"She won't do it."

"Make her," Cati said.

"She's forbidden everyone from leaving Lygan Hall," Liam said.

"All I can see in my mind are those monsters tearing apart my friends." Cati's voice caught in her throat. "There are more of them out there. If not croilach, then whatever the chivving bastard plans to have attack us next. Let me find them. Let me kill them."

"You can't," Liam said. "I'm sorry, but you have to stay here. Work on training the fighters. Bruise them all if you have to, but I need you here and alive. You're the best teacher I've got."

"That is going to stop being good enough," Cati said. "I am not a house cat, Liam. I cannot pace in the kitchen, purring. There are monsters out there, and I will slay them."

"I know," Liam said, "but right now, our worst enemy is already in the Hall. I need you here, keeping the men moving, watching for any hint of the traitor. I need you to be ready to help me kill the chivving bastard when we find them."

Cati looked up at the stone ceiling. A series of orange orbs had been set into the rock, leaving a glowing trail of light overhead.

"I have fewer than a dozen people I can truly trust within these walls. I am your Trueborn, and I need you here," Liam said. "Please, Cati."

Cati nodded.

"Thank you." Liam walked over to the window, looking down at the valley below.

I wondered if he knew who lived in all the houses and which trees produced what fruit. I wondered if he was remembering his childhood or plotting the best place to attack the traitor.

"How many has Wyman questioned so far?" Liam asked.

"Based on the ones who've shown up to the training ground," Cati said, "about half of us. The only one who's put up a fuss is Marta."

"Marta?" I gripped the arms of my chair. "Marta would never hurt anyone. There's not—"

Cati held up a hand to silence me. "She's refusing to leave the children. Gwen still isn't awake, and she doesn't trust the sorcerers to take proper care of Cinni without her watching over them."

"Does she need to be questioned?" I asked.

"If she wants people to trust her word on Emmet's innocence, then she should," Cati said. "Anyone who's fought by Emmet's side knows he couldn't have done this. The more people proven innocent who can shout it to the cowardly slitches who hide in Lygan Hall, the better off we'll be."

"I can go to the children," I said. "Cinni knows me. I can mind them while Marta's away."

Cati looked to Liam.

A crease formed on his brow.

"You can't keep her locked in here all winter," Cati said. "There are already rumors of the Trueborn's new beloved flying around the Hall. People are obsessed with whispering about the traitor. People want to gossip about Ena. We can't allow the two sets of rumors to get jumbled together. The more they see Ena, the less they'll envision her as a dark enchantress who's poisoned your mind."

"Is that what they're saying about me?" I looked toward the windows, as though I might be able to see the people peering through, trying to catch a glimpse of my wickedness.

"It's started a bit," Cati said. "On my way to breakfast, I was asked if it was true you'd appeared in camp in the wake of a terrible storm. Before I'd finished eating, I was asked if you were already carrying a trueborn child."

Heat rushed to my face. "Where are they getting any of this? Is it Nessa?"

"She's barely spoken since Shane died," Cati said. "The problem is everyone knows you're here, and that's all. They need something to say about you, and none of them know a hint of the truth."

"So what am I supposed to do?" I asked.

"Nothing," Liam said. "I don't want you involved in clan politics."

"Then you should've kept your pants on or left the romance in the woods like every other sensible tryst." Cati crossed her arms and stared Liam down. "Normally, I'd be a touch less forward, but I've been having a chivving awful week."

"It's not safe for her to go wandering around where people can see her." Liam paced by the window. He looked like a caged animal. "We can't leave Ena exposed while Orla's out for blood."

"I'll go with her," Cati said. "Between Ailis and me, we can take care of the Trueborn's mysterious lover. Then, if someone dares to attack, I'll get to stab them, and you know how much that cheers me up."

"It's too dangerous," Liam said.

"Hiding her now will only make things more dangerous down the line." Cati stepped into Liam's path, stopping his pacing. "Finding the traitor will not make the Hall safe for Ena if the people still believe she's a threat. Let them see that she's only a girl and not some evil magic given human form. I'll take her to the sorcerers' compound to visit the children. The sooner your people accept Ena as the one their Trueborn has chosen, the safer she will be."

Liam rubbed his hands over his face.

"Ailis agrees with me," Cati said. "We are your friends, Liam. We are sworn to you. Let us do our job."

"I want to go," I said. "I don't want to be lied about, and I need to visit the children. I've walked into a tavern full of soldiers and come out alive. I don't want to hide from the people I've joined."

"Fine," Liam said, "but I want a full complement of guards. Ailis can choose who."

"How long will that take?" I asked.

"A few hours," Cati said.

"Good. I will not meet the people who whisper about me without armor."

I thought when I asked to see the people who'd brought me clothes, I might be laughed at or given a plain *no*. But the women had bustled in with a new rolling trunk and laid out items far finer than what they'd offered when I was only Liam's guest.

When I asked for paints and powders, I was certain they'd say no such thing existed in Lygan Hall. Instead, a man appeared in less than ten minutes, bearing a tray laid out with more pigments and brushes than I'd ever seen in one place.

Cati sat on the balcony as I traced the kohl around my eyes and painted my lips a deeper hue.

I chose a black bodice and skirt from the stores the women delivered to go with a shift of deep blue, just a shade darker than the color the guards wore. The women tucked the rest of the clothes into one of the wardrobes in Liam's sitting room. I don't know if he'd told them to or if they'd heard rumors of me carrying his child and decided I deserved half his space.

Either way, the women smiled as they ducked back out into the hall.

"Are you quite ready?" Cati came back in from the balcony.

"I'm starting to regret choosing to accompany you over staying on the training grounds."

"I thought you needed to protect me from the horrible whispers." I dug into the pack I'd carried from the camp. A servant had shoved it into the corner, as though the shadows might hide the blood stains.

"I count you as a friend, but if I lose my chivving mind, I'll be of no use to anyone."

I pulled my knife from my bag. The weight of the blade calmed my nerves. I tucked the weapon into the ankle of my boot.

"You won't lose your mind." I dug deeper into the pack, feeling for thick fabric.

"You don't know that."

"I do." I pulled the heavy black material out. "You trained a camp filled with men, put up with Liam and my brother, stalked soldiers through the mountains, and that's just the bits I've been around for. The awful pictures in your mind are just one more enemy to be defeated. You're a warrior, Cati. You will survive."

"I hate to admit that you've made me feel a bit better."

I stepped in front of the long mirror in the sitting room and fastened the black cloak around my neck. The silver bird clasp glinted in the orange light. I studied the girl in the mirror.

She wasn't the girl from Harane or the girl from the camp. She wasn't even the girl from Frason's Glenn.

The dark hair and clothes gave me the look of one who'd become accustomed to death and was not afraid to face the shadows. I'd painted my face to perfection, as though I'd used my lips to lure Liam in.

If they wanted to think I was dark and mysterious, I would not fight them. Let them point to me and say my beauty bewitched him. I was magnificent and perfect, a mirage the people could not see through. I had claimed their Trueborn, and they would have to accept that he was mine.

The girl in the mirror was powerful and fierce.

I hated her. I did not want to depend on her for my survival, but I was wise enough not to reject any weapon.

Let them stare.

"Are we ready then?" I turned toward the door to the hall.

"Sure." Cati pulled the bolt aside. "Let's go flounce you about and see what new whispers we hear."

"As long as they don't whisper that I am helpless."

Cati pulled the door open, and Ailis stepped into view.

"Huh," Ailis said. "Not what I was expecting for a stroll across the valley."

"What were you expecting?" I asked.

"Clean clothes and combed hair," Ailis said.

"None of that for our Ena." Cati bowed me down the hall. Ten guards in deep blue coats stepped forward to follow us. "A quiet peace is not in her blood."

"Of course not." I spoke loudly enough for all the guards to hear. "I was born in Harane. My parents died in Harane. The Guilds murdered the woman who raised me. They burned my home. I lost my taste for peace when I learned it was a lie."

A guard darted forward and pushed open the door that led out of the hall.

Aside from the blue-clad guards, the statue corridor had only four people in it—three strangers and Finn.

"Ena." Finn looked at me, a knowing smile growing across his face. "Liam told me you were heading down to see the children, and I'd been planning to check in on them today. I didn't feel quite safe making the long walk with my arm all bungled. But if I could go with you, I know my dear mother would feel much better about my leaving the keep."

I bit my cheeks to hide my smile.

"Have you been questioned by Wyman?" Ailis said.

Finn's jaw tensed.

"He went before I did," Cati said. "Liam had Wyman go through all the marked first."

But not me.

"Fine," Ailis said. "Just know that if we're attacked, we've been assigned to protect Ena, not you."

"Fair enough." Finn stepped next to me and offered me his good arm. "I would gladly meet a horrid death to protect my beloved Ena."

"Hush, you," I whispered. "I'm trying to look like I'm brave and in control of my own chivving destiny."

"No offense, my darling," Finn muttered as we cut down a side passage and to a flight of spiral stairs, "but one look at you, and the men will dream of your tits while the women loath you for your beauty. Some of that may be a bit flipped, but you get the general idea."

"It's a little late to change now." I glanced down to make sure my breasts were relatively covered.

"You absolutely should not change. Just know that the whispers will be gales of speech by nightfall." Finn winked.

"Good."

It took a full ten minutes to work our way down the spiral stairs, past guards, through corridors, down more stairs, past a metal gate, and out into the open.

I took a deep breath of the crisp fall air. For some reason, the scent of the wind smelled sweeter and fuller from the valley floor.

Trees with bright white bark rose up on either side of our dark stone path. The edges of their leaves had been kissed with oranges and golds, giving everyone winter's warning.

Along the sides of the path, bright red flowers bloomed at the top of long stalks, like the ground had decided to make living torches.

I tried to look calm as Ailis and Cati led me down the stone path that cut out into the valley proper. The walkway wound through flowerbeds and looped around fountains grander than anything I'd seen in Ilbrea.

"I think the thing I'm most excited for this winter is the solstice feast." Finn gripped my arm hard, as though he sensed my urge to linger beside a fountain made of pure white stone—the figure at the center looked eerily like Liam. "I already feel much better after a few proper meals, but there is something about the feasting season that warms my heart."

"I'm excited to see it," I said. "I don't think I've ever been to a feast before."

"If you're unsure, then you haven't," Finn said.

We cut off the path before we reached the proper town at the heart of the valley. The houses were all made of dark stone, like the rock had been discarded as they dug the tunnels of the crag and keep.

My breath hitched in my chest, and I squeezed Finn's arm.

He kissed the back of my hand. "I know you're not one to revel in fine food, as I am wont to do."

"Really? I'd never noticed."

"But there is plenty of music and dancing as well." Finn fell silent for a moment, not speaking again until we reached a group of men who stood beside the path in a tight clump. "And, since Liam knows how much you love a rollicking dance, I'm sure there will be better music than ever. I don't know if he tripped over himself and fell head over heels for you because you laugh like a fool when you dance or because you killed a Guilded commander. Either way, I don't suppose it matters."

The men all stared at me as we passed. I met each of their gazes, not allowing myself to flinch.

"The important thing is that after months in tents eating sludge, longing for a decent bed, and trying not to be torn apart by croilach," Finn pressed on, "we're safe in Lygan Hall. If anyone has earned a bit of peace, it's you."

We moved beyond the hearing of the men and onto a path lined with white flowers.

"Did you need to lay it on so thick?" I whispered.

"No." Finn shrugged. "But I did enjoy it."

I kept my hand in his as we moved from one path to another.

Just when I'd begun to wonder if the valley reached so far we'd need to camp overnight to cross it, trees surrounded our path.

"A quick word of warning," Finn said. "I never try to be my charming self with the sorcerers. It's best to go with a strict *yes ma'am*, *no ma'am*, and hope they don't take offense at your breathing."

"This is who we've left the children with?" I squeezed Finn's hand as the shadows of the trees overtook our path.

"They aren't as bad as you think," Finn said. "Only, their magic seems to make them too stern to enjoy a good laugh."

The path lost its stone surface as we ventured farther into the trees.

I took a deep breath, trying to catch the scent of the forest, but another feeling filled my chest. It wasn't the longing I'd felt every time I'd been near the boulders that surrounded the camp. The sensation was more like the prickly feel of knowing a predator is waiting to pounce.

The pressure of my knife hiding in my boot offered me comfort as I searched the shadows, looking for any hint of what had licked cold against the tops of my ears.

I heard the voices before I even spotted the stone wall surrounding the compound. The unseen people spoke in low and even tones.

Maybe this will be a good place for Cinni.

Tree branches laden with bright green leaves dripped over the stone wall. A silver gate blocked our way as we reached the end of the path.

I didn't let myself lean forward to peer through the bars of the gate. I wanted to. The urge to catch a glimpse of what might wait for me made my fingers twitch.

"We've come to see the sorcerers." Cati called out as she stepped in front of me. "I've brought Ena Ryeland to visit the children she rescued from the Lir Valley."

The gate swung open without a sound or hint as to how the metal had moved.

I kept my hand in Finn's as we followed Cati into the compound.

33

The stone of the walls surrounding the sorcerers' compound was thicker than I'd thought it would be. Nearly five feet of solid rock separated them from the rest of the valley.

Are the sorcerers trying to keep something out, or are the normal people trying to lock something in?

The question sent fear prickling on the back of my neck.

The garden that greeted us inside the walls did not quiet my fears. There were no people in the garden, despite the voices I'd heard from the outside.

Flowers of deep hues surrounded the paths that branched off in every direction. Their color was richer than any blooms I'd seen in Ilbrea, almost as though an artist had thickened the pigment as they painted this world.

The trees that grew up against the wall had broad, straight trunks without any hint of deformity. Shorter trees, with fruit dripping from their branches, grew in front of the giants I'd seen from outside the walls. Paths led to the fruit trees, as though inviting me to come and taste their bounty.

I didn't want to consider what the penalty for stealing food from the sorcerers might be.

"Beautiful, isn't it?" Finn said.

"It looks like the Brien enclave." I tried to relax my grip on Finn's hand. I couldn't manage it. "Is that how Regan created her perfect home? Magic?"

"The Brien allow their sorcerers to travel outside their safe haven," Finn said. "Regan keeps a complement of sorcerers with her at all times."

"The enclave isn't the Brien's true home?" I whispered. "They have a larger, grander place than that?"

"Not grander," Ailis said. "Just better protected."

"I suppose that's the price of amassing power," Finn said. "You start to fear everyone is trying to steal it from you."

"With the state we're in, do you blame them?" Cati asked.

Three women stepped through the trees on the far edge of the garden.

The first acknowledged us with a nod and led the others in our direction. Before they'd made it ten feet, a squeal of joy shot from behind them as Evie tore out of the trees and raced toward me.

"Ena!" She plowed into my side. "I was starting to think we'd been abandoned here forever."

"You haven't been abandoned." I gave Evie a hug before tipping her chin up so I could look into her dark eyes. "I just needed to wait until you'd settled in before I could visit."

"You look fancy." Evie wrinkled her brow. "Why do you look so fancy?"

So they will not see how lost I am.

"Because we are in Lygan Hall," Finn said. "I will eat, Ena will primp, and we'll all give in to a little bit of folly and enjoy our time here."

"I haven't had any folly," Evie said.

"You'll have to forgive the child," the first woman said. She wore her gray hair twisted into a large bun and had eyes of a brilliant emerald shade I'd only seen once before. "It can be so difficult for children to settle into new routines. We don't normally accost guests when they enter the garden."

"But I could hear them coming," Evie said.

"What has that got to do with running through the compound without permission?" the emerald-eyed woman asked.

Evie pursed her lips.

"It's been a lot of new things for you lately." I took Evie's hands. "But now you're finally somewhere you can get settled."

Evie bit her lips together as though trying swallow her own face.

"I'm here to sit with the children for a bit." I looked to the emerald-eyed woman. "Liam sent me so Marta could pay a visit to Wyman."

Evie's eyes widened.

"Evie would be pleased to take you to her siblings." The woman smiled. "The guards will wait here."

"We'll be staying with Ena," Ailis said. "Sorry, Iona. Liam has his ways."

Iona stared at Ailis for a moment, as though wondering if it would be worth the trouble of using magic to get the intruders out of her garden.

"As the Trueborn wills it," Iona finally said.

"I'm so glad you're going to sit with us for a while." Evie bounced on her toes as she led us back toward where she'd appeared. "Cinni and Dorran will be happy to see you. Gwen still isn't awake, so I don't think she'll care so much."

"Has there been any word on—" I looked back to where the three ladies had been. They'd all disappeared.

"I like Marta." Evie dragged me through the trees. "She tells us stories and tucks us under our blankets. She did it at camp, too. Every night." Evie looked up at me. "All the time."

"It's nice to have someone taking care of you," I said. "You'll finally…"

We stepped out on the other side of the trees, and I forgot what I was going to say.

Somehow, we'd moved from the garden to the inside of a stone hall, but there had never been any sort of door. I looked behind to find a solid wall I had apparently walked through not a breath before. Only Finn, Cati, and I had entered the room, but as Evie dragged me forward, the rest of the guards stepped through the solid stone, too.

If any of them were amazed at the feat, their faces didn't betray them.

"It would be nice to live someplace that isn't in the compound." Evie led me between two long tables where young men and women sat, reading by the light of the lae stones hanging from the ceiling.

There were no windows to offer any sunlight to the room. The only breaks in the walls I could see were two corridors that cut out from the back.

"Wyman said we're all going to have to study very hard and learn to use our magic," Evie said.

"I know," I said. "You've been so excited to learn."

"I thought it would be the fun sort of learning." Evie sighed. "Like the kind Cati taught in camp. I want to learn how to fight, but Wyman said I won't be using any real magic for months. *Months.*"

Finn gave a low laugh.

Evie stopped and spun to face him. "You wouldn't like it if they made you sit still and read for months."

"I'll give you that." Finn shrugged.

"And I'm not sure what they're going to do about Cinni." Evie furrowed her brow. "She's smart, maybe smarter than all of us, but I don't think she can spend months reading. If she sits too long, she gets antsy. That's when bad things happen. She'd been kept inside for six weeks before she snuck out to the pond for a breath of fresh air. That's when she sank the man who tried to grab her."

The echo of the horrible crack as the ground split beneath our feet rang through my mind. I didn't want to even begin to imagine what Cinni might do to the valley if they kept her tucked away for too long.

"I'll talk to Liam," I said, "make sure we get all four of you out for some nice fresh air so you don't feel cooped up. Maybe we can get someone to play a bit of music for Cinni, too. I think she'd like that."

The creases in Evie's brow smoothed out. "I think she'd like the music a lot." Evie tugged on my hand, dragging me into a long stone corridor with wooden doors along either wall. "When Gwen wakes up, can you take us to see more of Lygan Hall? I want to see where you're living."

"It's not all that interesting in the keep," Finn said. "If you want to see the good bits of Lygan Hall, it's me you ought to speak to. I grew up here as a scabby-kneed troublemaker. I learned all the best places to snag a sweet and the cracks and corners children aren't supposed to know about."

"I'm glad you've grown into such a fine influence for children," Ailis said.

"Children need a bit of fun." Finn winked at her. "Helps keep the grownups on their toes."

Ailis raised one ginger eyebrow at Finn.

I'd never realized how alike they looked. I wanted to ask if they were related but didn't want to seem even more ignorant than the guards trailing behind me probably believed me to be.

Evie paused in front of a set of wooden double doors. "I think you'll like this part." She shoved against the wood with all her might.

The doors swung open, and Evie staggered forward into a courtyard made for a fairy story.

Unlike the garden just inside the wall, this place was blatant in its magic.

The same sorts of deeply-hued flowers we'd passed in the front garden grew in ground-level beds surrounding the benches and fountain at the center of the space.

Potted plants sat on stone slabs that hovered in the air, as though they'd been suspended by invisible strings. The tiers of flowers rose all the way up to the second balcony that surrounded the square. Crystal spheres as clear as drops of water dotted the open air. The sun shone down from above, bathing the space in warm light.

I could picture the courtyard in the dark, with all the crystals glowing like lae stones, making the whole place look like the stars had come down to watch the sorcerers work. I wished I could see that sort of beautiful magic.

The hum of chatter stopped as the people in the courtyard caught sight of us. I kept my chin high and my face calm but couldn't drag my gaze from the fountain in the middle of the garden long enough to actually look at the people staring at me.

A statue of a woman stood at the center of the fountain. The angle of her chin and creases around her eyes were too familiar for me to ignore.

"Who's the woman in the fountain?" I asked.

"A lady who funneled all her magic into the mountain." Evie yanked on my hand, tugging me forward. "They've told me the story three times, and I read it in a book, too. I still don't understand it, though. If a lady putting her magic into the rocks is why the sorcerers in Lygan Hall have magic, then who put magic somewhere for the sorcerers in Ilbrea to get? Don't try asking for yourself, though. All you'll get is scowls and told the same story over again."

I sensed the stares of the people tracking us through the courtyard and to an open door on the far side.

"I've brought Ena, Finn, Cati and a bunch of strangers," Evie called into the room.

"Why have strangers come to visit us?" Dorran stepped into the doorway, his arms crossed over his chest.

"If you're rude to strangers, you'll never make new friends." Marta stepped out beside Dorran. She smiled at me. Both her dimples appeared on her cheeks, but the expression didn't quite reach her eyes. "It's good to see you all."

"You too," Ailis said. "You've been missed."

"Thanks." Marta nodded, and her smile disappeared. "Come on in, Ena. Cinni will be happy to have you for a visit."

I took a breath, steeling myself for some horror waiting within the room.

It was a pleasant place, with three big beds, a table and chairs, and a big couch facing an empty fireplace. A stack of books and the remains of lunch sat on the table.

"The food is better here," Dorran said. "Not that it would take much after the slop from camp."

"We should—"

"Be grateful we never went hungry?" Dorran cut across Marta. "I know." He sat down at the table and pulled a leather-bound book toward himself.

"Gwen." Evie ran to the farthest away bed where Gwen lay peacefully, as though she'd been tucked in for the night. "If you wanted to see Ena, now would be a good time to wake up."

Two hands appeared from the far side of the bed as Cinni pulled herself up to look at her oldest sister. Cinni stared into Gwen's face for a moment before sinking back down onto the floor.

"Cinni's taken to hiding behind the bed," Marta said. "If that's where she feels safe, she can stay there for now, but she'll have to start on her studies soon."

There was no hint of a response from the far side of the bed.

"She won't come out until Gwen wakes up," Dorran said. "Keep trying if you like, but you're wasting your time."

"She should get out and walk around," Evie said. "We could have fun, Cinni. Finn said he'd take us to places we shouldn't be."

Marta shot Finn a glare, but there was still no sound of movement from Cinni.

"I was going to ask Liam to send a musician to play for you, Cinni." I walked slowly toward her, listening for any hint of her getting upset. "Would you like a bit of music? Maybe we can get a fiddler to come by."

I sensed her anxiety rather than heard it, almost like a subtle thrum of panic flying through the air. "Or not." I backed away. "Perhaps after all the excitement, a nice bit of quiet would be best. You can let me know when you're ready to hear a few tunes played."

"I should go for my visit to Wyman," Marta said. "The sooner I leave, the sooner I'll be back. I don't want to miss dinner with the children."

"I don't think you should go at all." Evie raced across the room and stood in the doorway, blocking Marta's path.

"Ena will be with you," Marta said, "and I'll only be gone for a while."

"I don't care," Evie said. "You shouldn't go to that man. You should stay with us. It's better for you to stay with us."

I stood very still, waiting to hear whatever sound had upset Evie.

"Evie"—Marta knelt to be eyelevel with the child—"sometimes, we are asked to do unpleasant things."

"It's a bit more than unpleasant," Evie said.

"And even if we don't want to, we have to be brave and face the task," Marta said. "If not for ourselves, then for the people we care about. I will be back very soon. So be good for Ena, and look after Gwen."

Evie bit down on her lips.

"Please, Evie." Marta stood and looked to me. "See you in a bit."

Evie didn't fight as Marta shifted her out of the doorway and stepped into the courtyard. She just stared after Marta, still biting her lips.

"It's not going to be so bad," I said. "I'm here. Finn and Cati are here."

Evie wrinkled her brow.

"Marta will be back soon," I said. "I promise you're going to be just fine."

"It's not me I'm worried about," Evie said. "I can hear them. The people Wyman questions. Their voices carry through the stone in the compound. I can hear all of them scream."

34

There was a certain strange peace to being locked inside Lygan Hall. The size of the valley made it easy to forget that none of us were allowed to leave. And the strength of the stone offered a false sense of safety that I was tired enough to accept.

For thirteen days, I visited the children every morning, letting the people watch me as I walked to and from the compound, always with a pack of guards marching around me. I went to the training ground every afternoon. Cati finally gave in to my request for her to teach me proper sword combat.

I hadn't ventured into the village. Liam was against my going. Cati and Ailis agreed. The village had too many corners, too many shadows where evil could hide.

Every night, Liam would tell me it would soon be over. They would find the traitor, and I would be allowed to walk freely among the people.

Still, the traitor had not been found, and my paths led me only to the training ground and to the compound.

Wyman had questioned everyone from the camp but me. I offered to be questioned, but Liam refused.

So the murderer walked free, and the rumors about Emmet and me kept growing.

We were sent by the Guilds. The King himself had trained me as an assassin. I'd killed Emmet and left him to rot on the western border of the woods. I'd bewitched Liam and forced him to make the croilach.

Finn was the only one who'd actually tell me what the whispers were. Everyone else held their lips tight and their weapons close.

Nights spent in Liam's arms were the only thing that kept me from raging at the gale of accusations.

He wanted to touch me. He wanted to hold me. He didn't think I was a murderer or an enchantress who had stolen his affection.

I would fall asleep tangled in his arms and wake to his skin pressed against mine in the morning. I wanted to spend my life waking up surrounded by his warmth.

I could have lived with the rumors if it meant being by his side, but there are some accusations that cannot be ignored.

"They're going to have to try something else." Finn set down his fork and leaned back in his chair. "It's been two weeks. Gwen should've woken up by now."

"I've already spoken to Wyman." Liam kept his gaze fixed on his plate. He'd barely touched his meal. "They can't help her. If they'd seen her use magic before, they might know enough about which bit of her burnt out, but if they just start guessing, they could do more harm than good."

"Cinni won't make it much longer," I said. "I managed to get her to listen to the fiddle player a few days ago, but now she's back to hiding behind the bed."

"We can try and get her out of the compound," Finn said. "Maybe some fresh air will do her good."

"Wyman won't allow it," Liam said. "And I can't say I blame him. We've all seen what Cinni is capable of. If something sets her off, people could die."

"Losing her mind from being trapped in that room, huddled by her unconscious sister could get people killed as well." I stood, went to the window, and looked down over the valley.

The angle of the morning light lent deep and mysterious

shadows to the now familiar scene. The thick cluster of trees that shrouded the compound didn't look like anything more than an innocent little forest, but I knew all too well what danger lurked within the stone walls.

"We could send my grandmother to them," Finn said. "Have her bring a pie around, let her dote on the children. That woman's got a comforting presence that would bring a bear to heel."

"I'll see if Wyman will allow it." Liam set his fork aside and dug his knuckles into his temples. "I should be able to do more. I should be doing something to help the children or protect the Hall."

"Don't be too hard on yourself," Finn said. "Orla's banned us from leaving to hunt for monsters. Colm is the Blood Leader, so setting up guards and watches is his territory. Wyman rules the sorcerers' compound with a magic-laden fist. And as best we can tell, the gods themselves aided the trueborn who made the croilach. As far as I'm aware, you can't use clan laws to punish gods, so there's chiv all we can do."

"I should spend some time on the training field today," Liam said. "Make sure the people from camp are keeping up. Orla will have to open the gates eventually, and we'll need to be ready when she does."

A faint thumping carried from the far side of the door.

"What a happy day that will be," Finn said. "I've always hated the winter hunts. Absolutely loathed getting snow packed into my boots."

The thumping got louder.

I walked toward the door to the hall, grateful for the knife pressed against my ankle.

"But," Finn sighed, "I would trek through snow with a song in my heart if it meant getting closer to the trueborn who started all this."

"There are people in the hall," I said.

A moment later, the sound of voices came through the wood.

"Get to the bedroom." Liam leapt to his feet and grabbed the sword that leaned against his wardrobe.

I opened my mouth to protest.

"Go." Finn drew his own sword.

My heart battered against my ribs as I stepped into the bedroom, the place that had become my sanctuary.

Bang, bang, bang.

A fist slammed against Liam's sitting room door.

Please do not take this peace from me.

"Who's there?" Liam called.

"Your Elder." Orla's voice cut through the door.

Neither Liam nor Finn relaxed.

"Get back." Finn shooed me into the shadows of Liam's bedroom. He didn't tell me to close the door. There would have been no point since there wasn't a lock.

I pulled the knife from my boot and pressed my back to the stone wall.

Liam stepped toward the hall door. The rasp of the bolt of being slid aside sent a shiver up my spine.

"Mother," Liam said. "What an unexpected surprise."

"Don't bother," Orla said. "No amount of sentiment or foolery will help you, Liam."

Footsteps moved closer to the door.

"Where's the girl?" Orla said.

"What do you want with her?" Liam asked.

"The only wish I have for that girl is for her to never have existed," Orla said. "I am not that lucky."

"No, you're not," Liam said. "If you've nothing more to do here than insult the woman I've chosen to share my bed, get out."

"Neither of us is lucky in that regard," Orla said.

Thumps came from the hall as though an army of men were approaching.

"Word has come from the Healy Clan," Orla said. "The blood leader they lost was murdered."

"We knew that," Finn said.

"Poisoned," Orla said. "His death looked like a blood fever until the very end. A handful of others took ill with the same symptoms though some of them survived. What a clever ruse, mimicking an illness to cover murder."

I gripped the hilt of my knife, but my hands would not stop shaking.

"The Healys have been searching for a culprit," Orla pressed on. "It took a while for the rumors on the wind to fly all the way to their fortress. Another military leader had been killed in much the same fashion. A Guilded commander, in fact. Two such similar assassinations cannot be a coincidence."

"Ena had nothing to do with this." There was a hint of fear lying beneath Liam's words.

I wanted to take his hand and promise that everything would be all right. I could not have stomached such a lie.

"The Healys have sent their grievance to the Clans Council," Orla said. "A trial has been called."

"This is ridiculous," Liam said. "Ena has never even met anyone from the Healy Clan. She'd never know how to find them."

"Ena has been summoned to stand trial before the clans," Orla said. "I hope you are happy with the woman you've chosen, Liam. She could very well cost you your life."

"If that's the price of being with Ena, then I will pay it."

"No." I stepped out of the shadows and into the doorway. "No, you can't. They want to accuse me, fine. But they can't drag you into this."

Orla looked at me. Her eyes were cold. I couldn't tell if the ice was born of hatred or terror.

"You will both be taken immediately," Orla said. "The escort leaves in an hour."

"I'll go," I said. "Liam can stay here. He can't—"

"You gave him your oath," Orla cut across my words. "You are bound to him. He accepted responsibility for your steps within the mountains. Your punishment will be his. Take them."

"Will you let your anger go this far?" Liam said.

Orla stepped out of the way.

A pack of blue-clad guards took her place.

"What will you do without an heir, Mother?" Liam asked. "If you let them push you this far, the Duweads will be nothing but filth beneath the boots of the other clans."

"If I do not obey the summons, it will be seen as an act of war," Orla said.

The guards entered the room, but none of them tried to grab us.

"You want to lead this clan with an Ilbrean in your bed, then prove her worth and her innocence," Orla said. "You have made your choices. Live or die by them."

The sound of Orla's starched skirt rustled down the hall, but none of the guards followed her.

"I hate to do this, Liam," one of the guards said. "Can you just come with us?"

Liam stayed silent.

"There's a full complement of guards outside this corridor," the man said. "You'll never make it past them. All you'd do is kill a mess of your own people."

"And the path?" Liam said.

The guard shook his head. "I'm sorry, Liam."

Liam handed the guard his sword. "Do not forget that I am your Trueborn."

"Your knife, Miss." The guard nearest me held his hand out for my blade.

Liam gave a tiny nod.

I flipped my knife and laid the hilt in the guard's hand, then reached down and pulled the sheath from my boot. "I would appreciate it if you kept them together. Cati gave me the sheath and blade as a set."

"I…" The guard looked to Liam and then back to me. "Yes, Miss."

"She and I will travel together," Liam said. "If you separate us, I will fight back."

"If Orla orders us—"

"We will not be separated," Liam said. "Am I understood?"

"Yes, Trueborn." The guard nearest Liam bowed.

"I'll just pack you a few things, shall I?" Finn replaced his own sword in its sheath on his hip. "It'll be quite a journey, and you know how the clan elders like to blather."

"You can't," the guard said.

"Why would that be?" Finn's fingers twitched as though he longed to pull his sword right back out of its sheath.

"You've been called upon to be a guard of the escort," the man said. "They looked for you in your rooms. Better toss a uniform on before Colm has a fit."

"Go," Liam said. "We'll meet you below."

Finn stepped between the guards and to my side. "I'll see you soon." He kissed my forehead and weaved back through the men and out of sight.

"Fetch someone to pack for Ena and me," Liam said. "I am the Trueborn of the Duwead Clan. I will not step in front of the council looking as though I have been abandoned by my people."

"Of course not." The man bowed. "I'll send word down and have someone take care of it."

Liam reached for me. I wanted to feel his hand in mine so badly, but still, it took me a moment to convince my feet to move.

I stepped between the two nearest guards and held my breath, waiting for one of them to run me through. I took another step, and still the blue-coated guards only watched me.

Liam took a step toward me, closing the distance between us.

"It's going to be a long journey." Liam took my hand in his. "We should start as soon as possible. The longer there are guards escorting us to the Broinn, the longer Lygan Hall will be vulnerable to attack."

I let Liam lead me into the corridor. Two-dozen guards filled the narrow space.

"Whoever you believe is responsible for the croilach attacks, understand there could be more out there," Liam said. "Any trueborn strong enough and desperate enough to create nine of the beasts would have no reason to stop there. Nothing but death can stop a murderer so filled with fury. Make sure all the guards who are staying in the Hall know how much danger this valley is in. Watch every shadow a monster might hide in.

"I don't know who unleashed this terror on the Duwead Clan, but it is up to the guards of Lygan Hall to protect its people. Do not let this be the end of our clan. Fight to the last man to protect the innocent lives here. And be prepared for battle when we find out which trueborn is responsible for the deaths of thirty of our people. They may think they are defeating us. They are only forging a fiercer enemy."

His words rang through the hall.

The posture of the guards changed. Their shoulders went back as they tightened their grips on their weapons.

"We will protect the Hall," a female guard with short hair said. "They will be taught the consequences of attacking the Duweads."

A ripple of nods went up and down the corridor.

I held tight to Liam's hand as he walked through the guards and into the room of statues beyond.

Another pack of guards waited for us. They added on to the flock trailing in our wake.

Liam didn't stop to speak to those guards as he led me down corridors and through rooms I'd never even seen before.

I may never see this place again.

I forced down the rising panic in my chest and swallowed the dozens of things I needed to say to Liam. I wished I could promise myself there would be time to speak to him later, but I didn't know if that was true.

"The children," I said just loud enough for Liam to hear. "Promise me they'll be safe."

"Marta is still with them," Liam said. "She'll look after them."

A knot pressed on my throat, making it impossible to speak. I nodded instead.

We stopped at a spiral staircase where ten more guards waited for us.

Liam nodded them down the stairs. We followed the blue coats, twisting around and around.

Orange lights had been set into the ceiling, but they didn't offer a cheerful glow. The hue seemed menacing, as though the flames of a battle were lapping at our flesh.

We followed the guards around and around until I was sure we'd gone far below the ground.

There hadn't been any windows to prove we'd gotten closer to the earth, or any doorways where others waited to join our path. Just a twisting descent that offered no clue as to when it might end.

The sounds of voices below were the first hint of there being anything to our journey besides plunging into the earth.

"I'll not have either of them traveling on foot." I recognized Tirra's voice. "You would do well to remember who your Trueborn is and the courtesy you owe him."

Gratitude replaced a tiny bit of my dread.

The stairs ended, and we stepped out into a tunnel forty feet wide and so long I couldn't see anything but darkness in either direction.

Tirra stood to one side. She held the reins of two horses while more of the animals pawed at the ground behind her.

"Liam." Tirra turned to him. "I have horses for you and Ena."

"Thank you, Tirra." Liam gave a tiny smile.

"I won't be accompanying you apparently." Tirra sucked in

her cheeks as though swallowing words she longed to shout. "That doesn't mean the two of you shouldn't be riding as your station demands." She shot a glare at a white-haired guard. "This mount should do well for Ena."

A horse with a pure black coat stepped forward as Tirra handed me her reins.

"Only fitting, I think." Tirra gave me a nod and passed the reins of a matching black horse to Liam. "See that you bring them back to me well cared for. These ladies are more than pretty. They're two of the fastest I've got."

"They'll be looked after," Liam said.

Tirra nodded and turned to the swarm of guards in the tunnel. "Who is going to be caring for the horses on this chivving mess of an expedition?"

"Me," a hesitant voice called over the sounds of the masses.

Tirra stormed toward whatever poor sap had been placed in charge of caring for her darling horses.

Liam led me down the corridor.

We passed a man with bright white hair and dark skin. He stood in the center of the guards, lording over their scrambling chaos. From the way the men nodded to him as they passed, it was easy enough to guess he was Colm, Blood Leader of the Duwead Clan.

But there was something different in the way the guards acknowledged Colm and Liam.

Liam nodded at the guards we passed and moved without waiting for anyone to give permission, even though we were both prisoners.

The guards nodded back to Liam. Some even stopped what they were doing long enough to bow. Even as they went about their tasks, everyone seemed aware of the presence of their Trueborn.

I had never walked anywhere in Lygan Hall with Liam, not

since the first day when he'd saved me from Orla's wrath. I hadn't seen the way the people reacted to him. Not really.

As we walked to the very front edge of the pack of guards, it was as though, in a strange way, Liam was still in control. Even as we were being forced to attend a trial where both of us could be killed, Liam was still the one they looked to for protection and permission.

I don't think he understood the power he emitted, just walking through his own people. Maybe that's what it's like for those raised to rule. They become numb to the respect and deference offered them.

Liam stopped when there was only a line of twelve guards in front of us.

The guards bowed to him.

He gave them a nod, then offered me a hand to help me onto my horse.

I wouldn't have taken it, but I could feel the stares of the hundreds of guards behind us.

Trust him. Let him show them the Liam they need to see.

I took his hand and climbed onto my horse.

She shifted her weight beneath me, as though longing to run.

Liam kissed the back of my hand before climbing into his saddle.

"Excuse me, Miss."

I looked down to find the young guard with the bald head and dark skin.

"I was told to give you this"—he held up my black cloak—"to keep you warm on the journey."

"Thank you." I threw the cloak around my shoulders and fastened the bird clasp. The metal of the closure was chill against my skin. The dark fabric matched my mount's coat.

I looked behind to the rows of guards, searching their ranks for any familiar faces from the camp. Finn's red hair was easy to spot, and Case stood right beside him.

I could not find anyone else I knew in the mass of blue.

All of them stared at me as though caught in some terrible trance.

I was not an orphan from Harane to them.

I was no longer chased by Death. I had become the fiend.

I would accept their fear if it meant saving Liam's life.

The mountain did not know that a stone heart can grieve, nor did she understand how deeply a human heart can be damaged by greed.

Long ago, after the mother trusted the mountain to save her child and funneled all her magic into the stone, the mountain learned those horrible lessons.

The mountain called the offspring of the child she raised deep within her stone back to the safety of her lands. The offspring came, bringing their spouses and the children they had born.

The mountain feared the spouses who did not hold her stone in their blood—they were intruders who would ruin her lands and steal from her beloved children—but love convinced her to save them all.

The mountain watched her people thriving in her embrace and learned what wonders the love between a human and her mate can create. The stone at the heart of the mountain felt hope for the first time.

Love and children. Generations of children who would prosper in her embrace. The mountain would never be lonely again.

The offspring gathered in the Broinn, living together and enjoying the bounty the mountain provided. There was a time of great peace and prosperity when the Black Bloods first came to their true home.

But wherever there is anything of worth, jealousy grows.

Fights over food, territory, and rank brought violence to the Broinn.

The mountain wept as the blood of her beloved children seeped into her stones. Her walls trembled and the ground cracked, but the children would not heed her warning and refused to cease their battle.

Magic surged through the mountain as she prepared to end her children's lives rather than watch them become murderers and monsters.

Most fled in fear.

Five mothers were brave enough to kneel before the mountain and beg forgiveness.

They had lived too close, too packed together. The women swore that if they had the space, they could keep their children from fighting each other.

The mountain heard the mothers' plea and gave in to their wishes.

She carved five tunnels leading away from the Broinn, giving each mother a path to follow with her children, granting each of them a home where they could be safe and let generations expand within the embrace of the mountains.

Each woman swore an oath of peace to the mountain and followed the path to the territory where they would build their clan.

The mountain was happy, for her children had found peace.

The mountain did not know how easily humans lie.

38

I'm not sure how long we rode the first day in the tunnel. There wasn't even a way to be sure when the sun had set far above us. It was as though the mountain had trapped me underground again, swallowed me whole and left me with no choice but to continue forward. Only this time, there were hundreds of people with me. I had felt safer alone in the darkness.

I knew Orla rode behind us, in the very center of the group beside Blood Leader Colm. Even glancing at the man's dark skin and bright white hair made me uneasy to have him riding out of my view. I could feel the prickle of stares on the back of my neck and wondered if one of those sets of eyes belonged to Orla or Colm. I did not turn around to check. I would not give Orla the pleasure of knowing that I wanted nothing more than to run from the demons marching behind me.

But Liam rode calmly at my side, and I could not leave him behind. I would not even attempt escape without him.

So I kept riding forward.

In the dim blue light of the lae stones, there was no warning of anything in front of us until the wall of the outpost came into view.

Six men in black coats stood on top of the wall, their arrows nocked and aimed at our escort.

My heart leapt into my throat as I waited for the soldiers to attack, but they did not loose their arrows.

"We've come to the outpost for shelter as we journey to the Broinn," a guard at the front of our pack called up. "We travel with Orla, Elder of the Duwead Clan, Liam, Trueborn Duwead, and Colm, Blood Leader of the Duwead Clan."

With a clinking of chains and creak of hinges, a door in the center of the wall swung down.

A great pool of orange light glowed on the other side.

I tightened my grip on my reins, still waiting for an attack. But the guards at the front of our group walked quickly forward, as though excited to pass through the doorway.

"We only got word you were coming a few hours ago," a man in a black uniform said as soon as the first of the blue-clad guards stepped under the wall. "We've the main rooms prepared, but the guards might have to find a spot and toss a blanket down."

"We can't blame you," one of the blue guards said. "We usually offer more than a breath of warning before coming to you in this number."

The blue guard sounded cheerful, despite the three feet of stone wall we'd ridden beneath to reach the inside of the orange-lit space.

If I hadn't been terrified, I might have been impressed enough to understand his relief.

The orange glow came from hundreds of orbs hanging from the dark stone, just as it had in Orla's council chamber. But this space was not as barren.

To one side, a stable had been carved into the stone wall. To the other, three layers of balconies reached up toward the stone ceiling. Across from the gate, far enough away that all the guards, both black and blue-clad, could have had a fine time dancing and never worried about bashing elbows, another high stone wall and wide door blocked our way forward.

A blue-clad guard stepped in front of me and reached for my reins.

"Kely, that is not how you treat a lady," Liam said. "You will respect her, or you will stay away from her."

"I'm sorry, Trueborn." The guard Kely bowed.

Liam climbed off his horse and offered Kely his reins before reaching up and lifting me down. He passed the reins of my horse to Kely. "Don't be sorry. Just spread the word to the other guards. Ena will be treated with the same respect given to me. You will make sure the guards at the Broinn understand this as well. Am I clear?"

"Yes, Trueborn." Kely bowed to Liam and then to me. "It is an honor to serve the Trueborn."

Liam didn't speak again until Kely had disappeared into the swarm of blue coats. "We should get to our quarters. Tomorrow will be another long ride."

"Of course." I kept my hand in Liam's, refusing to show a hint of the stiffness in my legs as I followed him toward the side of the outpost where balconies rose up the wall.

Four men in black uniforms stood at the bottom of a set of stairs that reached straight up to the third story. All four bowed and stepped out of Liam's path.

"The room at the end if you would, Trueborn." One of the guards gave Liam an extra bow.

Liam gave a stiff nod and stepped past the guards. He led me onto the stairs and nodded to me before beginning to climb.

I let my gaze slip out over the scene below as I followed Liam.

The horses were already being brought into the stable. Colm stood at the center of it all, watching as the gates shut us off from the tunnel back to Lygan Hall. Orla herself was nowhere to be seen.

At the top of the stairs, Liam led me all the way down the long balcony to the very last room.

I'd expected bars on the window and a giant lock on the door, but there was no sign at all that the room we'd been given was meant to be a prison.

Liam placed a hand on the back of my waist, ushering me quickly through the door and shutting it behind us. There was no bolt for him to slide into place.

We both stood staring at the room for a long while.

The bed had been laid out with blankets and pillows. A bottle of chamb and a tray of rolls, honey, and cured meat waited on the table. A circle of orange orbs had been set into the ceiling.

"What is this place?" I asked.

"The outpost. The halfway point between Lygan Hall and the Broinn."

"How far apart are they?"

"A bit over sixty-two miles."

"We did travel a long way today, didn't we?"

"Ena, I'm so sorry." Liam turned to me. Pain I could not bear to witness filled his eyes.

"Don't." I took off my cloak and laid it on the bed. "Why do the men here wear black?"

"They're members of the shadow guard. They take an oath to stay underground protecting the clan. The color is a sign of respect for their sacrifice. There are some below Lygan Hall, too, just nowhere you would've been."

"That is quite the sacrifice to make."

I tried to picture it. Willingly forsaking the sun to protect my home. I would have taken that vow if I could have spared Harane, but we were a village, not a mighty clan with hundreds of men and tunnels the Guilds would have to fight to breach.

"We should eat." I sat at the table and stared at the food, wondering if it had been poisoned. It would have been a poetic end. "Do you think it's safe?"

"Our own people prepared it." Liam sat beside me and poured himself a glass of chamb.

"The Healy Blood Leader probably thought the same thing."

Liam took a sip before passing the glass to me.

"If it were poison I'd brewed, you wouldn't be able to taste it." I sipped from the glass. The bubbles tickled my throat but offered no flavor of malice.

"Then I suppose it's a good thing I'm sure you didn't do this." Liam poured a glass for himself.

"There has to be a way out." My breath hitched in my chest.

"If Orla doesn't deliver us to the trial, it will be considered an act of war against the clans," Liam said. "A clan war would kill thousands of Black Bloods. We could lose all the work we've done in Ilbrea."

"Better to be executed than to live knowing you've caused that much pain." I took another sip of chamb to wash the sour from my mouth.

"They will not hurt you." Liam set his glass down and tipped my chin so I had to look into his dark eyes. "I swear to you, Ena, I will protect you."

"I don't know if you can." I forced my voice to stay calm. "But you have to find a way to save yourself."

"Ena—"

"There is no camp without you." I pressed my fingers over his lips. "The sorcis will be left to suffer. They will be taken by the Guilds. You can't let that happen."

Liam kissed my fingers and lifted them away from his mouth. "Our fates are tied. They cannot judge you as guilty without placing the same judgment on me."

"Then pull the stone back out of my ribs. You drew the mark on my side, take the magic out. Tell them it was only a rumor that I gave you my oath. Then you'll be—"

"It can't be done. There is no way to erase a mark, and removing the stone would mean killing you."

"Regan wasn't punished when that man touched me in the enclave." I pushed away from Liam and stood. "If that man had to die and she was left unharmed, there has to be a way to protect you, too."

"Violating you was a low offense."

"I had to kill that man." As soon as I had spoken, I wished I could swallow my words. I pressed a hand to my chest, feeling my pendant against my skin as I waited for Orla to come bursting in, gleeful of my confession.

A minute passed before I found the courage to speak again. "How can groping me be considered a low offense if he had to be executed?"

"His actions were not horrible enough to be considered offensive to the mountain. If Regan had defended him"—Liam stood and walked slowly toward me, as though afraid I might actually try and run from him—"if she'd hidden what the bastard had done, or tried to keep him from the clans' justice, then she would have been tied up in the woods and gutted with him.

"To murder a clan member in their own territory is one of the highest offenses in the Clan Treaty and goes against our covenant with the mountain. I could tie you up and hand you to the council, and it would not release me from the bond we both agreed to."

"There has to be a way." I made myself speak past the horrible knot of fear in my throat. "There's got to be something we can do. I will not let them hurt you."

"There's only one way out of this for either of us. We have to prove to the council that you're innocent."

"How? You've spent weeks searching for the one who betrayed us. How are we going to be able to do anything different in the Broinn than you've already done in Lygan Hall?"

Liam went still for a moment. I could see him tucking his own fear away so I wouldn't feel it.

"I swear to you I will find a way." Liam pressed his lips to my forehead.

"And if you can't?"

"Then I will shatter the stones above us, and we will flee."

"Across the Arion Sea?" I touched the creases by the corners of his eyes. "Or to the kingless territories?"

"Your path is mine, Ena. And we will walk side by side to whatever end."

I kissed him, trying to sink his taste so deep into my bones that not even fire could burn the memory away.

His hands roamed up my sides, as though he wanted to be sure I was still breathing.

I pressed myself against him, needing to feel every ridge of his body against mine. Needing to know that even as darkness surrounded us, he craved me as much as I did him.

His longing pulsed through me.

He lifted me, and I wrapped my legs around him, unwilling to be parted from him for a single moment.

I forgot about the guards outside as he pressed my back against the stone wall. He trailed his lips along my neck, and the violence of the world meant nothing.

His flesh found mine, and not even the will of the gods could have torn me from him.

39

I don't know who in Lygan Hall packed my things to travel. It could have been Nora, it seemed so much like the way she'd prepared me to leave Frason's Glenn. A small trunk had been stuffed to bursting with fancy clothes to match my black cloak and plenty of powders and paints to ensure I had armor strong enough to take on the Guilds.

A man in a black coat delivered our breakfast tray. A little glass bottle sat beside the rolls and cheese. The shadow guard stared at me as he placed the tray on the table.

I took the little bottle and drank its bitter contents while staring right back into his eyes.

A flush of red overtook the guard's face, and he fixed his gaze on his boots as he bowed back out of the room.

Men who will gladly fight demons will run from the truth of womanhood. I am grateful for the lesson I learned from that cowardly guard.

I rode by Liam's side through the darkness for another long day.

The blackness of the tunnel pressed in around me. The only

sounds were the pounding of the guards' feet and clopping of the horses' hooves.

I wasn't sure if time was racing as I neared my doom, or if it had stopped as the mountain tried to rob me of my sanity. Either way, the constant plodding developed a steady rhythm in my mind, and the rhythm developed a voice of its own.

He is mine.

He is mine.

He is mine.

If they touch him, they will burn.

He is mine.

He is mine.

The words offered a violent comfort.

When I had almost become convinced that the words were not born of my own thoughts, another wall came into view.

This wall did not leave a gap for men to stand on the top. The barrier reached from floor to ceiling with only thin slats for windows where archers could aim their bows.

Arrowheads glistened in the blue light as we stopped in front of the gate.

"We've come at the request of the Clans Council," a guard at the front of our pack called up. "We travel with Orla, Elder of the Duwead Clan, Liam, Trueborn Duwead, Colm, Blood Leader of the Duwead Clan, and Ena Ryeland, who will face the accusation of murder."

The metal gate in the wall began lowering to the ground. There was no orange glow to beam into the tunnel. But the sounds of voices and movement carried from the darkness beyond.

Even after the gate lay flat against the ground, the guard at the front of our escort remained still for a moment.

I took a breath, waiting for something horrible or magical to happen. But the guard only gave himself a nod before stepping up onto the back of the gate and leading us through the fifteen-foot long corridor under the wall.

We passed beneath the stone arch, and my whole body tensed as though the gods themselves were staring down at me, already declaring their judgment.

We reached the end of the passage, and a new feeling replaced the fear in my chest. A pull that started at the point right in front of my heart, right beneath my stone pendant.

Have they poisoned me?

The horrible thought raced through my mind before I recognized the sensation.

The longing, the need to follow wherever that pull in my chest led.

I looked to Liam. He rode by my side, his face made of stern stone like he wasn't feeling anything unusual.

We rode past orange orbs set into the wall, passing another set of balconies like in the outpost, before following a twist in the path that led to a wide-open space.

I searched the cavern, trying to find what the pull in my chest might be leading me toward.

There were tiers of seats carved into each of the five stone walls, all facing the center of the room where a pentagon-shaped table had been surrounded by five chairs.

Five tunnels led into the space, cutting in at the corners of each of the walls. A door had been carved into the base of each of the seating sections. All the doors had heavy metal bars crisscrossing their wood.

I studied each of the entryways, trying to find where the pull might be leading me.

Liam climbed off his horse and reached up to me.

I laid my hand on his chest as he lifted me down. His heartbeat thumped against my palm. The lure of him still made me want to drown in him, but the pull was there behind my longing for Liam, drawing me toward something I could not see.

"Don't be afraid," Liam whispered the moment before a ringing cut through the air.

He pressed my hand against the steady thumping of his heart as the bell tolled again and again.

The noise vibrated my ribs, shaking away the armor I had wrapped around my fear.

Sounds of movement came in the slim silences between the awful tolling. Soon, shadows appeared down the other four corridors. Hundreds of people entered the cavern.

Each set of tiers filled with armed guards dressed in a different color. Green, gray, purple, and burnt orange marked each of the other clans. When the guards had reached their places, three from each group would step toward the center of the room. One would sit while two stood behind them.

The bell did not stop tolling until all four sides had gone still, leaving only the Duwead Clan outside the chamber.

A shuffling of footsteps came from behind us, followed by the rustling of a starched skirt.

Orla stepped in front of Liam and me, then gestured the guards forward onto the bottom tiers of the empty section.

"She will not stand with you," Orla spoke under the sound of the guards' feet. "Play whatever games you like in the Hall, but if they see you treat her as though the customs of the clans do not apply to your petal whore, you will set the council against her before we begin."

Liam took my hand. For a moment, it seemed as though he might bolt up the tunnel, leading me to freedom.

There is no way out.

"Follow the last of the guards," Liam said. "Stand on the bottom tier, and wait to be called."

He squeezed my hand as the last of the Duwead guards passed.

I pulled free of his comfort to take my place on the bottom tier. The longing in my chest doubled in the absence of his touch.

He followed Orla to her seat at the center of the room, then stood behind her chair with Colm.

A woman with pale blond hair nodded to Liam from across the table. It wasn't until she smiled that I recognized Regan.

A wave of fury washed over my fear.

"Just hold still," a familiar voice whispered in my ear. "They'll blather for a bit, but the best thing you can do is let them argue."

I glanced over my shoulder.

Finn stood behind me, his gaze fixed on the people at the table even as he spoke.

"Don't react. They'll see it and hold it against you."

I exhaled, forcing my face to be calm.

A man in a gray jacket stood from his seat at the table. "As Elder of the Healy Clan, I call this council to order."

Fear dug into my spine.

"We have come here today to discuss the murder of the Blood Leader of my clan. Warner was a good man and a fine fighter who led the guards of the Healy Clan with honor for many years. He was denied the privilege of dying in battle by a coward who resorted to poison for a traitorous end. The Clan Treaty was broken. The one responsible will face the consequences, or the Healy Clan will seek justice of their own."

The gray-clad guards of the Healy Clan began stomping all together. The rhythm of their pounding quickened as though they were speeding their charge for my blood.

I kept my gaze locked on the table.

"Enough!" The woman sitting in front of Regan waved a hand through the air.

The Healy guards fell silent.

"We all received word of your accusation against a girl of the Duwead Clan," the Brien Elder said. "What evidence do you have of her guilt?"

None!

I wanted to scream the word, but Liam stayed silent. I pressed my hands against my thighs, willing my rage not to betray me.

"I believe we all know what the girl has done," the Healy Elder said. "Word traveled to all of us that Ena Ryeland, sister of Emmet Ryeland, had joined the Duwead Clan. But she was not ferried out of Ilbrea as a sorci running from the Sorcerers Guild. Ena Ryeland is but a normal girl. A normal girl who happens to have a strange skill for murder."

The word rang around the room. There was no stomping this time.

"Ena Ryeland joined the Duweads and less than a month later assassinated a Guilded Commander with a heartless poisoning plot. We all heard about it, didn't we?" The Healy Elder looked to each of the sections of tiers. "Every trader moving between clans carried with them the story of the Duweads' great victory, granted to them by an Ilbrean girl who just so happened to be an assassin. The tales did not warn us of how dark her deeds truly were." The Elder stared straight at me.

I did not flinch as I met his gaze.

"She did not just poison the commander," the Elder pressed on. "She gave people around him a vicious brew to make the commander's death look like an illness. Putting other lives at risk to kill her mark.

"We lost a great man when we lost Warner. I had every healer and sorcerer in my fortress try to save him. In the end, the best of them came to one conclusion. Poison. The symptoms looked like a blood fever, but there was no illness in his body. It was not a disease but an attack that killed my Blood Leader and claimed three innocent lives as the murderer sought her mark."

A rustle of tiny movements carried around the crowd.

"Eight of Warner's men fell ill at the same time he was stricken. Three died." The Elder pointed to me. "This assassin came from Ilbrea and is trying to commit the same atrocities she executed on Guild soil. We will not allow her reign of terror to continue here."

"I'm so sorry." Orla shook her head.

"It is a time of great grief," the Healy Elder said.

"No," Orla said, "not that. I'm sorry that I must be misunderstanding you. Or, rather, I believe you have misspoken."

"What?" The Healy Elder narrowed his eyes.

"You seem to have implied that there was some horror or monstrosity involved in the execution of Commander Drason," Orla said. "Perhaps you aren't familiar with his name, but I am. The man that girl killed was guilty of kidnapping magic born children and handing them over to the Sorcerers Guild. He was also guilty of taking the mothers of those children. We don't know where he took them or exactly what he did with them, but I believe any thinking person with knowledge of the Guilds will agree that his aim must have involved breeding."

There was a long silence as Orla sat and stared at the Healy Elder.

"I'm sorry again, Edric." Orla nodded to the Healy Elder. "Perhaps a woman needs to be completely blunt when speaking to a man. Commander Drason stole magically gifted children from their mothers. He then kidnapped the mothers and raped them to breed new children for him to steal. If you would like to argue that this man did not deserve death, then I suppose we will have to sit through it. If you do not have an argument to make on Drason's behalf, then let us not refer to his death as murder. It was an execution for crimes against innocents, organized and completed by the Duwead Clan. Would you like to accuse me of murdering an Ilbrean commander, Edric?"

"We are here to discuss the murder of my Blood Leader." Furious red crept up Edric's cheeks.

"Then please keep to the topic at hand. I hate being underground and would like to return to Lygan Hall as quickly as possible."

Edric worked his lips together for a moment before speaking. "There is only one person this council is aware of who is known to have brewed the sort of poison that killed Blood Leader Warner. This girl wheedled her way into the Duwead Clan under suspicious circumstances. It is my belief that Ena Ryeland poisoned Warner in an effort to begin a clan war."

"Why?" the Brien Elder asked. "Why would an Ilbrean born care about a clan war?"

"It is my belief that Ena Ryeland and her brother Emmet Ryeland are working on behalf of the Guilds," Edric said. "It is my belief that they desire to start a clan war so the Guilds can steal the land rightfully granted to the children of the mountain."

The rumble of whispers that flooded the hall sounded like an army of ghosts come to haunt me.

My mind stumbled back, sorting through everything I'd done in my life, trying to find one action that might appear as though I were trying to aid the Guilds.

"This is all very interesting," an elder with long gray curls said. "But do you have an ounce of proof, or just whispers?"

"I don't need proof, Elan," Edric said. "Ena Ryeland herself will prove me right."

I squeezed my hands against my thighs so hard I could feel bruises forming on my legs.

"Under the Clans Treaty, I have the right to question Ena," Edric said. "I have the right to question her in front of the full council. The treaty made no mention of an elder not being allowed to question an accused just because that elder was born a sorcerer."

40

The torrent of words that flew through the chamber was loud enough to drown out the questions in my mind.

I didn't understand why I wouldn't want to be questioned. I knew I was innocent. Answering questions in front of everyone seemed like a chivving wonderful way to clear my name.

But Finn stepped in front of me, his hand on the hilt of his sword, as Liam left Orla's side to join in protecting me.

"There is no rule in the treaty that forbids my questioning the one who murdered my Blood Leader," Edric shouted over the roar of the crowd.

"We cannot allow such a thing to happen." The Brien Elder stood. "You are using the gifts of your birth to grab at a power never meant to be offered in the treaty."

"Such nonsense coming from the woman who hoards all the magic she can steal from Ilbrea." An elder with a long black braid slammed his hand against the table.

"This is what comes of allowing a clan to have an elder that is not a trueborn," Elan said.

"There is nothing in the treaty that demands an elder be a trueborn," Edric said.

"The mountain created the order the clans should live by," Elan said.

"How has your clan fared with a sorcerer leading, Edric?" the black-haired Elder asked. "Has the death of your crops been enough for the mountain to demonstrate her displeasure? Will she have to collapse the stone over your heads before you finally learn?"

"Do not concern yourself with the covenant my people hold with the mountain, Ronin," Edric said.

"Silence, all of you," the Brien Elder held a hand in the air. "I did not come here to listen to two men preening and bickering."

"Then let us proceed with the questioning," Edric said. "The sooner I prove Ena Ryeland's guilt, the sooner justice will be served."

"The question you have raised is much larger than the murder of one blood leader," Orla said. "If you do this, if you use magic to influence the workings of this council, you will be endangering everything the treaty was created to protect."

The room fell silent as Orla spoke.

"If we allow this to happen, what will we become?" She looked to each of the tiers in turn. "What precedent will we set? If the Healy Elder wants to dive into your mind, all he will have to do is accuse you of a crime. He will be given the power to torment based on accusations with no witnesses, no evidence beyond rumors. Is this the choice you would make? If you are all this weak, I fear we have reached the beginning of the end."

"We should conference and vote," the Brien Elder said. "This choice goes beyond the matter of Ena Ryeland."

"There is no choice involved." Edric pointed a quivering finger at me. "That girl murdered my Blood Leader."

Liam stepped to the side, standing between me and Edric.

"The treaty gives me the right to question the accused," Edric said. "I will not allow council politics to steal the Healy's justice for Warner's death."

"We will conference," the Brien Elder said. "Those in favor?"

Orla, the Brien Elder, the black-braided elder Ronin, and Elan all raised their hands.

"I suppose the story keepers who blather warnings in my ear know their history after all," Edric said. "Not all treaties are made to last."

"And not all men are wise enough to rule," Orla said.

The Brien Elder swept her hand through the air before the uproar could begin. "The girl should be locked away."

"Of course." Orla nodded to the guards around me. "I have no qualm with justice being done, only with the ravings of a mad man."

A wave of sound exploded from the tiers of gray-clad Healy guards.

"This way, Miss." Kely stepped up beside Liam. "If I may, Trueborn?"

"I'll stay with her," Liam said.

"Don't," Finn said. "Not with all of them watching."

Anger flashed through Liam's eyes.

"She can survive anything, Liam," Finn said. "Trust me, I know." He took my hand and guided me away from Liam.

The other people in the stands were all funneling back into their tunnels, but that wasn't where Finn led me. He took me to the door at the base of the Duwead tiers instead.

Kely stepped around Finn and unlocked the door. The metal lock turned with a terrible thunk.

"It won't be long," Finn said.

"Take care of Liam." I stepped into the cell. "Do not let his anger make him foolish."

"I'll watch him."

The door swung shut, and for the first time in days, I was alone.

41

The cell was short. A person as tall as Liam wouldn't have been able to stand upright.

A wooden pallet lay along the back wall, as though it were meant to offer a prisoner a place to sleep. I could not bring myself to even sit on that surface.

The stench of the room was an awful mix of terror and human decay.

"He will not abandon you in here, Ena Ryeland." My voice bounced around the tiny room. "You have been trapped in fouler places than this, and you have crawled your way out of every one of them."

I paced in front of the door for a while, trying to calm my nerves with the rhythm of the movement. All I managed to do was make my cage seem smaller.

Pulling my cloak tightly around my shoulders, I stared at the door, willing Liam to come bursting through to tell me he'd found the murderer.

I stood there until my hands grew numb from gripping my cloak. I wanted to sit down, but sitting seemed too much like resigning myself to being trapped for a very long time.

They do not know what we are made of. A voice that sounded like Emmet's echoed through my thoughts. *They are made of stone, but we were born in fire.*

The rumble of Emmet's voice pressed against my ears, but I could not understand the words.

"You will not let them break your mind, Ena Ryeland," I whispered to myself.

The rumbling grew louder, until words carried through the door, and I recognized the unmistakable anger in my brother's voice.

"I've come to stand trial before the council," Emmet shouted, as though he knew I was trapped behind the door and desperate to hear his voice.

There was a moment of muffled speech before Emmet spoke again.

"Guilty men run from accusations. Innocent men clear their names."

I pressed my ear to the door.

"Where is my sister?"

An angry voice replied.

"Then lock me away with her, or question me now," Emmet said. "I have nothing to hide from any of you, and after what I've seen in Ilbrea, there is more important work to be done than sitting around in a cave, accusing people of crimes they couldn't possibly have committed."

A voice that sounded like Orla's spoke. "Will you and Ena willingly agree to be questioned by Edric, Elder of the Healy Clan, knowing that he is a sorcerer?"

I leaned closer to the door.

"Is that what you're all bickering about?" Emmet asked.

"I have the right to interrogate—"

Orla spoke over Edric, "But a precedent cannot be set if the questioning is entered into willingly."

There was a long silence.

I waited for Emmet to speak.

"My sister and I willingly submit to the Healy sorcerer's questioning." It sounded as though Emmet stood right outside my door. "That's what all you Black Bloods forget—children of stone may rule in the mountains, but Ena and I were forged in the ashes. Children of ash cannot be broken."

I held my breath, waiting for my cell door to open. But the tolling of the bell came instead. The rock around me did not dull the sound, but rather amplified it, as though the mountain herself wanted to see if she could shake me into pieces.

A thunder of footsteps pounded over my head as the ringing stopped.

When the footsteps went quiet, a voice spoke. It sounded like the Elder of the Brien Clan.

"Emmet and Ena Ryeland have freely volunteered to be questioned by Edric, sorcerer and Elder of the Healy Clan. This questioning takes place without the treaty being invoked. The findings of this questioning will be held as true before the council, and the fate of the accused will be determined from the truth held within their own minds."

"That isn't what—" Edric shouted.

"Do not press, Edric," the Brien Elder said. "It makes you appear too eager to quarrel. Some might even suggest you are trying to break the treaty between the clans."

There was a long silence before Edric spoke again. "I will examine them thoroughly. What I find shall be sufficient to determine the truth."

More voices spoke, but they were all too quiet to hear.

A rumble like a giant boulder being rolled across the floor grated against my ears.

I willed my heart to beat softly as I waited for Edric to ask his first question.

"Answer loudly, Emmet," I whispered. "I need to be able to hear."

Pressing my palms against the door, I shut my eyes, listening for any hint of speech.

A horrible scream came instead.

The cry held such agony that I could barely recognize my own brother's voice.

"Emmet!" I banged on the door, hopelessly trying to reach him. "Emmet!"

His screams changed pitch, as though shifting from pained to terrified.

"Stop it!" I slammed my fists against the door.

The pitch of his screams changed again. His anguish went beyond fear or pain. It had become the cry of one who had been robbed of everything they loved and wanted nothing more than to leave this world.

I kept beating against the door as my breath hitched in my chest.

"Emmet!"

I slammed my fists against the wood over and over, not caring that warm blood dripped down my arms.

When I thought my brother might choke on his own blood from screaming so loudly, the sound stopped.

The silence was almost worse than his screaming. At least then I had been sure he was alive.

"Emmet!" I pounded on the door. "Where is my brother? Emmet!"

Low voices spoke outside.

"Emmet!"

The lock on my cell turned with a heavy thunk.

A pale-faced guard opened the door.

"Where is my brother?"

"Ena Ryeland." Orla spoke too loudly for me to ignore. "We have been assured by your brother that you will submit to questioning without need of invoking the treaty."

I stepped out of my prison and into the vast room.

Liam stood behind his mother's chair. Pain and fear filled his eyes.

"Where is my brother?" I asked.

Orla did not answer, but Liam glanced over his shoulder toward the place I had stood before.

I followed his gaze.

Emmet had taken my place on the bottom tier. Finn stood right behind him.

A new patch of burns marked the side of Emmet's neck. His face was pale and sweaty, as though he'd been violently ill. He met my eyes and nodded.

Locked in my cell, I was afraid my brother had been broken. But the torment they'd unleashed on him was nothing to a child who had survived the Guilds.

"I am innocent." I spoke loudly, letting my voice ring around the cavern. "I have nothing to hide from the council and will be grateful for a chance to swiftly clear my name."

I glanced back to Liam.

He had his gaze fixed front, away from me.

"What a relief to make quick work of this," the Brien Elder said. "Come, Ena Ryeland. Whether you're guilty or not, I am anxious to start for home."

I kept my head high as I walked toward the table. I could feel the gaze of the hundreds of people around me, but I did not shy away from them.

The blood dripping from my hands was nothing more than another layer of armor, another illusion to keep them from seeing the real Ena Ryeland.

No one told me to stop as I stepped right up to the edge of the table. A cart carrying a giant stone basin of water rested beside Edric.

"On the table, if you will." The Brien Elder pointed to the center of the pentagon.

A blue-clad guard offered me his hand.

I ignored him and stepped straight up onto the table without aid.

"Remove your cloak," Ronin said.

I looked to him.

"It's best to not have any constriction around the throat." Ronin bowed his head.

I unfastened the bird clasp and let the cloak fall behind me.

The stares of the people surrounding me grew in their hunger.

Without the cloak, the curves of my body were exposed. I watched the people on the tiers. Lust, longing, jealousy—they all felt something as they stared at me.

"I submit this questioning for the consideration of the council." Edric stood and locked his gaze on me.

I stayed still, blood dripping from my hands, as I waited for his first question.

But a glimmer of light emerging from the stone basin drew my attention from Edric's face.

A sheet of gleaming water rose up and stayed floating in the air even as lights danced across its surface.

Fear.

The word echoed through my mind, but the voice was not one I recognized.

Show me your fear.

I looked to Edric.

A smile lit his face.

I thought for a moment that I had already lost my mind. Somewhere in the blood and chaos, all reason and sanity had vanished.

Then darkness surrounded me. Pitch black with the endless thumping of hooves driving into my mind.

I was trapped on the mountain road, and there was no escape. I would be stuck riding on that horse until I died, knowing it had been my failure that had killed my parents.

Bright sunlight flashed before me.

A soldier with silver hair stood behind our house. He smiled as he ran his sword through my father's gut.

Ester with blood leaking from her womb and a baby that would not breathe.

Jesep lying on the ground, surrounded by blood. Too much blood for one person to lose.

The clanking of chains filled my ears as darkness surrounded me again. The slats of a wagon covered me. I was locked beneath. Stored like goods to be sold.

Nantic. A sorcerer with emerald green eyes. But my fear of her didn't steal the world from me. There was a glimmer beyond her form. A sheet of light that showed the images of my horror as though my life were no more than a pantomime performed to terrify the masses.

A smith's forge. Emmet gone, missing.

I kept my gaze locked on the images of my fear as new shapes swirled into being.

Smoke in Harane. A hand at my throat. My body pressed against the side of a shop.

Lily.

Lily hanging in front of our home.

Lily gone.

Stinging in my eyes blurred the images. I lost sight of the water's pantomime as the scene surrounded me again.

A little girl screaming, but I could not save her.

Soldiers attacking unarmed innocents. Blood on my hands I could never wash away.

The man in the woods. His blood blossoming over my fingers. The warmth of his life staining my skin red.

Pierce. Nothing more than bones.

The croilach chasing me.

Torches chasing me.

Dogs chasing me.

Darkness swallowing me. Leaving me in a city long forgotten by the world. Doubt draining my courage as the darkness continued. Houses and fountains. The darkness would never let me go.

An entire city the world had forgotten, as I had been left in the dark, forgotten and abandoned.

Marta shouting. Doubt scarring my joy.

Croilach everywhere. Blood, so much blood.

Red to paint the entire world with Death's own brush.

Screaming and blood.

Cinni and screaming and blood.

Screaming. Horrible screaming.

My breath hitched in my throat.

Screaming and graves. A child making graves.

Liam. Liam afraid.

The darkness swallowed Liam's face, and the pounding of hooves shook all reason from my mind.

Show me your guilt.

A voice joined the darkness, but the black did not falter. The hooves did not stop. They pounded and pounded against the ground, shouting to the world how badly I had failed.

I'd created my own fate when I'd been too slow to save my parents.

Everything else, every other wound, had started there.

"Enough." A voice echoed through the darkness, but the black did not shift. "If there is anything else you want to see, do it. Otherwise, stop this spectacle."

Show me the lives you have taken.

My mother and my father sitting together at our table.

Ester's baby, still and pale.

Jesep laughing as he tried to dance. He'd loved to dance.

Lily, her hair blowing in the breeze as the rope twisted around her neck.

Marten. So many faces in Marten. Hundreds of eyes I did not get to look into before I caused them to close forever.

The man with the gray-blue eyes and the scar on his lip.

The man on the boat who looked afraid as I plunged my knife into his flesh.

The images rotated back to my mother. Red spots dotted her neck. Emmet lay by her side.

"Stop," a voice said. "Unless your aim is to prove how desperate you are, just stop."

The images faded, and the bright lights of the cavern bored into my eyes. I swayed, trying to keep my feet beneath me as fatigue washed through my body.

"I think we can all agree you found nothing to substantiate an accusation, Edric," the Brien Elder said. "Would you like to vote or humiliate yourself further?"

I looked to Edric.

He gripped the edge of the table. Sweat slicked his brow and stained the collar of his shirt.

"The houses, the darkness, what was that?" Edric said.

"Your question does not concern the death of your blood leader," Orla said. "You questioned her on the matter of murder. That vote must take place before other matters distract this council."

"Distract?" Elan had gone horribly pale.

I wondered if my failures had been so terrible they'd actually scared her.

"I am ready for a vote," Edric said.

"All who agree Ena Ryeland is innocent." The Brien Elder raised her hand.

Three more hands followed hers.

"My Blood Leader is still dead," Edric said.

"And you have no idea who killed him." Orla stood up. "Search your own clan before you draw all of us to the Broinn next time."

"You only want her to be innocent to protect your son," Edric said. "You're only concerned with the girl's fate so you can save your heir from execution."

Orla leaned across the table. "Are you going to criticize how I run my clan while your people go hungry? Look to your own troubles before coming after mine."

"Are you really both foolish enough to waste time bickering after the images Edric pulled from this girl's mind?" Elan said. "No petty grudge can be as important as the city below the mountains this Ilbrean saw."

"That was a part of Lygan Hall," Ronin said. "It's not surprising. I'm sure all of us have halls we've abandoned with time."

"Are there empty portions of Lygan Hall that vast?" Elan looked to Orla.

Orla stared stone-faced back at her.

"It wasn't Lygan Hall." My voice came out strong, undamaged by screaming. I wondered if I had screamed, or if it had only been terrible memories that echoed in my ears. My cheeks were damp, like tears had betrayed me. I wanted to touch my face, see if I really had cried in front of all those people, but I was too afraid my hands might shake if I moved them. "I was running from a Guilded sorcerer. He had soldiers and dogs with him. The mountain swallowed me, and I ended up in the city."

Silence filled the cavern.

"I'm not sure who exactly built the place I found," I said, "but it wasn't anything like Lygan Hall."

I waited for horrible images to flood my mind again, but the elders just stared at me.

"The girl is mistaken," Ronin said.

"Whatever you like so long as you believe I didn't murder a

Black Blood or betray the Duwead Clan." I waited for someone to bow me off the table, but no one moved. "I was trapped in those tunnels for two weeks. That's where I was before the blood leader was murdered, stuck in the darkness below the mountains, so there's no chance I could have had anything to do with a plot against the Healy Clan. I wandered around the underground city and found a compound beneath the mountains. My innocence is proven. Surely I am done here."

The Brien Elder waved a hand through the air. "The Ryelands deserve rest after the ordeal they've been through. Take them to their quarters."

"We have just heard heresy from someone standing on our table," Elan said.

"I agree, Bryana, the Ryelands do deserve rest." Orla nodded to the Brien elder. "The two taken in by my clan have been cleared of the false accusation of assassination. Stew on your own upset before you deliver your troubles to my door."

"How did you get inside the mountain?" Ronin leaned closer to the table.

I turned to Orla. My legs felt as though they might collapse beneath me. I met Orla's gaze and gave her a nod. "Shall I answer, or would you prefer I be taken to rest?"

"This matter cannot be ignored, Orla," Ronin said.

I kept my gaze fixed on Orla's face.

"There are so many matters that cannot be ignored," Orla said. "A trueborn has sent nine croilach to murder my heir. A blood leader has been killed, and we still don't know who is to blame. The mountain sheltered an Ilbrean born girl and showed her an impossible city. Which matter would you like to conquer first, Ronin?"

I waited for Ronin to respond, but it was Bryana, the Brien Elder, who spoke first.

"Nine croilach were sent after Liam?" Bryana asked.

"Yes." Orla looked toward Regan. "Would you like me to

accuse your Trueborn? She is the only one I can think of who would hold such a grudge against my heir."

"Don't be ridiculous," Bryana said. "Regan has been working with Liam to aid the sorcis for years."

"Until she demanded that Ena supply her poison," Orla said. "Liam refused to allow that folly."

A shadow passed behind the Brien Elder's eyes.

"The cooperation between the Duweads and the Brien is no more," Orla said. "Didn't you know?"

"Do you mean to tell me the Brien Trueborn sought poison and no one thought to inform me?" Edric smacked his hand against the table.

"You were so busy accusing the Ryelands, I didn't think factual information would matter to you," Orla said.

"I wasn't seeking the poison for anyone in the clans," Regan said.

If I hadn't heard her voice before I might not have noticed the hint of fear.

"There was a problem on the southern path," Regan said. "I wanted to deal with it quietly and requested the Duwead Trueborn's aid."

"And I forbade Ena to brew poison for you," Liam said. "She is sworn to me and had to obey. Whatever trouble you find yourself in, Regan, do not try to draw me into it with you."

"Then it's the Brien who came for my Blood Leader." Edric pointed a quivering finger at Bryana.

"Do not begin to imagine I will allow you to question my Trueborn, sorcerer," Bryana said. "I'd rather meet you on a battlefield than allow you to violate my daughter's mind."

Regan stepped closer to the back of her mother's chair.

"There is a murderer sweeping through the clans," Edric said. "They have killed my Blood Leader and attacked the Duwead Trueborn."

"Are we now on the same side, Edric?" Orla asked.

"How can you bicker about petty sides when the mountain has acted so strangely?" Ronin said. "The matter of men killing men is nothing compared to the mountain sheltering an Ilbrean girl."

"Ena Ryeland, when did you take to the Duwead Trueborn's bed?" Bryana asked.

"What?" The word caught in my throat as I faced the Brien Elder.

"When did you crawl into Liam's bed?" Bryana stared brazenly at me like she hadn't done anything wrong.

Heat rose up my neck. "That is none of your chivving—"

"Is there a chance you were pregnant with the Trueborn's child when the mountain sheltered you?" Bryana cut across my protest.

"No." I wanted to tear her eyes from her chivving head and grind them beneath my fancy new boots.

"Are you sure?" Bryana tipped her head to the side.

"There is no chance of it," Liam said. "Now, leave her alone."

"Hmm." Bryana narrowed her eyes at me. "What about another Black Blood? Could you be carrying a different Duwead's child?"

"Does it bother you that much?" I asked. "Is it that horrible to you that the mountain might have saved my life just because she could?"

"A simple yes or no will do," Bryana said.

"No," I spat the word at her. "I'm done here."

I jumped off the table, snatched up my cloak, and strode toward the Duwead entrance to the cavern.

"You are not done here," Elan said. "Guards, stop her."

A flock of green-clad guards charged down from the tiers to the right of the Duwead Clan.

Without a word from Liam, the blue-coated Duwead guards ran to stand between me and Elan's men.

"What?" I rounded on the table. "What more could you

possibly want from me? I have proven my innocence, let you dive into my mind, let you question whose bed I've chosen to share. What else do you want?"

"What you are saying of the mountain is untrue," Elan said. "She would not shelter an Ilbrean, would not lead an Ilbrean to hidden secrets."

"It's a mountain!" I spread my arms wide, shouting to the ceiling high above us. "I think a mountain can do whatever it chivving wants."

"What you think does not matter," Elan said. "What you are saying is blasphemous."

"I am only telling you what happened," I said. "I wouldn't have mentioned it at all if you hadn't gone poking about in my mind."

"We were wrong to vote so quickly," Elan said. "This girl has treacherously fooled the mountain who has protected and nurtured us all. She was clearly taught some vile magic by the Sorcerers Guild that allowed her to fool Edric."

"This is preposterous," Orla said. "Edric, is there any chance of an ungifted girl fooling a sorcerer."

"I…" Edric dried the sweat on his brow with his sleeve.

"Could she have fooled you?" Orla stood, staring Edric down.

"It is possible to fool a sorcerer if they gently examine a mind," Edric said. "I dug deep enough into the Ryelands' minds I would have found any lies."

"I call upon this council to hear charges against Ena Ryeland for treachery against the clans and the mountain herself," Elan said.

"What?" A hand gripped my arm before I could move toward the table.

"I've just told you the girl isn't lying," Edric said. "Everything I showed you is true."

"Then the Ryelands have placed us all in more danger than I feared." Elan took her Blood Leader's hand and climbed up onto the table. "Are none of you capable of seeing the damage this girl has done? This Ilbrean has employed some dark trickery to make the mountain grant her shelter."

"I didn't make the mountain do anything!" An arm wrapped around my waist, holding me back.

"If the mountain was fooled into sheltering an Ilbrean, will she next offer our sacred pathways to the Guilds' army?" Elan shouted over me. "This girl has done horrible damage to the bond between Black Blood and mountain. There are already Guilded soldiers prowling through the western outskirts of our woods. If they are given a pathway, they could march straight into our homes."

The room fell silent. Elan took a long moment looking at each group around the room.

"The death of a blood leader and an attempt on a trueborn's life are nothing compared to the horror of having Guilded soldiers diving deeper into the mountains." Elan spoke softly, forcing everyone to stay quiet if they wanted to hear her words. "We must find out why the mountain accepted her. We must find out what foul deception this girl is guilty of. We are Black Bloods, and we will protect our home!"

A cheer shot around the crowd, starting with Elan's own people before flying through every group but the Duweads.

"We need to go," a voice spoke under the shouts.

I glanced over my shoulder as Emmet began dragging me back behind the crowd.

"Do not let that girl leave." Elan's command carried over the cheers, changing the pitch of the sound from approval to a battle cry.

"Form a line and defend!" Liam raced toward me, but he didn't have a sword. They'd taken his weapon from him.

I fought against Emmet's grip as he pulled me farther away.

A streak of red and blue dove into the horde of men racing toward us.

"Finn!" I shouted his name, but he'd already disappeared into the throng.

A clang of metal on metal came from the right.

"Stop, all of you!" Finn leapt onto the table and shouted over the masses. "For the sake of the mountain herself, stop."

A crack shook the cavern. Dust fell from the ceiling high above.

"Hold your attack!" Finn bellowed.

I don't know if it was the mountain cracking or Finn's plea that made the two groups pull apart.

"We all know the story of how the mountain sheltered a child," Finn said. "We've always believed that we are special, beloved by the mountain. But we've been wrong."

Finn looked to me and held my gaze. There was no fear in his eyes, only a blazing determination that drained the warmth from my body.

"I found mountain stone in Ilbrea," Finn said. "In the Lir Valley, far from where our legends say the stone should be. The stone that we have worshiped does not belong solely to us. Whatever magic our people have been granted was not born of a pact with the mountain. It exists in Ilbrea as well.

"You say that we are in danger of the Guilds infiltrating our mountains. They already have. I have seen them. I have fought them. Would you rather waste your time fighting over a legend or work together to find a real answer to our problems? The Guilds are coming. They will try to take our land and our lives. Will you stand against the paun, or will you hide belowground, bickering while the world burns?"

"Do you dare—"

"I've faced the Guilds, Elder Elan." Finn jumped off the table. "Yes, I chivving well dare."

44

"We're going." Emmet pinned me to his side and lifted me off my feet, carrying me away from the cavern.

Finn strode after us, holding his sword aloft but not looking at the guards he passed.

"Guards, to our corridor," Liam ordered.

A sea of blue followed Emmet back toward the gate.

"Put me down." I pushed against Emmet's arm. "Put me down. I can walk."

Emmet let my feet touch the floor but kept a firm grip on my arm, dragging me forward.

I clutched my cloak to my chest, taking comfort in its unchanging weight even as the world went mad.

"We can't leave." Orla caught up to us.

Six guards with swords drawn surrounded her as she moved quickly enough she had to lift the hem of her starched skirt.

"My sister has been cleared of murder," Emmet said. "We're leaving."

"I won't leave without Liam," I said.

Emmet didn't reply. The wall blocking the path to Lygan Hall came into view. The horses had been stabled on one side, but there was no hint of anyone in the warren of rooms on the other.

"No one is leaving," Orla said. "The gate opens at my pleasure."

"I came in without your permission," Emmet said. "Will you really make us prisoners?"

"Your sister just triggered an avalanche, and I am not sure any man is strong enough to stop the fall," Orla said. "I offer you shelter. If you've ever held any allegiance to the Duwead Clan, you would willingly stay."

"If the Duwead Elder appreciated the people who put their lives on the line for her clan, then none of us would be here," Emmet said.

"I didn't have a choice." Orla veered toward the wall of balconies.

"There's always a choice," Emmet said. "Some are just too cowardly to see the true path forward."

I expected Emmet to drag me toward the closed gate, but he followed Orla instead.

The room Emmet hauled me into looked more like a fancy dining room than a place that belonged deep underground. A long, wooden table reached down the center of the room as though Orla were expecting twenty people for dinner. A bookcase took up most of the back wall. The bindings on the books were old, as though they'd been underground far longer than I'd been alive.

Orla sat at the head of the table, facing us.

I could hear the sounds of men rushing about outside, but it didn't sound like fighting.

"Are you all right?" Emmet eased his grip on my arm.

"Fine. You?" I looked up at him. The burns on his neck looked worse than they had from a distance. "Has anyone even looked at those?"

I reached to shift his collar away from the wound. Blood still dripped from my hands.

"Hopefully there are some proper healing supplies here." A knot pressed against the front of my throat.

"We'll sort it out."

I just nodded. I couldn't think of anything to say.

Emmet lifted the cloak from my grip and kissed the top of my head.

I leaned my cheek against his chest, and he wrapped his arms around me. I'd forgotten how comforting and solid my brother was.

The agony and fear of everything Edric had shown all those people dug at my chest, like a tiny, vicious monster was picking parts of me away. My breath hitched as pain pierced my lungs.

"You're going to be fine." Emmet held me tighter. "You are strong enough to survive armies and fire. Those chivving bastards are nothing to people like us. You'll be all right."

I wrapped my arms around Emmet, not caring that I was dripping blood on him. "Thank you for looking for me."

"I was getting ready to sneak into Ilara." Emmet laid his cheek against the top of my head. "But I went to Mave's first. I needed help finding supplies. She told me you'd left for Lygan Hall."

"When you tell Marta where you were, be sure to emphasize needing supplies before mentioning Mave."

Emmet took a step away from me.

"She was worried sick about you," I said.

"I'll fetch a healer." Emmet didn't meet my gaze before going out the door and leaving me with Orla.

"This underground city," Orla said, "what did you see?"

I stood at the opposite end of the table from her, watching her for a moment.

"Was Edric wrong?" Orla said. "Did you fool him? Does the place not exist?"

"I didn't see everything that's down there. At least, I don't think so. When the mountain swallowed me, I followed a long path. Then I was so thirsty, I could barely keep going, and I found a fountain and plants. Edible plants growing that far underground. There was a beautiful statue in the fountain, like the one in the sorcerers' compound. And houses, I don't know how many. I kept to the path, just trying to find a way out.

"Sometimes, I would walk for days and see nothing, like there were bits of the countryside no one had chosen for their homes.

"I found a manor with a walled garden. It looked like the people had packed up and moved on, but there was no sign of trouble. Then, when I thought I'd go mad from being alone for so long, the mountain let me out, and I was back in the forest."

"And the stone Finn spoke of?" Orla asked.

"He found the shard in the mine below the Lir Valley," I said. "I don't know if that's what Lir is mining or if they just found it by accident."

The door swung open behind me.

Finn walked in, followed by a livid Liam.

"Just in time," Orla said.

"And you never once mentioned it to me?" Liam shut the door behind him. He looked at me, and for an instant it seemed like he was going to reach for me. But then his face grew hard and he went back to glaring at Finn.

The pain in my chest dug deeper.

"What should I have said?" Finn asked. "I found a bit of stone and I'm afraid we've been lied to all our chivving lives?"

"It would have been better to hear it from you before you leapt up onto the council's table," Liam said. "You could be charged with heresy. Gods and stars, Finn, what were you thinking?"

"That they were going to keep trying to pin every sort of misery on Ena!" Finn shouted. "That we were one against four with those guards charging at us, and I didn't like the odds of the people I care about staying alive. And the stars can blame me if they like, but people have a right to know that what we've been taught is a chivving lie."

"Finn," Orla said.

"I'm sorry, Orla," Finn said, "but I can't reconcile the existence of the Black Bloods with there being mountain stone so far away from the eastern mountains. Not if everything I've been taught is true.

"If the magic that protects us was created by the mother funneling her magic into the heart of the mountain, then this stone"—he reached into his pocket and pulled out a folded cloth—"shouldn't be anywhere near the Lir Valley. If we really are standing right beneath the summit, in the womb the mountain formed to raise the child, then there shouldn't be a random mine of magical chivving stone far west near Ilara."

"Let me see it." Liam held out his hand.

"I'm right, Liam. I'm certain of it." Finn unfolded the cloth and placed the shard of stone on Liam's palm.

The tiny bit of black rock lay against Liam's skin.

For one blissful moment, I thought Finn had been wrong.

But Liam gasped, and the tiny shard glowed a brilliant, pale blue.

Orla stood and hurried to her son's side.

"Give it to me." She held her hand next to Liam's.

Liam stayed staring at his palm, as though seeing something I could not.

"Now, Liam."

Liam picked up the sliver of light and placed it on Orla's palm.

"How could this be?" Orla tipped her hand, examining the bit of impossible magic.

"I don't know," Finn said. "But I found it in Lir's mine. The man owns an entire valley and is powerful enough to ward the Guilds off his land. The two can't be a coincidence."

"Why didn't you come to me immediately?" Orla looked away from the light in her palm to study Finn's face.

"With the Ryelands being accused of treachery, it didn't seem like a good time to cause a fuss," Finn said.

"And the middle of a council meeting did?" Liam asked.

"It stopped the fight." Finn shrugged. "Besides, people deserve to know."

"What will happen now that they do?" I asked.

Liam turned to me.

He looked at my face and the blood on my hands. There was distance in his eyes I'd never seen before. "I'm so sorry. I'm sorry this happened to you." He reached for me.

I lifted my hands away from him, holding them close to my chest. "Don't be." I forced myself to give him a quick smile. "I've been through far worse before."

The door swung open, and an old man burst in with Emmet close behind him.

The man bowed to Orla before looking to me. "I hear you've hurt your hands."

"I'm fine," I said. "Emmet's got burns—"

"You're bleeding, Ena," Emmet said. "My burns are old. A bit longer without care won't make a difference."

"At the table, if you will." The healer pulled out a chair for me.

"Emmet." Liam stepped toward him. "I'm glad you're back."

"I never should have gone anywhere," Emmet said. "I never should have left Nantic. I should have stayed in Ilbrea where I could look after my sister."

"Emmet." I stepped between him and Liam.

"I asked you for one thing, and this is where you've landed her," Emmet said.

"I love her." Liam placed his hand on the back of my waist.

For the first time, his touch did not bring comfort.

"I am doing everything I can to keep her safe," Liam said. "Her being called here was not because of me."

"You should have taken her and run," Emmet said.

"You shouldn't have volunteered her to be questioned by a sorcerer," Liam said.

"If you were truly a man of your word, you would be across the Arion Sea by now." Emmet's voice was low and dangerous. "Then I wouldn't have had to take the only way out she had left."

"Emmet, stop it." I sat and laid my bloody hands out on the table. "I am chivving well capable of making my own choices, and we've got bigger problems right now than both of you thinking you know what's best for me."

"We'll get this bandaged up for you," the healer said. "Won't take long at all."

"I can do it myself if you'd like to tend to my brother."

"There's a healer here," Emmet said. "Just let him do his work."

"We all have our own work to do," Orla said, "and I fear our tasks have just become monumentally difficult."

"What do you mean?" Emmet said.

"The council is in uproar," Orla said. "We are as close to fracturing the treaty as I have seen in the last twenty years."

"What should we do?" Finn said. "You can't deny that Ena and I both spoke the truth."

"First, we send Ena and Emmet back to Lygan Hall," Liam said. "They can take the two horses they rode here."

"I'm not leaving you." I pulled my hand from the healer's grasp.

"If you could hold still, Miss," the healer gripped my wrist.

"The Hall is no safer than the Broinn," Orla said. "Not when we still have a murderer lurking among us. And it would be wrong to remove the one person who's seen the city belowground when people will have so many questions."

"You would have Ena placed back on trial?" Emmet said.

"You cannot be placed on trial for telling the truth, despite what Elan thinks," Orla said.

"Do you think any of them will stay here after the way the council meeting crumbled?" Finn asked.

The healer spread a stinging salve onto my fingers. I'd cracked through the skin on my knuckles and torn the sides of my hands.

"Ronin might leave," Orla said. "The whole Davin Clan has always been prone to dramatics. Bryana will stay for fear of missing information. Edric is still worried about his dead blood leader. Elan will be terrified of this information being accepted and ruining her idea of what the Black Bloods are meant to be. She won't risk the truth getting out without putting up a fight. The bells will be rung again in the morning. Until then, we all stay in this corridor. Colm will see to the guards."

"We should plan," Liam said. "Look at what the best path to peace might be."

"We've thrown a knife at a monster's hide," Orla said. "All we can do now is wait to see how badly we've angered the beast."

45

Someone had laid out a clean shift for me. I stood next to the bed, staring at it for a long while.

I wanted to know if they had laid it out while the worst horrors of my life were being displayed for all to watch, or after. Had they waited to see if I'd be found guilty before bothering to find me something to wear that hadn't been stained with my own blood? Had they only done such a kind thing because they'd seen the horrors in my mind and felt sorry for me?

Everyone in Lygan Hall will know my secrets. I can't hide from them any longer.

"Do you need help?" Liam asked.

"What?" I spun toward him and backed away from him all at the same time.

"Your clothes," Liam said. "With the bandages you've got on, I thought you might need help getting changed."

"I can manage." I turned away from him to untie my bodice. Pain throbbed through my fingers, and I could feel the newly scabbed wounds cracking. But I made quick work of the knot and loosening the laces.

"Are you hungry?" Liam asked.

"No." I shimmied the bodice over my head and knelt to untie my boots.

"I'm sorry there's not a better place for you to wash up."

"I don't mind. I'm too tired anyway."

"A cup of tea then, to help you sleep."

"I've just said I'm tired." I kicked off my boots and unfastened my skirt. The heavy material pooled around my feet as it fell.

"Right. I'm sorry."

I yanked off my dark blue shift and pulled on the clean, cream-colored one.

"If there's anything I can do to make you more comfortable, please just—"

"Which one is it?" I cut across Liam.

"What?"

"Which horrible memory of mine bothered you so badly that you don't want to touch me?" I untied the string from the bottom of my braid, grateful for the stinging of my hands as I shook my hair free. "You already knew about the ride to Nantic, so it can't be that. Was it actually seeing the faces of the people I failed? Seeing my parents? Or was it the man I stabbed on that boat? I never told anyone about murdering him."

"You wouldn't have done it if you'd had any other choice."

"I could have screamed." I dug into my trunk for my comb. The bandages shifted as I searched through the fabric, leaving my wounds exposed. "I could have hit him on the head or shouted for Finn. But I killed him instead. Just like I killed the man in the Brien enclave."

"You didn't have a choice."

"There is always a choice!"

"No one can blame you for any of that." Liam laid a hand on my shoulder.

I pulled away from him. "Was it being captured to be sold to the highest bidder? I'd have ended up a whore in a far worse place than Mave's. Did that make you realize how little I'm worth?"

"You're worth everything." Liam held my comb out to me. "I love you, Ena Ryeland."

"Don't." I stood and backed away from him. I couldn't even make myself accept the comb.

"I do. I love you. And no horror, no nightmare, nothing from your past could ever make me stop loving you."

"You deserve someone better." Pain sliced through my throat. "Someone whole and untainted. Orla's right to hate me."

"I've told you before. You are the bravest, strongest woman I've ever met."

"I don't want you to care for me out of some twisted sense of sympathy." Heat stung my eyes.

"I'm sorry for all the terrible things that have happened to you. If I could erase them, I would, but I cannot pity the woman who's survived so much. You are not weak. You are not tainted. You are fierce, Ena. You are a survivor. You are an inferno that will blaze through the evils of this world. I only hope I will be lucky enough to stand by your side to see the flames."

"I'm not brave." A tear raced down my cheek. I raised my hand to wipe it away, but my bandages had shifted, and blood covered my skin. "I'm afraid. I'm always chivving afraid. And people die, and it's my fault."

"No, it's not." Liam reached forward slowly, as though waiting for me to back away. "You may feel fear, but it doesn't control you. You are brave. You are courageous and powerful. You've saved lives, Ena. That is more than most people ever manage."

He wiped my tears away.

"I'm sorry for what Edric did to you." Liam stepped closer. His scent surrounded me. "I'm sorry I let Bryana question you like that. But you are not diminished by their evil. There is no force in this world strong enough to do that."

More tears spilled down my cheeks as Liam fixed my bandages.

He led me to the bed and pulled back the blankets.

I curled up on my side, feeling like a little girl, lying in Lily's loft, too terrified to sleep.

Liam pulled the blankets up to my shoulders.

"Don't go." I caught his hand before he could move away. "Please don't go."

His boots thumped against the floor as he kicked them off.

He kept his hand in mine as he climbed under the blankets, his body cradling mine as though giving a fresh promise to keep the nightmares at bay.

46

I sat between Emmet and Finn at the long wooden table. We'd finished eating our breakfast an hour before, but the bell still hadn't rung. Orla and Liam had left as soon as someone came to take our plates away, but Finn, Emmet, and I had been abandoned to sit.

I stared at my bandaged hands on the table. The healer had come and re-dressed them. The wounds felt better than I'd thought they would. I wanted to know what the healer had used on my skin.

Emmet wore a bandage on his neck that gave off an earthy scent I didn't recognize. I wanted to know what ointment held such an odor, as well.

"Do you think they all left?" Finn said. "Maybe they've all cleared out, and we can just pack up and go home."

"We're not that lucky," Emmet said.

We sat silently for a few more minutes.

When I couldn't stand sitting anymore, I went to the bookcase in the back of the room.

"I think things will be better now," Finn said. "If we can get Black Bloods to believe there's mountain stone in Ilbrea, maybe they'll see that what goes on out there really does have something to do with them. It could rally enough people that we can finally fight."

"Maybe." I ran my fingers along the spines of the books. None of them were titles I'd encountered in Harane.

"I…"

I looked back to Finn.

He ran his hands over his face before speaking again. "I don't think the legends are true. I don't think all Black Bloods are descendants of a child raised by stone, but I am certain there's something special about the mountain."

"There has to be," I said. "Normal mountains don't save people."

"Then there's got to be a reason for it," Finn said. "The mountain wanted us to find the stone and you to see the city. This is how it's meant to be. Everything is happening according to the mountain's plan."

I opened my mouth to argue, but there was something in the certainty in Finn's eyes that I didn't want to test. I had only believed in one person the way Finn trusted the mountain. Losing that faith had nearly broken me.

"Whatever the stars have planned, we'll keep fighting." Emmet clapped Finn on the back.

"I'm glad we're good at it." Finn smiled.

A ringing echoed down the tunnel.

"They didn't all leave then." I could barely hear Finn's words over the tolling of the bell.

"Right." I stared at the door. I'm not sure if I was waiting for someone to come in or deciding if I really was brave enough to go out and face the council again.

"Come on." Emmet stood up and held out his hand.

"Right." I nodded. "Better to get it done."

I took Emmet's arm, careful not to crack the scabs on my hand.

As soon as we stepped outside, the sound of the bells began vibrating in my lungs, and I could feel the pull again. The longing hitched onto the front of my chest, drawing me toward the cavern.

"Miss." Kely, who'd taken my horse, stepped in front of me and held out my cloak. "They cleaned it as best they could," he shouted over the bells. "I thought you might want it."

"Thank you." I gave Kely the best smile I could and took the cloak.

He bowed before running to join the line of guards gathering at the end of the corridor.

I let go of Emmet to fasten the cloak around my neck.

"Ena," Liam called in the silence between the tolls.

He'd reached my side before I could turn toward him. They'd given him a sword to wear at his hip. I wished someone had thought to give me a knife—any sort of weapon.

"To the cavern," Colm called from the front of the pack, his words barely discernable over the throbbing in my ears.

"I'll protect her," Emmet shouted over the din.

"Finn and I will both stay with the two of you," Liam shouted back.

He met Emmet's gaze, and something passed between them. Some understanding I did not share.

Emmet nodded.

Liam stepped in front of me while Finn and Emmet stood on either side.

"Where's Case?" I leaned close to Finn's ear.

Finn pointed toward the front of the group where the guards had pulled their swords from their sheaths. "Colm's orders."

What does the Blood Leader think will happen?

The front of our group started forward. The movement rippled across the pack of guards until the whole Duwead flock began moving toward the cavern.

They were not this ready to defend when my life was at stake.

I scanned the crowd, searching for Orla. She traveled at the back, surrounded by black-clad guards.

I squeezed Emmet's arm and glanced back toward Orla.

He followed my gaze.

"Will there be anyone left at the gate?" I leaned close to his ear.

Worry mixed with anger creased the corners of Emmet's eyes, but he didn't answer.

By the time I could see into the cavern, three of the five sides were mostly filled.

Ronin's section was completely empty.

The first line of Duwead guards stood in front of the tiers, their weapons still drawn. The rest of the guards filed up onto the steps behind them.

I waited for Liam to walk toward the pentagon table at the center of the cavern, but he led me to the corner of the tier where I'd stood the morning before, placing me behind him with Emmet and Finn still standing on either side.

Orla and the shadow guard didn't enter until the rest of us were still.

The three elders already seated said nothing as Orla, Colm, and ten black-clad guards approached the table.

The bell stopped tolling as she reached her seat. My ears pounded in the silence, but still, I could hear the rustle of Orla's chivving skirt.

"Has your Trueborn decided not to join us?" Bryana asked, staring pointedly at Liam standing in front of me.

"My clan was attacked yesterday in this very chamber," Orla said. "And let us not forget the attempts on my Trueborn's life."

"Should we all call guards to stand behind our seats?" Edric said. "Will we resort to petty threats soon?"

"You have no space to judge after your actions yesterday, Edric," Orla said.

"The traditions we have in place hold a purpose," Elan said.

"Bringing armed men with you to our table? You are trying to destroy everything the Black Bloods should cherish."

"I am only seeking my own safety as I offer you all the truth," Orla said.

"Have you decided to admit to killing my Blood Leader?" Edric leaned forward, as though ready to pounce.

"I offer physical proof that what Finn told you about the stone under the Lir Valley is true."

"That is blas—"

"And presents a larger threat than I had hoped to face in my lifetime." Orla ignored Elan and reached into her pocket. Finn's worn cloth had been replaced by a square of black silk. Orla unfolded the fabric and placed the tiny shard in her hand.

The extraordinary blue light flared to life, glowing brighter than it had the night before.

"What is this trickery?" Edric stood and leaned over the table, peering into the light.

"You would not be able to see it," Bryana said. "You're a sorcerer, not a trueborn."

"What does that—"

"The stone calls to trueborn," Bryana said. "You see a shining light. We see the blazing potential of magic. We feel its pull in our blood, see its vibrancy in a way you can't begin to imagine. This is mountain stone. This is the essence that runs through our veins."

"This stone was found in a mine far outside our mountain range," Orla said. "In an Ilbrean mine. The enemy we have all feared for years has access to this precious resource."

Bryana pressed her fingers to her mouth, looking afraid for the first time. Regan reached forward and placed her hand on her mother's shoulder.

"The stones that we use for protection," Orla said, "that we alter to create light, that had been used to create the terrifying weapons our own treaty banned—the Guilds have access to this stone."

"Lies," Elan said. "Is this how desperate you've become to interfere with Ilbrea? The Black Bloods' place is in the mountains. The Guilds have nothing to do with us."

"Do you suggest I created this stone?" Orla stood and held the blazing light high.

"You could have gotten that anywhere," Elan said.

"Why would I do such a thing?" Orla asked.

"Desperate people are prone to disgusting acts." Elan stood up. "I did not think I would ever see an elder treat the covenant we hold with this mountain with such disregard."

"I value the bond we Black Bloods have with the mountain above all," Orla said. "But we cannot turn away from the truth, not when we are even more vulnerable to an attack from Ilbrea than we feared."

"You say the stone was found in Ilbrea," Edric said, "prove it. Let us all see where the stone was discovered."

My chest seized as the horror of being asked to let that man display images from my mind stripped away my senses and left me with nothing but a will to flee.

Emmet took my arm, as though preparing to grab me and run.

"I'd be happy to let you prance through my memories." Finn waved. "You'll see a lot of dark tunnel, but I'd like to think my attention to detail will give you all a decent show."

Orla did not look surprised or angry as she turned to Finn. She gave him a formal nod before speaking. "Do you freely volunteer?"

"Absolutely." Finn squeezed my hand before stepping down and through the line of sword-bearing guards.

"I will not stay to watch this masquerade of lies." Elan strode away toward the Hayes corridor. "May you someday remember the duty that comes with the stone in your blood."

"Black Bloods deserve to know the truth." Finn looked to each of the four groups on the tiers as he walked toward the table. "I am grateful for the duty I owe the mountain."

Elan disappeared, unwilling to watch what the rest of us had to witness.

"Can you get someone to fetch the giant bowl?" Finn leapt up onto the table. "I'd prefer to—"

I didn't hear the buzz cutting through the air. I should have heard it, but I didn't. I didn't notice anything at all until blood sprayed from Finn's back, coating Orla and the shadow guard.

A hand gripped my arm, but I wrenched free, diving through the line of guards to reach Finn's side.

"Protect your Elder!" Colm's voice cut above the screaming.

The shadow guard surrounded Orla, rushing her away.

A bellow carried from the far side of the cavern as the green-clad Hayes guards charged the Duweads.

Still, I ran forward. I had to reach Finn.

Nothing in the world mattered but reaching Finn.

Only one person ran faster.

One streak of blue sprinted toward the wall of green.

I slipped in Finn's blood as I reached the table.

Finn lay on his back, gasping for breath, his eyes wide and his gaze fixed on the crack in the ceiling high above us.

"You're going to be all right." I climbed up onto the table and knelt beside him. The warmth of his blood soaked through my skirt. "Look at me, Finn. You're going to be fine. I just need you to keep breathing."

Finn turned his gaze to my face as I tore the sleeve from my shift and pressed it to the wound.

He gasped in pain.

"I need the healer!" I shouted as loudly as I could. "Someone get the healer."

There was no one to hear me.

Liam had charged straight for the attacking Hayes and fought on the far side of the table, trying to keep them from reaching Finn and me.

But a pack of Hayes had gotten past him, all the way to where the tiers met the Duwead corridor.

Emmet fought at the bottom of the steps, slashing through men as he tried to reach me.

"It's fine," I said. "We can hold on. We can wait."

I kept pressing on the wound with one hand while I unfastened my cloak and draped the thick fabric over Finn.

Boom.

A wave of light flew from Edric's side of the table, knocking both Duweads and Hayes aside, leaving Edric and his men a clear path to flee. But the Brien had joined the fight, pushing the bulk of the Hayes guards back toward their tunnel.

"Case." Finn's hand trembled as he pointed.

"Don't move." I took Finn's hand. "You've got to hold still. Just keep breathing. That's all you have to do."

"Case." Finn gasped.

"Case!" I shouted. "Case!"

I looked away from Finn to see if Case had heard me. It only took me a moment to find him, standing in the middle of the Hayes guards, fighting alongside the bastards as they tried to flee.

"Emmet!" I screamed his name.

"Ena."

I looked toward Emmet's voice in time to see him slash through the throat of a Hayes guard.

"Stop Case." I pointed toward the crowd.

Darkness devoured my brother as he spotted the traitor. He wasn't the boy I had worshiped or the man I had hated. Emmet Ryeland was a demon born of Death himself.

He did not give them the warning of a battle cry as he raced into the crowd of green-clad men. He sprinted silently toward them, blood already dripping from his blade.

"Emmet's fetching him." I looked down at Finn.

His eyes had gone blank. There was no fear on his face, or pain. He'd laid his hand on top of mine as I'd pressed on his wound. I hadn't even felt his touch.

"Finn."

I pressed my fingers to his neck, searching for a hint of life.

"Finn."

The world went silent around me as a sob banged against my ribs.

"Please, Finn."

No amount of love can bring a person back from death. There is not a soul in this world who is that strong.

My tears dripped onto Finn, marring his face.

I wanted to see him smile one more time. To hear him laugh just once so I could try to memorize the sound.

My hand trembled as I let go of the wound.

I took Finn's hand in mine and pressed my lips to his forehead. "I will make them understand. I will burn Ilara. I promise."

I laid his hand back on his chest and pulled his sword from its sheath.

The battle still raged around me. Guards in blue, green, black, and purple all lay dead on the ground, but the ones left standing seemed determined to fight.

Liam faced a line of green-clad men with purple Brien guards fighting by his side.

Emmet had pierced the pack of Elan's men, leaving the others fighting on our side struggling to follow in his wake. But none of Elan's cowards seemed eager to get near my brother.

A green-clad guard dared to slash his sword for Emmet's side.

Emmet dodged with the slightest lean as he swung his own blade, severing the guard's head from his body. The guard's body fell, toppling into the men behind him.

I leapt off the table and ran toward Emmet.

A green-clad guard had a Duwead pinned to the ground.

My ears rediscovered sound as I drove Finn's blade into the Hayes' back. My arm felt the effort it took to stab the man, but my heart felt nothing as I yanked my blade free and kept running toward Emmet.

A glisten of red-coated metal caught the corner of my eye.

I brought my blade up before I saw who was attacking.

The Hayes guard glared at me with hatred in his eyes.

"Blasphemer." He spat the title like it was worse than *murderer*.

I let my blade sink under his blow.

He raised his sword to swipe for my chest.

I kept my own blade low and sliced through the side of his knee.

The man cried out as his leg collapsed beneath him.

I slashed my sword through his gut and kept running toward Emmet.

The other Duwead guards had finally managed to catch up to him, and the Brien had blocked off the Hayes corridor, preventing the bastards from retreating.

There was no talk of surrender as Emmet's blade pierced the chest of another Hayes.

I reached the back of the pack of Duweads. There was no one there for me to fight. I wanted to get to the front of the crowd, to find someone else to sink Finn's sword into, but the Duwead line was thick, and they would not let me through.

"Keep Case alive!" I shouted. "Keep the chivving traitor alive!"

"Miss." Kely appeared by my side. Blood coated his right arm, and he held his sword awkwardly in his left. "The path to our corridor is clear. You should join Orla."

"I'm not going anywhere until they've captured the traitor," I shouted over the chorus of rage and agony.

"The Trueborn wants you safe," Kely said. "I'm trying to help you."

"If you want to help me, go fetch the healer. The longer he stays hidden, the more good people will die." My own words punctured my bloodlust.

"I can't leave the fight."

"Liam said to treat me as you would him. I am ordering you to fetch the healer. Drag him here if you have to."

Kely nodded and ran toward the tunnel, still awkwardly gripping his sword.

I looked at the cavern.

Finn lay on the table beneath my black cloak. Blood had been smeared across the dark stone of the floor. All around, guards lay on the ground, wounded or dead.

This is not the last fight.

I ran toward the nearest blue-clad guard who was still conscious. He'd been stabbed through the shoulder.

A hand reached out and grabbed my ankle. The man wore a green coat. I thrust my blade down through his throat.

"I need you to sit up if you can." I knelt beside the blue-clad guard.

"I can't feel my arm," the guard said.

"That's all right." I laid my sword by my side and ripped the other sleeve from my shift. "If we get you upright, you'll lose less blood. Can you manage it?"

The guard bit back his scream as I helped him to sit. I used Finn's sword to slice away the bottom of my skirt and made two bundles to tie against the wound.

I grabbed my sword and ran to the next guard. He had a horrible slice through his calf. I tied another strip of my skirt around his leg. I hoped he wouldn't blame me when he lost the limb.

The chaos on the far side of the cavern had quieted.

The next guard was a Brien. Pink frothed at the corners of his mouth.

Panic has never helped anyone, Ena Ryeland. Lily's voice echoed through my mind.

Tears blurred my vision as I lifted the guard just enough to fasten his own thick leather belt around the wound in his chest.

Footsteps carried up the Duwead corridor. I hadn't realized it was quiet enough for me to hear something so small. Two women charged out of the tunnel, each carrying a heavy pack. The old man who had wrapped my hands trotted after them a moment later.

"No!" The scream came from the Hayes side of the cavern.

The fighting had stopped. There was no more clanging of weapons, just the one terrible cry.

"Let me go! I'm one of you. Let me go!"

Emmet broke free of the crowd, dragging Case by his bound wrists. Case flailed along the ground, but Emmet either didn't notice or didn't care.

"Open the cell," Emmet ordered.

Kely limped as he ran past Emmet, pulling a heavy set of keys from his pocket. He opened the door, and Emmet threw Case into the cell.

I heard the smack as Case hit the ground.

"Lock him in and leave him for Orla's justice," Emmet said.

He looked my direction and met my gaze.

We were the same, my brother and I. We'd both been born into a world of flames and come out of the ashes with a blazing fire devouring our souls that not even vengeance could calm.

Emmet gave me a nod and strode toward the Hayes corridor. "Who wants to make sure there are no rats left in the warren?"

A roar rose up from the men.

Both Brien and Duwead followed my brother into the darkness.

I stood and moved on to the next wounded man. He'd been sliced through the gut and was beyond my aid.

"Ena," Liam said.

I couldn't make myself look at him. I was too afraid of turning around to find him wounded and on the edge of death.

"Ena, are you hurt?" Liam knelt in front of me. A small bit of blood stained his side, and a larger wound still bled on his leg. "Are you bleeding?"

"We need to wrap that." I sliced another strip of my skirt away with Finn's sword.

Liam took my hands in his, stopping me from reaching the wound on his thigh.

Blood covered my hands and arms. The red stained the pale skin above my bodice and soaked through my skirt.

"Were you wounded?" Liam tipped my chin up and made me look into his eyes.

"Please let me help you." My words cracked against the knot in my throat. "I can't lose you, too."

Liam sat back and let me wrap the tatters of my finely made skirt around his thigh.

"How?" My hands shook as I tied off the bandage. "How could this have happened?"

"I don't know. But we will find out."

I laid my hand against Liam's chest, needing to feel his heart beating.

"Finn loved him," I said.

"I know." Liam pressed my hand to his chest. "Finn loved you, too."

Everything inside me shattered. There was no joy left to bind the fragments of my soul together.

Liam held me close as I wept for the friend I had loved with reckless abandon.

49

By the time Emmet led the guards out of the Hayes corridor, all the wounded had been tended to and the dead separated by clan.

Finn still lay on the table. They had tried to move him, but I'd shouted like a madwoman until they'd backed away.

I couldn't bear to look at him, but I didn't want him clustered with the others. I didn't want them taking him away where I couldn't find him.

When Orla finally appeared, she wore a fitting air of grief and disgust. She'd changed her clothes and washed Finn's blood off her skin. It seemed wrong that she could undo the damage the battle had inflicted on her so easily while Finn would never come back.

I pressed the terrible pain into the dark void and tucked the blackness behind layers of rage and vengeful fire. It was the only way I could stay standing.

Regan and Bryana returned not long after Orla. They too bore no mark from the fight.

They all clustered with their blood leaders in front of the door to Case's cell, staring at the wood.

Liam kept my hand in his as he went to join them. I think I

would have started screaming again if they had tried to separate me from him.

"This is an act of war against the clans," Bryana said. "There is no coming back from this."

"I hope you do not count the Duweads amongst your enemies," Orla said.

"Is the traitor sworn to you or Liam?" Bryana asked.

"No," Liam said.

"Then our enemies are the Hayes and this traitor," Bryana said. "We should tell Edric and Ronin. Make sure they know what demons have swept through our lands."

"I'll send runners down both passages as soon as the execution is finished," Orla said.

"We need more information from him," Liam said. "How did he keep in contact with the Hayes? Who was he feeding information to in Ilbrea?"

"Is there another traitor, or was he working alone?" I gripped Liam's hand as a thick silence swooped through our cluster.

"Case knows the fate that awaits him," Orla said. "Do you think you'll be able to pull information from him?"

"Could a sorcerer do it?" I asked.

"He's already fooled one sorcerer," Liam said.

"Then I'll do it," I said.

"Have the Guilds trained you in assassination and torture?" Regan asked.

"No, only desperation. Leave him in there until I get back."

I turned away from the door to search the cavern.

A healer knelt beside a man with a slice through his side. The man bit down on a strip of leather as the healer cleaned the wound.

Liam stayed with me as I crossed the stained floor.

"Can I borrow something from your bag?" I asked.

The healer glanced up at me. "What?"

"Yarrow tincture if you have it," I said.

"Bottom pocket." The healer furrowed her brow at me. "Why?"

"Liam needs stitches in his leg, and you should clean the wound on his side as well." I let go of Liam's hand and pulled the little glass bottle from the bag.

"What are you doing?" Liam asked.

"Who here might have a bit of frie on them?" I said.

"Colm." Liam furrowed his brow. "Why?"

"A desperate person in a cage can only want one thing," I said. "So, I'll give it to him."

"You can't," Liam said.

"Finn is dead."

"Things are already bad enough."

"And I want to know who is responsible," I said. "Do you trust me to do this or not?"

Liam shut his eyes for a moment. "Promise me you won't untie him."

"I promise." I gripped the bottle in my hand and pressed my lips to Liam's cheek. "Don't let them interrupt me."

I strode back toward Colm. He'd made someone bring him a clean coat to cover the true horror of the day.

Blood still coated my skin. Finn's, our guards', their guards'.

Their blood offered a new form of armor. I was not a grieving girl. I was a warrior. An avenging demon.

Case had started this horror. If he hadn't betrayed us, Finn and I would have been in Lygan Hall eating pie and laughing while looking up at the bright blue sky. There were others to share the blame, but Case would be the first to die.

"I need your frie." I held my hand out to Colm.

"What?" Colm had the nerve to look insulted.

"Just give me the frie, and let me get the answers you can't."

"Do it," Orla ordered.

Fixing me with an angry glare, Colm pulled a little waterskin made of fine leather from his pocket. He winced as I pulled the stopper out with my teeth.

I dumped the full bottle of yarrow tincture into the frie, pushed the stopper back in, and shook the mixture up.

"Now let me in," I said.

"This is ridiculous," Colm said. "The Hayes are to blame. We'll find out who else aided them when we storm the Hayes citadel."

"Citadel?" I said. "Sounds like that cacting slitch really does trust in the mountain to protect her. Now open the door. I am not patient enough to wait for armies to move before I have answers."

"Let her try," Regan said. "Torment and evisceration wait for him either way."

"Open the door," Orla said.

Kely stepped forward and opened the lock with a heavy thunk.

I paused in front of the door. "Don't let them take Finn away. I don't want him discarded in the darkness."

Orla laid a hand on my bloody arm. "I promise you each of my people will receive a hero's funeral. Finn will be cared for."

I nodded, pushing the tendrils of pain back into the void. "Thank you."

I wrenched open the heavy door and stepped into the darkness.

50

Someone pushed the door closed behind me.

Thunk.

I didn't look back as they locked me in. My gaze was already fixed on Case.

He sat on the wooden pallet at the back of the room, his hands still tied in front of him. The orange light of the cell almost hid the moment when the hatred in his eyes shifted to worry.

"Where's Finn?" Case asked. "Have the healers seen him?"

"Finn's dead. It was quick though. He didn't suffer much."

Case shut his eyes, and his shoulders curled in toward his chest.

"Did you actually care about him?" I asked.

"I loved him, and those bastards—"

"Don't bother lying." I stepped closer to him. "There's no way you're making it through this day alive. You betrayed your clan and the man who loved you. You deserve to die."

"If you believe that, then why are you in here?"

"You tricked a sorcerer. How? How did you fool Wyman?"

"I didn't trick anyone. I'm innocent."

"What's the punishment for being a traitor?" I asked.

Case stared silently at me.

"No really, what is it? I don't know."

"Burning with coals, breaking with hammers, and evisceration." He swallowed like he might be ill on the floor.

"Seems fitting." I shrugged. "You got my friend killed and ripped my heart out—they rip your guts out."

Case turned to the side and vomited on the floor.

I waited for the retching to stop before speaking again.

"Finn loved you. And I think you loved him, too, at least a little."

"He was a wonderful man. He never should have been involved in any of this. He should have stayed in Lygan Hall."

"I want to hurt the one who shot a stone through his chest, and I want you to help me find them."

"I don't know anything."

"Lying won't save you from a horrible end. Nothing can save your life, but I can smooth out your final moments." I held up the skin.

"You hope to buy me with frie?"

"Widows brew." I pulled the stopper with my teeth and held the skin close enough to Case that he could smell its scent over the pungent odor of his own sick. "It's a fast end. You'll get a bit dizzy, maybe a little warm, then fall asleep, and you won't wake up."

"You're lying."

"Poison is my specialty. I'm offering you a kind end in exchange for information. Would you like to tell me how you fooled Wyman, or would you like your guts ripped out?"

Case stared at the waterskin. "Wyman was looking for fear and trying to be gentle. He poked around to see what I'd felt when the croilach attacked. All he found was terror. I didn't know Elan was going to send any beasts after us and certainly not a herd of them. I didn't want the monsters to rip through my clansmen. I never wanted them anywhere near Finn. He saw how genuine my terror was and let me go."

I swallowed my rage, forcing air into my leaden lungs before speaking again. "How were you communicating with Elan?"

"Stone birds, like the ones Liam uses. She sent me a batch of them before I left for the camp. I just had to write notes and tell the birds to fly."

"Did she send messages back to you?"

Case nodded. "There's a landslide about six miles north of camp. I'd go whenever I could sneak away and find birds there, waiting for me."

"And you told her everything? Where the sorcis we were trying to save were hiding? Where we were fetching supplies in Ilbrea?"

"I didn't know where everyone was going." Case stared down at his hands. "But when I did, I'd send a bird. Finn always told me where he was headed. He told me about the poison he helped you mix and the things you gave Gabe for the other soldiers. I told Elan about that, too."

I shut my eyes, pressing my self-loathing away.

If I'd never offered poison, so many lives would have been spared.

"Why did they mimic my poison?"

"I don't know. Elan never sent me information, only instructions."

"Why did you tell her what I'd done?"

"Why didn't you give Drason the widow's brew?" Case nodded toward the waterskin.

"It tastes awful. You'd never get someone to drink it without them knowing."

"I don't mind a bad taste." Case reached for the skin.

"Not yet." I moved the skin behind my back. "Who was the Hayes contact in Ilbrea?"

"I have no idea." Case pushed himself to his feet. "I only had a way to send messages to Elan."

"That's it?"

"She always pressed for information about things near Frason's Glenn. I think her contact must have been there if she was so eager for news. Maybe Elan had a dozen people in Ilbrea, I really don't know. Now please, give me the poison before they decide to come in."

"Why did she kill the Healy Blood Leader?"

"I don't know anything about that. All I did was send messages."

"Did you love him?" I shouldn't have asked, but I couldn't help myself.

"Yes, I did." Case looked to the ground.

"Then how could you do this?"

He looked up at me with determination in his eyes. "My love for one man cannot be greater than the love I have for the Black Bloods. Our place is here, honoring the covenant we hold with the mountain. Interfering in Ilbrea will do nothing but bring destruction to our land. I had to stop it."

I nodded and handed him the skin.

He pulled out the stopper with his teeth and drank greedily.

I knocked on the door. My blood still stained the wood from the day before.

"How did Elan find you?" I asked. "How did she know that a Duwead would be willing to betray their clan?"

"It's not hard to find like-minded people if you know where to look." Case sat on the pallet. "I'm not alone in my beliefs. The old ways will return, and the mountain will watch over those who have sacrificed to protect the people descended from the stone-raised babe. No amount of torture could make me turn in the others who are willing to risk everything to protect the Black Bloods."

"We'll see," I said as the door opened. "I'm willing to bet Regan is good with a knife."

"What?" Case stood.

I stepped out of the cell.

The guard caught hold of Case as he tried to attack me.

"May your death be everything you deserve."

Fire cannot shatter a mountain's stone, but ice can.

Innocent drops of water sneak into the cracks during the fine rains of summer. No one notices such a meaningless little intrusion. The mountain is too great to fear water as it should.

Winter comes, and the water turns to ice, growing and forging tiny new fissures in the stone.

It may take a hundred winters, but the stone will be defeated. The mountain will crumble.

Fire cannot tear down a mountain.

It's the cracks in the mountain's own stone that will be its undoing.

The journey back to Lygan Hall took longer as the living carefully carried the dead.

Three hundred men and women waited below Lygan Hall at the end of the long corridor to help us carry the fallen Duweads into their home.

Orla opened a massive stone door, and we walked up a long ramp and into the pale light of dusk.

Mountains of snow covered the ground. By some magic, a path of perfect green had been left for the mourners to tread.

The rest of the people of Lygan Hall waited by the edge of the woods, surrounding a field of emerald green grass.

Emmet squeezed my hand before leaving my side.

A tiny prick of joy managed to reach my heart as he walked across the field to Marta. Tears coursed down her cheeks as Emmet gave her a nod and took his place next to her.

Evie stared up at him before looking across the field to me, poking Dorran in the ribs, and whispering something in his ear. Cinni and Gwen stood hand in hand beside their siblings. Gwen offered me a tired smile.

I watched as the guards laid the shrouded dead on the ground.

I knew which one was Finn—Liam had been helping to carry our friend home.

He knelt beside Finn, caressing his head and saying something no else was meant to hear before standing and making his way through the field of bodies to stand beside me.

It was fully dark by the time the last of the families had bade farewell to their dead.

As an elderly woman escorted Finn's mother away, a faint gleam shimmered in the sky.

"We should begin." Orla took her place by Liam's other side.

A man with dark gray hair stepped forward and held his hands flat over the ground. He spoke no words, and the ground made no sound as the earth shifted, and the mountain reclaimed her beloved children.

Liam took my face in his hands and looked into my eyes. I could see his love for me right there. Behind the courage, behind the anger that drove him to face the horrors ahead, his love for me floated beneath it all, keeping the soul of a wonderful man from collapsing.

His kissed my forehead before stepping out onto the empty field.

"People of my clan." Liam's voice rang through the darkness. "The treaty that had long protected us has been broken by the Hayes Clan. Our enemies in Ilbrea are stronger than we knew and diving deeper into the mountains than they have ever dared before."

I looked up to the sky. The shimmer had become a dancing band of green light that swayed without care for the troubles of the men far below.

"We have two choices," Liam said. "We can barricade ourselves in Lygan Hall and hide while the world crumbles. Or we can fight to protect our clan, our families, and these mountains!"

A roar shook the ground as the people of Lygan Hall chose to launch themselves into a deadly battle.

Liam met my gaze and I nodded. I would follow him.

His path was mine, and we would walk side by side to whatever end.

Ena's journey continues in Feather and Flame. *Read on for a sneak preview.*

SOME BATTLES CANNOT BE WON

Continue reading for a sneak peek of *Feather and Flame*.

I wish I could give you a different ending to my tale. I wish the words I had to offer brought comfort and joy.

I am not powerful enough to change the path I have tread, and I will not lie.

I will not allow myself to commit that awful offense that ripped my heart from my chest and left me less than human.

I am only an orphan from Harane.

I am broken beyond repair.

There is no other truth for me to tell.

2

The scent of charcoal filled the little room, and a low rumble carried through the door.

I listened carefully as I ground the black lumps into fine powder. The sound from the corridor stayed steady.

Deirdre had brought flowers from the sorcerers' garden. I would need to use a fresh mortar and pestle to grind the petals once I'd finished with the coal.

The rumble grew louder.

If I made good time, I'd be able to finish a fresh set of inks in the next few days.

"That answer is no longer acceptable." The rumble of voices grew into actual words.

The reply was not loud enough for me to hear.

I set the mortar and pestle aside and went to the washstand in the corner. Someone had left sweet-smelling soap and fine, white cloths for me to dry my hands on.

"It's been months!" The angry shout rattled through my door. "If Colm can't manage it, then send someone who can."

I dried my hands on a cloth, leaving pale gray streaks across the pristine white. I didn't feel guilty for leaving a mess. I'd find fresh white cloths in my workroom in the morning no matter how badly I damaged the fabric.

"I don't care about the clans' rules. This war is a chivving waste of time, and you know it."

I fastened my cloak around my neck. The heavy fabric held a chill from being hung against the stone wall.

"Are we just supposed to wait for more people to die?"

I squared my shoulders before opening the door.

Emmet stood in the corridor, glowering at Ailis.

"What exactly do you want me to do about it?" Ailis asked, not bothering to glance my way.

Emmet didn't look in my direction either.

"Take me up to see Orla," Emmet said. "Let me at least try to convince her to allow us to join the fight."

"She wouldn't—"

"You can't tell me you're content to stay locked in Lygan Hall." Emmet spoke over Ailis. "There is a war going on. We should be at the front, making sure Colm does more than drink frie and let the siege continue."

Ailis pursed her lips and gripped the hilt of the sword at her hip. "Orla has chosen to sequester herself while the clan is at war. She is our Elder. There's nothing—"

"We're running out of time," Emmet said. "Spring will be here soon. We have to be ready to go out into Ilbrea. We can't let Colm drag out the fight with the Hayes."

"What a pleasant afternoon, Emmet." I stepped out of my workshop and into the hall.

The guards lining the corridor bowed to me.

I dug my nails into my palms, fighting to hide my hatred of their deference.

"Are you ready for our walk?" I asked.

Emmet stayed glaring at Ailis.

She ran her tongue over her teeth before speaking. "I'm getting really sick of having this fight with you."

"Then let me see Orla," Emmet said.

"Are you going to wade through the whole argument again?" I looped my hand through Emmet's arm and tried to steer him down the hall.

He wouldn't budge.

"Orla won't come out of her chambers," I said. "You're not allowed into her chambers. Even if you were, you and I still wouldn't be allowed to join Colm in fighting against the Hayes Clan."

"You shouldn't—"

"I should stay safely in Lygan Hall, I know." I yanked on Emmet's arm. He finally started walking down the corridor. "The Hayes want me dead, and my going into their territory would only be offering myself up for the slaughter. Besides, my place isn't fighting in the clan war anyway. I am very aware of your opinion, brother."

He didn't respond. The only sound the hall offered was our footsteps against the stone floor.

"Now it's Ailis's turn to speak," I said. "She'll tell you there is no argument she could make to convince Orla that Liam's people should join the war, even if she could get into the chamber to see our Elder."

"It's true." Ailis followed behind us with the rest of the guards. "Liam's duty is to protect us from the paun. The clan war is not his battle, and our place is at our Trueborn's side."

The guards' footsteps echoed through the hall as well, ruining my chance of hearing anyone approach.

"Then Emmet will say something about there being evil in the world and how only cowards hide while innocents suffer," I pressed on. "Ailis will say again that we can't chase after Colm. Our place is with the Trueborn, and his duty lies in Ilbrea."

"We are useless here," Emmet said.

"I'll tell you that, no matter how many paun were creeping into the mountains when you came to Lygan Hall, there's too much snow between us and Ilbrea to attack the Guilds, and you'll sink into a silent rage that will terrify everyone we pass."

A guard who looked barely older than fifteen scurried forward to open the door for me.

I nodded to him before stepping into the wide corridor beyond.

Benches lined the walls, and flames leapt cheerfully in a massive fireplace. Cold swept in through the wide windows overlooking the valley, but it was my presence that froze the people who'd been passing by.

I let them stare at me for a moment, but I couldn't bring myself to acknowledge them.

"Come on," Emmet said softly.

I fixed my gaze on him as we cut through the gawking Black Bloods. "Have I missed a part of the daily argument? Is there anything you'd like to add?"

The long scar on my brother's left cheek twitched.

"Well?" I bumped my shoulder against him.

"You're annoying when you do that," Emmet said.

"I'm your sister," I said. "It's my duty to annoy you. And we all must do our duty."

Neither of us spoke again as we wound the familiar path through the maze of corridors, down three sets of spiral stairs, and to the raised garden just outside the crag.

A sparkling layer of snow covered the ground, laying a blanket of white over the paths. But the fierce winter storms hadn't harmed the blooms of the garden. The Duwead sorcerers had seen to that.

Brightly hued flowers grew up from the snow, as though the summer sun still beamed down upon them every day. The garden was a beautiful thing to behold, but strolling through the blooms brought me no joy.

People stopped and nodded as I passed, always granting Emmet and me the path.

I fought to keep my face pleasant as we walked. Not angry, not joyful, just a blank canvas that would not feed any of their rumors.

We circled the garden twice before Emmet steered me to a bench under the drooping branches of a weeping tree.

Without a word, the guards fanned out around the tree, each with a hand on their sword, none of them seeming to mind the freezing air that whipped through the valley.

I bundled my cloak around me as I sat on the bench. The material was thick enough to block the worst of the wind. But the frozen ground still chilled my feet, and the air raised goose bumps on my neck.

"How was the training ground this morning?" Emmet asked.

"Much as you'll find it this afternoon," I said.

I stared up through the branches to the bright blue sky. I didn't want to talk about how empty the training ground was with most of the Duwead guards off fighting the Hayes. I didn't want to say that Cati looked like she might go mad at any moment either.

"We're not exposed enough," I said in a voice barely loud enough for Emmet to hear.

"I know," Emmet whispered, "but I needed to talk to you first."

"Why?" I twisted in my seat, leaning over to examine the rose-bush beside the bench.

"There are too many places to hide around the path you want to take," Emmet said. "If they come for you—"

"Then I'll have eleven people protecting me. I am not naïve, and I am not helpless."

"We should go back inside. Think through another plan."

"We've tried all our other plans, and none of them have worked. We take the path we've chosen, and that's final."

"Do not push me, Ena. I am not some Black Blood who will fall at your feet."

"No." I turned to Emmet, locking my gaze onto his eyes rather than letting it drift to the burn scars on his neck. "You are my brother, which means you know me well enough to understand that I will keep going with or without your help."

"I could tell him what you're up to."

I stood and brushed the dusting of snow off my cloak. "If you want to rat me out to Liam, so be it, but you'd have to speak to him to do it."

"There is nothing I wouldn't do to protect you," Emmet said.

"I am protecting myself." I pressed my hand to the knife hidden at my hip without meaning to. "Pretending danger doesn't exist will not make me safer. Locking me up won't get rid of the people who want me dead. I will do this with or without your help."

Emmet stared up through the leaves as I had.

I doubted he was studying the hue of the sky.

"If I tell you we're turning back, I don't want to hear a chivving word of argument," Emmet said.

"Of course." I took Emmet's arm. "But it's such a fine winter's day, a nice long walk seems like a lovely idea."

I led Emmet back onto the path.

Ailis stepped up to my side, eyeing the people between us and the entrance to the crag.

"I'd like to walk a while longer," I said. "Since there's no snow coming down, it would be a shame to waste the sunlight."

"We can circle the garden." Ailis gave me a nod.

"I'm going into the village." I longed to run but kept my pace even as I headed toward the stairs that led from the garden to the valley below.

"Is there something you need?" Conn stepped up to flank Emmet.

I looked to the guard.

Conn had such a bland face, I couldn't tell if he was trying to be helpful or was furious at my suggesting we venture into the village.

"Nothing that you can help me find, Conn." I offered him a smile.

"If you need one of the ladies from the Hall to fetch you something—"

"There are things I need to see for myself," I cut across Conn. I didn't want to watch the corners of his eyes scrunch up and not know if he was in pain or only squinting in the sunlight.

I didn't pause at the top of the sweeping staircase.

A group of women stepped out of my way, pressing their backs to the carved stone rails to give me the path.

I wanted to curl up inside my cloak and hide as the women reverently lowered their eyes.

Emmet placed his hand over mine as we passed the women.

They bowed to him.

"When did the Ryelands become objects of awe?" I whispered.

"When you found a city under a mountain and defied everything they thought they knew," Emmet said.

"Do not leave yourself out of this mess," I muttered, nodding as an older man bowed to us at the bottom of the stairs.

"All I've done is torment paun," Emmet said. "I'd be bowed to in half the taverns in Ilbrea if folks were brave enough and there were no Guilded soldiers nearby."

I swallowed my laugh as we reached the valley floor.

My shoulders tensed as we walked between the banks of snow along the dark stone path, though I didn't catch sight of anything dangerous.

"If you'd like to take a walk, maybe the sorcerers' compound would be a better destination," Ailis said as the path weaved between snow-covered flowerbeds. "I'm sure the Lir children would be happy to see you."

"I'll visit them later." I veered onto another path, one I had not been allowed to tread before.

Barren trees flanked the narrow lane, and mounds poked through the snow where bushes would bloom come spring.

I knew what was hiding beneath the blanket of white, but the mounds still seemed foreboding, as though monsters might leap out to devour me.

Emmet lifted his arm from my grip and let his hand hang by his side, closer to the hilt of his sword.

I strained my ears, listening for whatever might have set him on edge.

The blanket of snow muffled the sounds of the valley.

I am here. All you have to do is attack.

I sent my silent call out onto the wind.

We passed more Black Bloods on our way to the village. All their reactions to my brother and me were the same.

I hated it.

Their reverence seemed like a part of a terrible lie that I was somehow guilty of telling. But I had spoken only truth in the Broinn.

I had found an abandoned city below the mountain. I had been protected by the mountain, even though I was not a Black Blood.

I had spoken only truth, and still, my friend had died.

My breath hitched in my chest.

"Are you all right?" Emmet glanced down at me.

"Fine," I whispered.

"We should go back," Emmet said.

"I won't sit in my room, waiting to be murdered. If someone wants to attack me, they can chivving well do it in the open."

We reached the edge of the village. Despite my own words, I hesitated just before the first of the black stone houses.

"If you really want to go into the village, we should wait for more guards," Ailis said. "I'll double the lot assigned for tomorrow. We can come back then."

"Are the ten of you not enough?" I squared my shoulders and took my first steps into the village of Lygan Hall.

Order your copy of Feather and Flame *to continue the story.*

ESCAPE INTO ADVENTURE

Thank you for reading *Ice and Sky*. If you enjoyed the book, please consider leaving a review to help other readers find Ena's story.

As always, thanks for reading,

Megan O'Russell

Never miss a moment of the magic and romance.

Join the Megan O'Russell readers community to stay up to date on all the action by visiting https://www.meganorussell.com/book-signup.

ABOUT THE AUTHOR

 Megan O'Russell is the author of several Young Adult series that invite readers to escape into worlds of adventure. From *Girl of Glass*, which blends dystopian darkness with the heart-pounding danger of vampires, to *Ena of Ilbrea*, which draws readers into an epic world of magic and assassins.

With the *Girl of Glass* series, *The Tethering* series, *The Chronicles of Maggie Trent*, *The Tale of Bryant Adams*, the *Ena of Ilbrea* series, and several more projects planned for 2020, there are always exciting new books on the horizon. To be the first to hear about new releases, free short stories, and giveaways, sign up for Megan's newsletter by visiting the following:

https://www.meganorussell.com/book-signup.

Originally from Upstate New York, Megan is a professional musical theatre performer whose work has taken her across North America. Her chronic wanderlust has led her from Alaska to Thailand and many places in between. Wanting to travel has fostered Megan's love of books that allow her to visit countless new worlds from her favorite reading nook. Megan is also a lyricist and playwright. Information on her theatrical works can be found at RussellCompositions.com.

She would be thrilled to chat with you on Facebook or

Twitter @MeganORussell, elated if you'd visit her website MeganORussell.com, and over the moon if you'd like the pictures of her adventures on Instagram @ORussellMegan.

ALSO BY MEGAN O'RUSSELL

The Girl of Glass Series
Girl of Glass
Boy of Blood
Night of Never
Son of Sun

The Tale of Bryant Adams
How I Magically Messed Up My Life in Four Freakin' Days
Seven Things Not to Do When Everyone's Trying to Kill You
Three Simple Steps to Wizarding Domination

The Tethering Series
The Tethering
The Siren's Realm
The Dragon Unbound
The Blood Heir

The Chronicles of Maggie Trent
The Girl Without Magic
The Girl Locked With Gold
The Girl Cloaked in Shadow

Ena of Ilbrea
Wrath and Wing
Ember and Stone
Mountain and Ash

Ice and Sky

Feather and Flame

Guilds of Ilbrea

Inker and Crown

Printed in Great Britain
by Amazon